A CONSUMING FIRE

ALSO BY LAURA E. WEYMOUTH

The Light Between Worlds

A Treason of Thorns

A Rush of Wings

A
CONSUMING
FIRE

LAURA E. WEYMOUTH

Margaret K. McElderry Books
New York · London · Toronto · Sydney · New Delhi

✌50

MARGARET K. McELDERRY BOOKS · An imprint of Simon & Schuster Children's Publishing Division · 1230 Avenue of the Americas, New York, New York 10020 · This book is a work of fiction. Any references to historical events, real people, or real places are used fictitiously. Other names, characters, places, and events are products of the author's imagination, and any resemblance to actual events or places or persons, living or dead, is entirely coincidental. · Text © 2022 by Laura E. Weymouth · Jacket illustration © 2022 by Kim Ekdahl · Jacket design © 2022 by Simon & Schuster, Inc. · All rights reserved, including the right of reproduction in whole or in part in any form. · MARGARET K. McELDERRY BOOKS is a trademark of Simon & Schuster, Inc. · For information about special discounts for bulk purchases, please contact Simon & Schuster Special Sales at 1-866-506-1949 or business@simonandschuster.com. · The Simon & Schuster Speakers Bureau can bring authors to your live event. For more information or to book an event, contact the Simon & Schuster Speakers Bureau at 1-866-248-3049 or visit our website at www.simonspeakers.com. · Interior design © 2022 by Simon & Schuster, Inc. · The text for this book was set in Yana. · Manufactured in the United States of America · First Edition · 2 4 6 8 10 9 7 5 3 1 · Library of Congress Cataloging-in-Publication Data · Names: Weymouth, Laura E., author. · Title: A consuming fire / Laura E. Weymouth. · Description: First edition. | New York : Margaret K. McElderry Books, [2022] | Audience: Ages 14 up. | Audience: Grades 10-12. | Summary: Born to be a sacrificial Weatherell girl like her mother, Anya Astraea instead sets out in search of vengeance against the mountain deity who claimed the life of her twin sister. · Identifiers: LCCN 2021058871 (print) | LCCN 2021058872 (ebook) | ISBN 9781665902700 (hardcover) | ISBN 9781665902717 (paperback) | ISBN 9781665902724 (ebook) · Subjects: CYAC: Sacrifice—Fiction. | Revenge—Fiction. | Gods—Fiction. | Sisters—Fiction. | Twins—Fiction. | LCGFT: Novels. · Classification: LCC PZ7.1.W43757 Co 2022 (print) | LCC PZ7.1.W43757 (ebook) | DDC [Fic]—dc23 · LC record available at https://lccn.loc.gov/2021058871 · LC ebook record available at https://lccn.loc.gov/2021058872

FOR MY MOTHER
AND OUR FOREMOTHERS—
THE ONES WHO WENT

ONE
Weatherell

O nce upon a time, when Anya Astraea and her sister, Ilva, were small, they made a habit of walking out to Weatherell's final clearing together. The clearing marked the edge of the village's woodland—beyond it there was only the uninhabited New Forest, with its birdsong and bluebells and wandering piebald ponies, and past that, the forbidden expanse of Albion, which had been the Roman province of Britain before the last of the centurions left, some five centuries ago. While few raised in the village of Weatherell ever saw what lay outside the wood, none born and bred in Albion ever left the great island's shores.

In Weatherell's final clearing, at the edge of everything Anya knew, there stood a beech tree with golden leaves. Old charms crowded its branches, hanging so heavy they might have been a strange and jangling crop of fruit. They'd been made by the people of Weatherell, from glass and chestnut hulls and old coins dug up from the forest earth, which bore the faces of long-forgotten lordlings and Caesars. But the most vital of Weatherell's charms—the ones wrought for protection, not for beauty—were strung with bits of sun-bleached bone. Anya and Ilva would lie on their backs and look up at the spinning charms and try to guess which of the Weatherell girls each bone had come from.

Was it Gabrielle, who'd given her face to the god of the mountain, returning home indelibly marked by a mask of deep scars?

Was it Leya, who'd given her right leg at the knee, and joked until her death that at least she had another?

Was it Florien, who'd given her memory, and known not a soul when she'd come back to the village?

Was it Moriah, who'd given her thumbs and been considered lucky, because the god might certainly have required more?

On and on they'd guess, naming girls who'd gone out from Weatherell to serve as living sacrifices to the god of the mountain. It was Ilva's game, really. She found that naming the girls was a painless way of remembering Weatherell's history—a recollection with its teeth taken out. But it hurt for Anya even to remember people who'd lived and died before they were born. Perhaps those girls were shadows and stories and the bones in charms now, but to Anya, they still lived. She felt the weight of their sacrifice hanging over her every day.

And though most of the Weatherell girls who'd gone out into the world were dead, the god himself was still very much alive on his faraway mountain. His divine sleep could only be renewed with the sweet taste of abnegation—of a living sacrifice offered by a righteous lamb. Nothing but the willing pain of a

Weatherell girl could soothe and sate the god and keep all the vast isle of Albion free from his ruthless predations.

"Someday, I'm going to go," Ilva would whisper to Anya, spinning a story of her own as they lay side by side in the soft fallen leaves. She'd clutch her greatest treasure as she did—a strange trinket, washed ashore from Gaul to the east or Hibernia to the west, no doubt, and carried inland by some creature. Made for stringing upon a cord or chain, it was a little cross-shaped pendant wrought of crude metal, a girl with a babe in arms on one side, a suffering man on the other. Wounds were visible upon the sufferer's hands and feet, and a twisting band of thorns stretched across his brow. Ilva loved the small relic because it was part of an unreachable world. Anya loved it on account of the sufferer—because for once, it was not the girl or the child who bore the wounds.

"When the eighteen years of grace Mam purchased with her sacrifice have passed, and it's time for the next of us to travel to the god again, I'll go," Ilva would announce to Anya and the little graven sufferer and the bones of the girls who'd gone before. "I'm the strongest and bravest—they'll send me if I offer. If I do, then you won't have to leave, or anyone else, and when I come back we'll have a story to tell. You'll take care of me afterward if I need it, won't you, Anya?"

"I don't want you to go," Anya protested staunchly every time, at which Ilva would only laugh.

"Someone has to go, little moon. Better me than you."

"I don't want it to be either of us."

"Who then?" Ilva would press. "Who would you send instead? Elsie? Min? Amara, perhaps?"

Every time, Anya shook her head. "None of them. I don't want anyone to go. It isn't fair, and it isn't right."

"It's the way of things," Ilva answered with a shrug. "The way they were and are and will be. It's not for us to change the working of the world, only to make it a safer place."

"It isn't fair," Anya repeated sullenly, though she gave in to Ilva in the end. She always allowed her sister to have her way sooner or later—Anya had come into the world hard on Ilva's heels, tiny fingers wrapped around her ankle, and had been trying to keep pace with her ever since.

Secretly, though, Anya harbored doubts as to her sister's motives in going to the god. Ilva was a restless soul and a wandering spirit. While Anya would never say so out loud, she sometimes wondered how much Ilva's longing to go had to do with sacrifice, and how much of it was simply a desire to leave Weatherell in the only way afforded to the village's girls. If she were braver, Anya often thought, she'd tell Ilva no when her sister spoke of going to the god. She herself was the most dutiful, the most restrained, the nearest to righteousness of all Weatherell's daughters. The most fit for a sacrifice. But she was afraid and unwilling, and Ilva was not. Anya felt a deep-seated sense of wrongness and revulsion at her core when she considered the journey and the offering. Ilva felt only eagerness and expectation at the prospect of leaving Weatherell, despite departure's agonizing price.

Perhaps that was all that mattered, in the end.

The last time Anya walked out to the final clearing with Ilva, it was to say goodbye, because her sister had laid hold of the one unspeakably costly freedom available to her. At midwinter, when the Arbiter and his selectmen called for a living sacrifice to renew the god's slumber, Ilva alone stepped forward. So there'd been no selection process, no testing of her faith or drills from the Cataclysm, the god's inscrutable holy book. There'd just been Ilva, set apart for the offering from the moment she took that fateful step and spoke her name.

On their last morning together, Anya and Ilva stood alone under the beech tree. Their mother, Willem, had said her terse farewells back in the village, and refused to walk out to the edge of Weatherell's bounds. Willem hadn't wanted Ilva to go, and the two of them had fought over it for weeks. The fighting left Anya trapped between them and nearly torn in two, because while she would never naysay Ilva, in her heart of hearts, she agreed with their mother. Though she did not have the courage or conviction to take her place, nevertheless, Anya did not want her sister to go.

Ilva wore a heavy and practical canvas pack slung over her shoulders, full of the things she'd need on her journey to the mountain. She'd cut her brown curls off at the chin to make for less bother on the road. And a band of supple scarlet leather wrapped around her neck, marking her out to all of Albion as a Weatherell girl—as righteous, and a sacrifice.

Anya had sewn the scarlet band on herself, because Willem could not. The night before Ilva's departure, Anya knelt behind her sister in their small, firelit cottage, fingers trembling against

Ilva's warm skin as she tried to steady herself. But all Anya's efforts had not been enough, and the needle slipped. Tears welled in her eyes, blurring her vision, and she heard Ilva take in a soft breath. When she blinked back the tears and could see again, a drop of blood stood out, stark red against her sister's white skin.

"It doesn't matter, Anya," Ilva said. "You're doing very well."

Anya glanced over at Willem, who sat by the hearth, watching. Willem's leather-and-iron hands lay on a table across the room, and her scarred, handless wrists rested in her lap.

"It's a bad omen," their mother said sternly. "Bones are for protection, but blood is for ill luck."

"Stop." There was steel in Ilva's voice as she spoke to their mother, and it left Anya breathless. Only Ilva dared stand up to Willem's anger, which sometimes burned low and other times flared hot, but was always present. It had grown worse in the past months, though—Anya had been warned that the women who'd once gone to the god were always affected so. Until another girl sated the god of the mountain, his baleful influence reached across Albion to touch those who'd been sacrifices before, rendering them restless and short-tempered, however hard they strove for kindness.

"I don't believe in luck or superstition, and you know it," Ilva said with defiance, fixing her eyes on Willem until their mother quailed. Ilva had been an unstoppable force since her acceptance as Weatherell's sacrifice, and Anya thought that between the reflected heat of Willem's anger and Ilva's resolve, she might catch fire and burn away to ash.

But she'd found it in her to finish sewing on the band, and

pressed a kiss like a prayer to the back of Ilva's neck when she'd completed the task.

"Be brave, little moon," Ilva whispered to her, so low that Willem could not hear. "I know you'll find your courage without me."

And then their last hours together were at an end. They stood under the beech tree one final time, the branches above them flush with the new green of spring. The twisting path out of the wood was already beneath Ilva's feet, and the trail back to Weatherell beneath Anya's.

"I'm glad it's me," Ilva said fiercely as Anya clung to her. "Not just on account of seeing the world beyond the wood. I couldn't have lived with myself if they'd sent you. I've always known that—always known it would have killed me to watch you go."

"Hurry on the road," Anya begged, tendrils of guilt unfurling in the pit of her stomach. "Hurry away, and hurry home. I'll be lost until you're back, Ilva, truly I will."

Ilva held her sister at arm's length. Her eyes were dry and glittering with suppressed anticipation, while Anya's were dim with tears. In addition to the scarlet band, Ilva wore a long braided cord around her neck, and Anya knew without seeing that the otherworldly pendant must hang from the end of it, the mother and child and sufferer tucked away against Ilva's pale skin.

"Will you keep your promise, and look after me once I've come back from my adventure?" Ilva asked. "Will you care for me as well as you've done for the rest of the ones who went—for our mother and Sylvie and Philomena?"

"I will look after you until the day you die," Anya swore.

"And when that day comes, when we're old and full of stories, I'll break up your bones with my own two hands, to be turned into Weatherell's charms. No one else will touch you."

Ilva smiled. "You're very sure of that. But I'm only a minute older than you—who's to say I'll go first?"

Anya wanted to be brave and lighthearted like Ilva, to find levity in the face of death and disaster. But when she opened her mouth to return the joke, her humor withered and died. She could only manage to stare at Ilva, and shake her head in dismay.

"Be brave," Ilva told her again, and with a last swift embrace, she turned her back on Weatherell and her face toward all of Albion, which lay beyond the wood.

Anya watched her sister set her shoulders and take the first steps of a journey dozens of girls had undergone before. She stood and looked after Ilva until the trees swallowed her up. And in the moment Ilva disappeared, Anya knew that though she herself had not set out to go to the god of the mountain, he'd nevertheless reached inside her, rendering her somehow broken instead of whole.

† † † †

Once upon a time, Anya Astraea stood under the golden beech tree in Weatherell's final clearing and watched her sister, Ilva, go to the god of the mountain. Now every afternoon, she stood under it alone and waited for her return.

As spring wore on to summer, she hurried through her morning's work each day. Through brushing her mother's hair and washing her gently with a soft cloth; through buckling on Willem's useless leather-and-iron hands and murmuring rote prayers to the god of the mountain together. The prayers were more a lullaby than anything else—a way of placating the god through soothing words and staving off his appetite for pain and self-denial.

Then Anya would hurry to fetch their skittish black-nosed sheep from the sheepyard at the village's center, beneath the overarching boughs of unfathomably ancient trees. And when she brought their ewes to the Weatherell boys who followed the flocks, she'd bring Philomena and Sylvie's few lambs as well.

Along with Willem, Philomena and Sylvie were Weatherell's three still-living ones who went, who'd gone to the mountain as girls and given of themselves to the god. They served the village as a reminder, and as an ongoing sacrifice—it was said in Weatherell and beyond the wood that the lives of the ones who went served as the purest of prayers. That they were bound to the god, and their connection to him continued to ensure peace for Weatherell, even after their offering had been made. It was why Willem had never been allowed a more functional substitute for the hands she'd given—Arbiter Thorn declared that equipping her with such a thing would be to flout the will of the god.

This spring, however, Philomena was surely doing the lion's share of the peacemaking. She was often unwell but had been worse than ever since the year of disfavor began. Long ago, the god asked for her ability to bear children, which she'd given to him, and she'd suffered from internal complaints ever since. It seemed to intensify her pain, that fathomless miles away, the god she'd once knelt before was restless and waking.

When Anya ducked into Philomena and Sylvie's cottage after tending their sheep, she found the interior dim and cool—no fire on the hearth, not even a candle burning. Sylvie sat hunched in the shadows in a far corner of the cottage's single room, swathed in blankets to ward off the chill. The oldest of the ones who went, she had a wrinkled face that sagged and drooped against the place where her eyes had been, though she turned her head toward Anya at the sound of the girl's voice. Even in the gloom, Anya could make out the black latticework of unreadable script that had been inked into Sylvie's skin, spreading across her neck. Anya knew that most of it ran in orderly rows along her back, though Sylvie refused to speak of it, except to say that the markings had been done to her beyond the wood, and against her will.

"What about a fire?" Anya asked Sylvie briskly, and set about making one. As she knelt before the hearth, she could hear Philomena behind her, struggling to get out of bed. But Anya did not turn, or offer to help. If there was anything the ones who went all had in common, besides their journey to the mountain, it was a fierce pride and a determination to remain independent whenever possible.

Slowly, the sound of Philomena's footsteps drew closer. Anya glanced up and smiled as the woman reached the hearth, dropping into a wicker chair with a trembling sigh.

More so than Willem, Philomena was a mother to Anya. Threads of silver twined through her chestnut hair, and the crow's-feet around her eyes deepened with each passing year, but Philly was a gentle and hospitable soul. It was to her Anya went when she needed to confess troubles or talk over fears. It was Philly who'd held Anya close and let her sob after Ilva left, keeping the girl together when she'd thought her heart would surely break. Even the year of disfavor seemed unable to temper Philly's kindness, though it brought her bodily pain.

"Good morning, Anya," Philomena said, though there was a tense, tormented note behind the words. "Do you know what day it is today?"

Anya nodded, turning back to her work at the hearth. She felt Philly reach out a hand and settle it briefly atop her head like a blessing.

"Two months since Ilva left," Anya answered. "Today I can start watching for her return."

Two months was the quickest any Weatherell girl had made the journey to the mountain and back. They crossed nearly all of Albion and its disparate patchwork of feuding fiefdoms and provinces, all ruled over by petty lords grasping at power. But the island's true overseers were the Elect, who tended souls in the world beyond the wood and guarded the well-traveled and safe high roads from the New Forest through the countryside beyond. Under the Elect's careful watch, Weatherell girls went north, keeping well away from the forbidden metropolis of Old Londinium, and fording the River Thames at a place called Godstow. Then there was mile after mile of plains and hills and moors that led to Banevale, the city at the foot of the mountain called Bane Nevis, where the god of the mountain dwelt in power.

Frida held the record for the fastest journey north. Ten girls ago she'd gone out to the god and returned with her mouth a gaping hole—lips and teeth and tongue torn clear away. But she'd been the fastest, in spite of her injuries.

Secretly, Anya had hoped Ilva would beat Frida's record.

Hurry on the road, she'd said, after all. *Hurry away, and hurry home.*

When Philomena spoke again, warmth and good humor eclipsed the pain in her voice. "You say you can start watching for Ilva today as if you haven't done so since the moment she left. All of Weatherell knows you've been looking out for her, Anya. It will be a while yet, I'm sure—the burden of the god's unease still lies heavy on your mother and Sylvie and me. But I don't think any girl has ever been as fortunate in her family as Ilva, or left behind someone so eager for her return."

Anya flushed. She'd never thought of herself and Ilva as fortunate in their family. Neither of them knew who their father was—Willem had called them Astraea, after him, but would never say more than that she'd met him beyond the wood. And Willem herself was not a warm or devoted mother in any sense. She'd been furious when Ilva put her name forward to go, and refused to speak of her since her departure. Every night Anya wept over her sister in careful silence, because when Willem overheard her tears, she said sharp and cutting things that haunted Anya for days.

If you'd had her courage, you'd be walking now instead of crying.

I'd rather it had been you. You count costs in ways she never does.

It was no use Anya trying to reassure herself that Willem's temper was the result of the god's restlessness, either—her mother had always been harsh. The year of disfavor only honed an edge that had already been there. It coupled with a gnawing guilt over Ilva's going that Anya had felt since her sister's departure and left her in constant misery, though she tried to hide it.

In truth, it was not only eagerness over Ilva's return that took Anya out to the final clearing each day, though she'd plenty of that. There was also the need to see Ilva first: to look her over, and learn what she'd given to the god, and grapple with the low, relentless regret Anya now carried. She knew it would not abate until Ilva was safe beside her again, an offering triumphant, who had purchased grace and peace for all of Albion and had an adventure besides.

After starting Philomena and Sylvie's fire and fixing them a late breakfast, Anya took to the woods. She slipped out of Weatherell's village proper without a backward glance, because she knew every inch of what lay behind her. How each cottage had been built up against the trunk of a tall, spreading tree. How every door had been painted with a protective rune, to ward off ill luck. How the branches overhead glittered with charms, which stirred when the breeze picked up and filled the village with intermittent hollow sounds.

Weatherell was everything Anya knew. She'd never left the village, and never would. There she'd been born, and there she'd die. The Elect, which Weatherell's Arbiter and selectmen were part of, said it must be so. How else could a girl be born every eighteen years to serve as a sacrifice and a spotless lamb, free of the pride and failings that ran rampant in the country beyond Weatherell's bounds?

But such things were not for Anya to worry on. Holiness and boundaries were the province of the Arbiter and the Elect. Sacrifice—the making of it and the surviving of it, the raising of daughters who might be fit for it—was the province of girls like Anya Astraea and her sister, Ilva, who had gone to the god.

Though perhaps elsewhere things were different, Anya sometimes thought blasphemously. Perhaps elsewhere, sacrifice belonged to the sufferer with his band of thorns, and the girl and her child were left intact. Perhaps there might one day be a world in which she did not constantly catch glimpses of bones overheard and feel a sudden stab of regret, and of an indefinable wrongness.

The path to the final clearing looked entirely different now than it had when Ilva left. When she'd gone out to Albion, the woods had only hinted at summer to come. Now everything was green and lush and full of life, smelling of rich earth and growing things.

Anya ghosted down the trail, running her hands along the velvety tops of wildflowers and hardly having to look to find her way. Two months to the day since Ilva had set out from home. Longing and fear and guilt pooled at Anya's core. How much more time would pass before her sister's return? And how had she fared on the mountain? How would the pieces of their new life fall into place?

When she stepped into the final clearing, wind was combing through the branches of the beech tree, setting its charms to chiming. The long grass stood sweet and green, dotted with white flowers, and overhead stretched an expanse of blue sky ringed by tree branches. It was as much of the sky as Anya had ever seen, and today soft clouds and a few distant birds scudded across it. Anya took a breath of good clean air and thought to herself that the worst must surely have passed. She'd survived two months of Ilva's absence. Two months alone with Willem, and her sharp, inexorable tongue. Two months of feeling like half instead of whole. It could not be long now before Ilva completed her work and returned to Weatherell to take her place among the ones who went.

And when Anya drew closer to the beech tree, her heart leaped painfully in her chest. Though Philomena had said it could not be so, Ilva sat among the roots of the tree, leaning against its trunk.

As Anya ran to her, Ilva's face lit with a fleeting smile. Then Anya's arms were around her sister and she was sobbing, all the tears Willem had scorned pouring out of her in a flood. Ilva was everything she'd hoped for, everything she'd longed to have back, everything she'd ever wanted to be.

"I hurried," Ilva whispered. But she did not put her arms around Anya in return.

As the force of Anya's relief calmed, she rocked back on her heels.

"I hurried," Ilva said again, her voice a quiet rasp. As she spoke, Anya saw for the first time that her sister's skin was flushed, with fever and a pair of angry scars that crept up from under the collar of her woolen shirt. Ilva's breath came shallow and fast, and her eyes were dim and unfocused. Her hands, resting on her lap, would not stop shaking.

Anya fumbled with the neck of Ilva's shirt, loosening its drawstrings until she could see her sister's chest and the place where the god had touched her. Her breath caught at the sight of a vicious red handprint, inhumanly large, burned into the skin over Ilva's heart. There was no sign of the sufferer's pendant, though the scarlet band that marked a Weatherell girl still wrapped around Ilva's neck.

"What is it? What's wrong? What did you give?" Anya asked, the words coming out in a panicked jumble. "Ilva. *Ilva.* Show me what's the matter. Show me so I can fix it."

For a moment, Ilva's eyes rolled back and fear cut deep at Anya's core. But her sister rallied, catching her breath with a pained hitch and fixing her gaze on Anya with an effort.

"Everything hurts," she breathed.

"What did you give?" Anya asked again.

Ilva swallowed and winced, as if even that small action pained her. "Nothing. I gave him nothing, in the end. He told me there was no sacrifice he'd accept. When I said I would give him whatever he asked for, he reached out a hand. And oh, Anya. He is so terrible. It's a struggle even to stand before him."

For a long moment, Ilva fell silent, her breath coming hard

and fast as the feverish color drained from her face, leaving her gray and drawn instead.

"He reached out," she whispered, "and placed his hand on my heart. And when he spoke, all his anger and his fire and his bitterness went into me. I can feel them in me yet, eating up my insides, and everything good and alive went out of me and into him, too. He touched me, and I knew it was the beginning of the end."

Tears pooled in Ilva's eyes, and her voice was barely audible, even above the scant breeze stirring the grasses. "Just when I thought I would die, he turned away. But I gave him nothing, Anya. Do you understand? I gave him nothing, because he *took* from me instead."

Ilva's hands in Anya's were no longer trembling like delicate leaves. Now they shook like the earth beneath Weatherell, which occasionally rumbled and shifted. As Anya watched in horror, the shaking spread. All of Ilva shivered and jerked, as if caught out in the bitterest cold.

Anya drew her own hands away and sat helplessly by, with one fist pressed to her mouth and the other to her middle, as some unseen, insidious force wracked her sister.

At last, the shaking stopped and Ilva was still.

"Ilva?" Anya asked.

No answer. Froth stained one side of Ilva's face, her head had tipped back as she shook, and her lips parted a little. Anya had seen many a dead thing in the woods around Weatherell, and her sister had the aching, unnatural look of something life had left behind.

"Ilva?" Anya's voice broke on the word.

With the shallowest gasp, Ilva's chest rose and fell again.

"Don't go." The warning came out ragged, cobbled together from caught breath and splintered bones and the last dying embers of Ilva's once-indomitable will. "Whatever happens, don't go."

"I'm right here," Anya sobbed.

"No. That's not . . . don't go. Don't let *anyone else* go. Promise me."

Anya took Ilva's hands in her own again. "I promise."

"Be brave, little moon," Ilva said, her eyes fixing on Anya's one last time. "Will you . . ."

Her voice trailed off, and Anya waited.

But Ilva was still.

She did not move.

She did not blink.

She did not breathe.

After a few moments, Anya Astraea, who had sent her sister out to be a living sacrifice, curled up on her side with her head on Ilva's lap. Everything inside her had gone still too—still as stone, or as the frozen forest earth at midwinter.

Anya lay motionless until the sun went down. Then Philomena got up from her place by the hearth and led the people of Weatherell to the village's final clearing. They found Anya there, lying beside the cold, stiff body of their failed offering. Anya would not rise, and had to be carried back to the village, for when Ilva left her again—this time irrevocably—her scant courage had utterly failed, swallowed up by a sea of guilt.

She dared not move.

She dared not blink.

She dared not breathe.

TWO

Anger in the Bones

Two months later, Anya Astraea knelt at the heart of an entirely different clearing.

It was smaller, and crowded around with thick, branching pines. They lent the air a wild, spicy smell and shut out all but slivers of the sky. Fallen needles, dead and golden brown and sharp-tipped, carpeted the clearing floor. There were no charms among the tree branches here, and the quiet spread out like a damp blanket, eerie and stifling.

The villagers of Weatherell stood among the trees at the clearing's edge, clad in the gray robes and hoods that the devout and the Elect wore on solemn occasions. The Elect kept to handed-down Roman styles—long robes bound at the waist with a length of cord, cloaks secured at the shoulders with metal clasps. They looked like a part of the forest itself, as if they had grown up from its soil and would stay rooted there forever.

At the center of the open space lay Ilva's bones.

Her body had been set out for the wind and rain and small

woodland creatures to tend to, and they'd done their work admirably. All that remained of Anya's sister now was her skeletal frame, and the only thing left to be done for her was to break up those bones and place them one by one into the hands of the people of Weatherell. Then Ilva, who had been meant for a sacrifice in life, might carry on safeguarding the village as the very last of her became warding charms in death.

It should have been Willem who undertook this last rite, and it was a rarity in Weatherell for anyone young to do this final piece of kinwork. That task was reserved for elders—for those whom time and experience had fortified against the knife-twist of loss. But Anya, in a vain attempt at assuaging the guilt that ate away at her, had begged to do the job. Though Philomena had offered to care for Ilva in Willem's place, there was the matter of Anya's promise, too. She'd told Ilva, before her sister left, that someday she'd break up her bones herself.

Neither of them had expected this day to come for years. Decades, even. What fools they'd been. What fools the god had made of them. And if Anya had only been less afraid, less beleaguered by her own quiet, heretic convictions, if she'd been willing to contradict her sister and go to the mountain instead—it might never have come to this. So however much it hurt Anya to see the last rite through, she knew she could not bear another moment of cowardice, or hold another drop of regret.

Ilva's bones seemed featherlight as Anya began to work them apart, snapping strands of sinew and the worn but resistant tendons. She did her work carefully, meticulously, not wanting to damage a single leftover piece of Ilva if it could be avoided. But wretched tears swam in Anya's eyes as they always did, and her hands set to trembling. She cursed herself for her weakness as with a small splintering sound, a frail bone in one of Ilva's spiderlike fingers shattered.

Anya stared at the ragged shards on her palm, and a sob rose up in her throat. She fought desperately to force it down, but it tore its way out of her with a strangled gasp. Then shame poured hot and liquid through her as she began to cry harder than she'd ever cried before, until she retched and choked and could not draw breath, and all the while the people of Weatherell stood watching.

A whisper of movement stirred the air as someone crouched in front of her, kneeling with a pained sigh. Philly's face swam into view through the fog of Anya's heartbreak and humiliation. The woman's kind brown eyes glistened with tears, but she was restrained, dignified, controlled even in the midst of grief.

Everything Anya was not.

"Anya, my love. You can do this, I promise."

"We're not supposed to die," Anya whispered.

Philomena frowned, failing to catch the thin thread of her words. "What, my darling?"

Anya lifted her head, slowly, stiffly. Her gray hood fell back, but she paid it no mind. Digging her hands down into the pine needles and the forest soil beneath, she fixed her eyes on Philly, and on the knot of waiting villagers.

"We're not supposed to die," she said, her voice louder this time—brash and defiant, as it had never been before.

"I know," Philly soothed. "I know. Let me help you, Anya."

But Anya looked at the villagers beyond Philomena, all alike in their funeral garb, and she could see *him* in every one of them: the god of the mountain, his eyes gleaming at her from the shadows. Watching the spectacle of Anya's pain. Taking in the brokenness he'd wrought.

Forcing her fingers farther into the earth until it scraped and stung against her skin and the pine needles pricked like thin blades, Anya took in a deep breath. She filled her living lungs with air, and as she did, a fire caught within her, fueled by the tinder of her wretched guilt and her shattering conviction that *no one* ought to be sent to a god capable of such cruelty. That fire blazed from the crown of her head to the soles of her feet, a vast and all-consuming force.

"We're not. Supposed. To die."

The words tore out of her in a ragged, furious shout, and she knew how she must look—filthy and exhausted and wild-eyed before the bones of her dead sister. But she had gone far, far past caring.

Philomena faltered. She edged away, uncertain in the face of Anya's wrath, and rejoined the waiting villagers.

"Anya Astraea." When Willem spoke, her voice was sharp as a switch. The filtered light gleamed off her leather-and-iron hands, setting her apart from the others in their robes. "Finish your work."

Anya shut her mouth. She wiped her face on her sleeve. And

she obeyed her mother, because all her life she had been taught to give way, to choose the path of least resistance. She broke up the rest of Ilva's bones with hands that no longer shook. Then piece by piece, she surrendered her sister to the waiting villagers, who each took their bones with murmured thanks but could not meet Anya's eyes.

When she'd finished, Anya went and waited at Willem's side as Arbiter Thorn stepped into the center of the clearing, to the place where Ilva's bones had been. But Anya had not given up all of her sister as she'd been meant to—she'd secreted the broadest of the bones from Ilva's right arm away in her sleeve. At the last, she could not bear to be parted. Not wholly. Not forever.

Solemnly, Arbiter Thorn opened the thick, leather-bound holy book he was seldom without. Anya knew from frequent glimpses that it was written in Divinitas, the language the Romans had brought with them, and which none but the divine or the Elect could now speak or read. It was an odd-sounding tongue, ushering from the nose and the front of the mouth, and the script was stark and angular. The Arbiter leafed through his book steadily before stopping with a finger pressed against his chosen text. He alone wore black, and stood like a shadow beneath the pines. When he read aloud, it was not in Divinitas. Instead, he translated into Brythonic as he went, the words comforting in the softness of their consonants and vowels and in their wavelike lilt.

"I beseech you therefore, sisters," Arbiter Thorn read, clearly and deliberately, "by the mercies of the god, that ye present your bodies a living sacrifice, holy, acceptable unto the god, which is your reasonable service."

A charge filled the air as the Arbiter looked up. It was not their customary funeral benediction he'd read, about ashes to ashes, dust to dust, bones to charms. But everyone in the village recognized his words. Everyone knew the passage that summoned a lamb from among their number.

"A living sacrifice," the Arbiter said softly. "And yet our last Weatherell girl did not live. She was found wanting, and she failed."

Something sick and bitter churned in the pit of Anya's stomach to hear the Arbiter speak so of Ilva. Reluctantly, she tore her gaze from her own two feet and looked up.

Only to find her sister standing behind the black-robed Arbiter. Or rather, a semblance of her sister—this Ilva was not as she'd been in life, or in the moments of her dying, or even now, reduced to bone. She looked as she must have during the long slow weeks of her decay, flesh hanging from her in ribbons, bone showing through in places, eyes a milky, unseeing ruin.

Anya caught her breath with a hitch and stole a surreptitious glance at Willem and Philly, but they watched the Arbiter with impassive faces, appearing not to notice the apparition of Ilva. As if this manifestation of her belonged solely to Anya—a visible outworking of her unrelenting guilt over not just Ilva, but all the Weatherell girls who'd ever gone to the god.

"Will we be protected by a faulty offering?" Arbiter Thorn asked. "Will we be spared the judgment of our god, if his sacrifice no longer lives? His wakefulness and displeasure will surely spread across Albion as he wanders from the mountain, and one day, he will reach this village. When he does, how great and terrible will be his coming. How many lives will be lost as he visits righteous judgment on the world and our wood. Unless . . ."

The Arbiter paused, and in the silence, Anya watched. Despite the hesitation, there was a certainty about him, and for the first time she realized that his words were never improvised, but always rehearsed. Behind him, Ilva stood impassive, eyes withering in their sockets and skin sloughing from her bones at a preternatural rate.

". . . unless another brave girl will step forward, and offer herself for the good of Weatherell, and all of Albion besides?"

There it was, the request spoken as if it pained him, and as if it had only just occurred to him to ask. But Anya was sure he must have spent weeks planning for another departure with the selectmen. There were provisions to assemble, a new leather band to be made, travel alms to collect. Sending a Weatherell girl out from the wood was no momentary decision.

No one seemed willing to move, or speak. Only Anya found it in her to glance about, for she was an empty shell in the wake of her wild grief over Ilva, impervious to pain or fear or shock at the sight of her sister's ghost. But she saw pain and fear aplenty when she scanned the faces of the people of Weatherell.

Every family with daughters huddled closer to one another, their gazes haunted, their lips pressed into thin, anxious lines. They'd all been able to breathe in the months since Ilva left. The shadow of this year, the eighteenth year between sacrifices, had passed over. Ilva had taken it with her, wrapping it about herself like a shroud.

Now the shadow had fallen again, and for the second time in that cursed year, the unimaginable happened.

First, Ilva had gone to the mountain and died for her trouble.

And now, when the Arbiter spoke, no girl stepped forward.

Silence washed over the clearing. Never in Weatherell's long history had an Arbiter called for a sacrifice and failed to find a willing offering. But never in that history had a girl gone out to the god and lost her life for it, either.

Anya knew why. She knew it with a deep, heartsick ache. It was not Ilva who'd been found wanting and failed. It was Anya herself, who had both the temperament and virtue necessary for an offering, yet through conviction and cowardice had not gone in her sister's stead, and had lost her as a result.

Arbiter Thorn shifted his weight from one foot to the other as the silence dragged on and grew agonizing. Even Anya's heart, torn to pieces in her chest, began to beat a little faster. Then the Arbiter spoke again and confirmed her suspicions, that he had planned for this moment, that he had known the girls of Weatherell would need a push. Behind him, Ilva had begun to speak, her half-skeletal mouth moving in a soundless refrain.

"Selectman Callis?" the Arbiter said, his voice little more than a murmur. "Would you step forward and read the account you brought back last week, from out beyond the trees?"

Selectman Callis did as the Arbiter asked. He was tall and burly and served the village as a blacksmith. No one had thought anything of it when the week before, he'd vanished for a few days—the selectmen were always coming and going, maintaining the ties between Weatherell and those of the Elect who served in the world outside the wood.

Now Callis drew a folded and smudged sheet of parchment from his pocket and smoothed it out. Anya could see the unreadable marks marching across the page—it had been written in Divinitas, just like Arbiter Thorn's holy book and the strange words inked into Sylvie's skin. As such, not a girl or a woman in Weatherell could read them. They spoke only Brythonic, and from childhood learned instead the branching runes of plainscript, which were used elsewhere in Albion and might be of service if they were to become one of the offertory girls.

"From First Arbiter Thelon of Banevale,'" Selectman Callis read, "'the city in the shadow of the god.

"'Dearly beloved brothers and sisters of the wood, we received your living sacrifice this spring with joy. As we've done for centuries, we offered her whatever hospitality she required and treated her honorably. We found her acceptable, if a little enamored of the world and her surroundings. But it is no surprise that a spotless lamb from Weatherell would find much distraction beyond the borders of your wood. In spite of that, your offering stayed the course and climbed the mountain, and presented herself to the god.

"'But there she was found wanting, and the terrible and righteous divinity we serve refused her. We can only assume that in the course of her journey, your lamb fell afoul of some temptation and sullied herself in a way the god could not abide.

"Since then, we have lived stricken with fear. Our god grows restless now, without the accustomed sweetness of self-sacrifice to maintain his rest. His fire can be seen on the mountaintop nightly, and unless a fit offering is made, the last of his bonds will surely be loosed before long. I fear we cannot bear the full weight of his impending judgment, and beg of you to send another sacrifice. A pure-hearted girl, who will not turn aside from her task.

"'Make haste, brothers and sisters. The god's anger builds and his righteousness is a consuming fire. Should he go unsated, none will be able to stand before his touch.'"

The last words of the letter seared into Anya like a brand as she stood far away from the fabled peak of Bane Nevis and the dreadful god who dwelt at its summit. She thought of Ilva, dying before her very eyes, and of the things her sister had said.

He touched me, and I knew it was the beginning of the end.

I gave him nothing, because he took from me instead.

Inside Anya, the fire that had flared to life as she broke up her sister's bones grew brighter, hotter, unendurable. It licked at her insides, until she was sure she must go up in smoke. All around her, the people of Weatherell still stood, ashamed but immoveable.

For centuries, they'd sent their girls to the god. But it seemed that even in Weatherell, there was a limit to what could be endured, and while the village could bear up under living sacrifices, death was a step too far.

"We will draw lots," the Arbiter said at last, impatience and frustration creeping into his voice.

A firestorm raged beneath Anya's quiet exterior as she looked from one face to another, at the grief and fear, the resignation and remorse awakening among the villagers of Weatherell as they realized that they were on the cusp of breaking with age-old tradition. Of separating themselves from generation after generation of girls who'd gone willingly to the god.

Echoes crowded Anya's fevered mind.

None can stand before his touch.

I gave him nothing, because he took from me instead.

Be brave, little moon. I know you'll find your courage without me.

A whispering grew audible in the clearing. An eerie, cold sound like wind in bare branches, and it took Anya a moment to realize that the words Ilva's watching ghost was speaking had become audible.

Don't go, she repeated, over and over, desperation in her plea as she twined her skeletal hands together. *Don't let anyone else go.*

Ilva's words fell on the fire blazing in Anya like lamp oil, burning away the constant chill of fear. For the briefest moment, she felt a flash of courage and clarity, and saw the path ahead—a way to honor the last request Ilva had made. To put an end to the wrongness Anya had always felt when she thought of the god of the mountain and his long line of tormented girls. Without hesitation, Anya took a step forward. Leather and iron brushed against her sleeve, but Willem's mechanical hands were powerless to hold her. She took another step.

Every villager had fixed their eyes on her, and though under other circumstances, their attention would have mortified Anya, this day she did not care. This day, she'd already swallowed her ration of shame.

Crossing the clearing, Anya knelt before Arbiter Thorn. Behind her, a collective sigh went up. A letting out of the breath, in relief over being spared yet again. Before her, the Arbiter's face was unreadable, and beyond him, the graying strands of Ilva's flesh were knitting back together in a gruesome semblance of life.

"I will go to the god of the mountain," Anya said softly. "My sister was meant to serve us as a living sacrifice. But as she was unable to satisfy the god, I will serve in her stead. I will finish what she began."

Inside Anya, the firestorm still raged—a bitter inferno of sorrow and trust betrayed. It slicked her palms with unspent fury. But she bowed her head before the Arbiter, knowing what was required of a Weatherell girl. To be strength clothed in meekness, determination bent on brokenness, purity tempered with self-destruction.

When the villagers applauded her bravery, the sound was muted and uncertain, muffled by the pines. Anya got to her feet and turned. She searched for her mother in the little crowd, unsure of what she'd find in Willem's face. Grief. Anger. Relief, perhaps, to be freed of her weakest daughter.

But she found none of that. Willem had gone.

And when she turned back to the Arbiter, Ilva's ghost had gone too, leaving her bereft once more.

All the rest of the morning, Anya wandered in the trackless forest. She carried those unholy flames inside her that had lit when she grieved so fiercely over her sister. They burned harsh and hot, and Anya feared that if she touched another living soul, she might set them ablaze.

At noon she settled under a spreading oak near a stream. She still carried Ilva's last bone, clutched tight against her skin. Now she took it out and turned it over in her hands. As she did, the fire in her burned hotter, until she thought it might send sparks snapping from her fingertips.

There was only the faintest whisper of Ilva in this fractured, yellow-white thing. It had been a part of her, yes, but she was in it no longer. And Anya's desire to keep it whole dissipated, going up like smoke before the heat inside her. Scrambling over to the stream, she chose two river rocks and retreated to the base of the oak tree. Then she began to work.

She broke up Ilva's final bone with care and precision, shaping it into a strong, pointed shard. Then she ran it over the rock time and again, honing the shard to a cutting edge. With each careful stroke, a little of the fire in her burned lower and became more manageable. She did not stop until she'd fashioned herself a long, slender knife that gleamed like pearl, with a dull end that could be wrapped in cordage for a handle.

Only once night had fallen and the moon tangled itself among the branches of the trees did Anya pocket her bone knife and turn for home. She slipped through Weatherell's village proper and in at the door of the cottage where once upon a time Ilva had lived with her and Willem.

It was pitch-black and cold inside. Anya knelt before the hearth and began the task of laying a fire. She'd done it so many times before that she'd no need of a lantern—her hands easily found what was required.

"You shouldn't have come back," Willem said from somewhere in the dark. "I swear to the god, Anya Astraea, handless though I may be, I will smother you in your sleep if you spend the night under this roof. Your sister leaving was bad enough, but I will kill you myself before you go to him."

Anya struck sparks from her patch box. With a small, serpentine hissing noise, the tinder she'd laid out caught the sparks, and light flared in the darkness. Quicker than ever before, the fire took. Anya waited patiently until she was sure the flames would not die out. Then she got to her feet and turned, facing her mother.

Willem stood with an all-too-familiar anger etched across her face. Firelight picked out the white network of scars that spread across the bare stumps of her wrists.

"I will kill you," Willem said again, and it wasn't a threat, but a promise. Was it the god's influence working in her, Anya wondered, that made her say such things, or was it only her own implacable nature?

"You won't," Anya answered quietly. She went to one of the cottage's back corners and took out the canvas pack Ilva had brought to the mountain. Anya set to work filling it with provisions that had already been left at the cottage for her: hard cheese and apples and dried mutton. From among her own belongings, she added a length of twine to wrap the handle of her knife.

Willem watched. As she saw the deft way in which Anya moved and the certainty in her posture, confusion grew in Willem's eyes.

"What is it you're doing, child?" she asked, with something like hunger in her voice.

Anya smiled a faint, bitter smile. She'd known it wouldn't be long before her mother sensed the thing that had flared to life within her.

"What are you doing, little moon?" Willem asked again, taunting Anya with Ilva's old endearment.

Anya stuffed a blanket into the pack. "You tell me, Mother. What am I doing?"

Willem stared at her, dark eyes following her daughter's every move. "I don't know. But I do know this—there was sacrifice in your sister. There was righteousness in her. I could see it, no matter her faults or her foolishness. I see none of that in you."

Anya stopped her work. She let her hands fall still and turned to her mother, so that they stood face to face in the ruddy firelight.

"I'm going to be a Weatherell girl," she said. "Like you were. Like Ilva. Like Philly and Sylvie and all the girls before us. I will leave the wood, and walk the length of Albion, and journey to the god on his mountain."

"And when you get there?"

"When I get there," Anya continued, blood and bones aflame inside her, "I will kill him. Because he cannot be righteous after what he did to Ilva and you and all the others, and I can't find a way to feel guiltless, not so long as he lives. If I'd been brave or good, I'd never have let Ilva leave here, but I couldn't have let anyone else go either—I need a way to make that right. I need . . . a penance, to take this guilt from me."

For a moment, Willem was silent. Then she took a single step back.

"Are you certain?" she asked. "Because in Weatherell or beyond the wood, folk will string you up for blasphemy if they learn the truth behind your going. The Elect will kill you, and make your very name a curse."

"*Vengeance is mine,*" Anya said, quoting the Arbiter's holy book. "*I will repay.*"

There was a sound of burning in her words, a taste of fire on her tongue. "I've never been sure of much, but I'm sure of this. I swear it on Ilva's bones."

Silence again. But when Willem did speak, her voice caught Anya short. There was something in her tone the girl had never heard there before.

Approval.

"Good," Willem said. "Very good, my little moon."

This time the endearment was no mockery, and tears stung Anya's eyes to think that this was what she must do to earn her mother's regard.

THREE

Out of the Woods
and into the World

Anya's departure from Weatherell was as unlike Ilva's as it could possibly be. There were no long weeks leading up to it as the last of the spring flooding receded, leaving dry forest earth in its wake. Nor was there a gathering of villagers to see her off, as they'd done for Ilva. Instead, Anya stepped out of the cottage door before dawn with her sister's pack on her shoulders and called to Philomena, who was up and crossing the open ground of the village proper, returning from the distant shared privies.

"Philly."

Philomena stopped, raising the lantern she held. She smiled at the sight of Anya, but it did not reach her eyes.

"Anya, my love. What can I do for you? Surely you're not off already? It's not—it's not too late to change your mind." Philomena's gaze faltered, as if she was ashamed to be suggesting such faithlessness but unable to keep from speaking the words.

By way of an answer, Anya held out her hands. In one, there

was a strip of thin crimson leather embossed with Divinitas script. In the other was a needle and thread.

"I've no one to sew on my band," she said simply.

At a gesture from Philomena, Anya knelt on the forest floor, feeling the knees of her trousers growing damp as Philly stitched the ends of the leather strip together at the back of her neck. Before her, Ilva's ghost wavered into visibility bare inches away, kneeling just as Anya did, with small white worms crawling among the hollow places between her fraying skin and bones.

"They told your sister, but I'm not sure if they reminded you—this band will mark you out to others," Philomena said, her voice and her hands both gentle. "It will speed you on your way. You need never stop to earn your keep while you're wearing it—people out there will know you're for a sacrifice. They'll give you shelter, and whatever you need for supplies, so that you can hurry on to the mountain. And the Elect will be able to keep watch over you—to ensure your safety until you reach journey's end. There are unscrupulous people beyond the wood. Lords and their lackeys, all hungry for power, but they've never yet proved a match for the Elect."

Anya stared down at the ground, the back of her neck prickling with discomfort beneath Philomena's fingers. No matter where she went, she'd be lying about her purpose from the moment anyone laid eyes on her. The thought rankled—Anya had always been more scrupulously truthful than Ilva. Her sister perpetually landed the pair of them in trouble, only to talk herself back out of it again with charm and wit and half-truths. It was Anya who quailed at deception, and if a lie would save her, she'd bite it back and take her punishment in silence.

But Anya was still angry and it burned this newest twist of guilt away. She let the anger force her upright, onto her feet. With a faint choking tug, Philomena severed the thread and left her band whole, a bright red circlet around her neck.

"I'll look after your mother," Philomena promised Anya. "You won't have to worry about her while you're gone."

"You've already got Sylvie to care for," Anya said with regret. "And Philly—who will look after you?"

"The village and our god." Philly twined her hands in front of her, like a child reciting answers from the god's Cataclysm.

Anya stifled a sigh. All that was tainted for her, and had been for years, if she was honest—the faith and the fear and the long slow march of time that led from sacrifice to sacrifice. Her unquestioning belief had faltered long before Ilva died. It wasn't in her, to trust a god who dealt in blood and brokenness and shattered lives.

"Goodbye, Philly," Anya said. "I'll miss you more than anyone else left in Weatherell, I think."

Philomena stepped forward, her arms outstretched, and Anya shied clumsily away, burdened by the pack.

"No, please don't," she begged. "I couldn't bear it if you touched me. Not now. Not just as I'm leaving."

With a sad smile, Philomena nodded. "You know, Anya, you've always wanted to be your sister, but there's more of your mother in you than you think. And whatever Willem's faults, she was made for living. So in two months' time, I'll be looking for you. Hurry home to us."

That last nearly undid Anya, it so perfectly matched her parting words to Ilva. For a moment she thought her knees might give way.

Instead, she turned her back to Philly. Letting out a long, steadying breath, Anya squared her shoulders. She would not show weakness just as she was leaving. She would not allow Philomena to see the way her heart had shattered, or how the dry, broken bits of it had become kindling for a blasphemous fire.

Dearly beloved, avenge not yourselves, but rather give place unto wrath, the Arbiter's voice said in the labyrinth of Anya's mind.

Vengeance is mine; I will repay, the unrelenting anger inside her answered.

And so Anya Astraea took a step, and then another, and another, and with each step came the echo of Ilva's ghost following along at her heels. By the time she looked back, the village had fallen behind. Only the sympathetic, whispering trees and her sister's restless soul kept her company now. Ahead of her stretched the thin brown ribbon of the path that led away through the woods and out into the country beyond.

As Anya stood with the road before her and Weatherell at her back, she realized with a sudden dull pang of conviction that if she truly committed to the course she'd chosen—if she saw her task through to its end—one way or another, she would likely never return home. Either the god would overpower her in his fury at her betrayal, or she would drag him into death along with her, or the impossible would happen, and she would meet with success. Anya was under no illusions. She knew that if she managed the impossible, it would make her an enemy of the Elect forever, and that they punished heresy and blasphemy most stringently of any sins.

But she had become both heretic and blasphemer already, profaned by her own unspoken desires and the unholy fire at her core. For a moment, Anya shut her eyes and could almost imagine she heard Ilva's living voice calling her name. Her sister's spirit waited, silent and spectral, ahead of her, until Anya let the ghostly remnants of Ilva draw her on.

† † † †

By midmorning, the forest had thinned. There was a strange emptiness beyond the trees that Anya caught wider and wider glimpses of, and then quite suddenly, the wood ended and everything beyond it began.

Anya stopped beneath the protective eaves of the forest and stared. Never had she imagined that such vast expanses of open space could exist. She stood alone on a little rise, Ilva's ghost having vanished some miles back, and before her lay hill country. The land undulated up and down, dotted with trees, but they were sparse and spread out among green fields, or separated by dry stone walls. The sky overhead was an impossible blue dome, higher even than the billowing white clouds that sailed along, casting their shadows across the meadows. The remote black shapes of birds wheeled across the sky too, dipping and swooping and gliding closer to earth, where they resolved into swallows and sparrows.

Away and away and away the land stretched, to what must surely be the world's farthest rim. *Horizon,* Sylvie had called that edge, where the last hills met the sky and vanished in a hazy union of earth and air. She'd warned that it was unreachable—that as you traveled toward it, more hills and more road appeared.

Anya could not imagine that. Could not fathom, in this moment, that there could possibly be *more* to Albion besides all that lay before her—and then the world beyond Albion, too. But one field over lay a relic of the thousand years of Roman occupation—the bend of an old high road that Anya must follow, snaking away northward.

North was where she needed to go.

As Anya stood and attempted to gather her flagging courage, an ominous crashing and snapping of branches sounded from the wood at her back. With her heart pounding in her chest, she pivoted, only to catch sight of a blurry, entirely living shape leaping past her. Bounding out into the open field beyond the wood, the creature stopped and sat, and resolved into a dog.

It was one of the few shaggy, disreputable mongrels that had attached themselves to Weatherell—beasts of no particular origin or ownership that eked out a living on scraps and kicks and not much else. Ilva had always, with an impish grin, referred to them collectively as *the Weatherell bitches*. This particular dog had a rakish look about her, with mottled gray and black and white fur and curious pricked-up ears. She tilted her head to one side and regarded Anya happily, swishing her tail through the grass.

It was as good as an invitation, and Anya let out a sigh.

"All right," she said, casting an uneasy glance back at the forest. "I suppose I can't let you outdo me."

And for the first time, she put one foot in front of the other and left everything she'd been born to behind. Fresh guilt rose within her as she did—Anya was, as far as she knew, the only Weatherell girl ever to depart the village under false pretenses. *On our knees, within the trees, lest we give of these, our blood and bones,* the children of Weatherell would sing as a skipping rhyme. Yet here was Anya, leaving the wood with no intention of giving. Instead, she was bent on taking. On stealing, as she had been stolen from.

The dog let out a few staccato barks and raced ahead, tearing through the wheat and launching herself over a wall to reach the overgrown, cobbled road. Then she settled into a fluid trot, setting the pace a few steps ahead of Anya. The plume of her tail served as a beacon and Anya followed, fiercely subduing the urge to glance over her shoulder, or to turn and run back. Back to the village and the Arbiter, to confess her blasphemous intentions and accept a penance to make right her wrongs, before she'd cut off all hope of ever returning home.

But this wasn't the sort of journey undertaken with the return in mind. Anya must fix her eyes on the mountain and her vengeance and dare to look no further. She must set her back to the forest and everything she'd ever known. For the briefest moment, with the road stretching before her, Anya could picture her sister whole and well and happy, setting out for adventure with a smile on her face and the wind in her honey-brown hair.

The image, however, was quickly subsumed by Ilva's ghost, which stepped out of thin air and seemed more spectral and gruesome than ever in full daylight. Unable to bear looking at it for long, Anya put her head down. Forcing back her innate fear and faintness of heart, she moved forward and let the road lead her north, toward vengeance or death—whichever awaited her on the god's blighted mountain.

† † † †

Not long after noon, a flock of houses appeared, nestled in one of the wide valleys as Anya crested the hill above it. They gave off a smell of woodsmoke and refuse and, even from a distance, seemed much too close together, as if they were trying to scramble atop one another, or huddle up for protection against some unknown threat.

Anya eyed the town doubtfully. She was shy of people even in Weatherell, where she knew every living soul. And meeting several farmers driving market carts along the high road had not helped matters. They'd nodded respectfully but then caught sight of her band. One or two looked quickly away and hurried their horses along, as if hoping Anya would not realize they'd seen who she was. But several had bowed so low Anya thought they might fall from their wagon boxes, and that made her flush and grow awkward. Ilva would have greeted them with more grace—stood straight-backed with the wild elegance that was

uniquely hers, and accepted gestures of respect as if they were
her due.

Despite Anya's discomfort, the road she followed ran through
the town. All around was nothing but empty fields and bare hill-
sides. And the waymark beside her with the name of the town
spelled out in spidery Brythonic runes bore a crimson arrow. A
sign left wherever Weatherell girls might hesitate, to point out
their way.

"What do you think?" she asked the dog, who still trotted
along with her, keeping a few paces ahead. It settled Anya a bit,
to have something living with her, rather than the dead. The dog,
for her part, sat sniffing the air with an enchanted look on her
clever, narrow face, as if the stink of the town were fragrant as
new blossoms.

"All right then," Anya said reluctantly. "Forward we go. But
you've got to have a name if we're to keep on together—what
about Midge?"

The dog looked pleased, though she seemed to look so always.
Still, the name suited her, with her trim gray persistence.

From closer up, the town was less unpleasant than Anya had
feared. A little stream ran through it, and she passed a mill with
a ceaselessly turning waterwheel. The houses were tall and thin
and pressed up against each other, but their walls were softened
by ivy and made all of warm yellow stone. The footbridges arch-
ing over the stream were stone too, and Anya's shaggy companion whined eagerly at the sight of cats lazing in the sun on their
raised ledges.

But the streets were strangely empty, besides a few figures here and there hurrying toward the town's center. With a frown, Anya followed after them.

She found herself at the edge of a small crowd, in an open square half filled with empty livestock pens, and Anya supposed it must be where they held auctions on market day. Philly had told her of such things, making them sound noisy and exciting.

What hung on the air now was not so much excitement as tense anticipation. A sullen mutter rose from the waiting crowd, and Anya turned to the bystander nearest her, ignoring the nervous things fluttering in her stomach long enough to speak.

"What's going on?" she asked the thin, gray-haired woman at her side. With a single glance, the stranger took in Anya—her trousers and braces made specially for traveling, her hair shorn to chin length for convenience on the road, her overstuffed pack, and the scarlet band about her throat. The woman's eyes widened, and she swallowed visibly before answering.

"They caught a thief red-handed, stealing from Arbiter Boldwood's safe, of all places. You think he'd have known to pick a better target, but the boy seems a right heathen. They've just finished the sentencing and are about to bring him out for his punishment."

"... which is?" Anya pressed.

The woman craned her neck, trying to see through the crowd. "The same as always, for thievery. Do you not have thieves in your Weatherell?"

Anya shook her head. "No. If you do anything in Weatherell

that might harm the community, you're turned out. So hardly anyone does."

The woman beside Anya sniffed and mumbled something under her breath.

"What's that?" Anya asked politely. "I didn't catch what you were saying."

The older woman at least had the grace to look shamefaced as she answered. "I said *righteous as a Weatherell girl*. There's a reason sacrifices to the god of the mountain come from your lot and not ours. But you'd best get used to a world where thieves—and worse—exist. The boy being charged is certainly the former, and I don't doubt someday he'll end up the latter as well."

Anya winced at the woman's words. She didn't feel righteous, with vengeance burning like a torch inside her. Neither had Ilva seemed righteous—she'd been good, yes, and strong and free, like a summer wind in the treetops. But righteous in the way that Weatherell girls were so often painted? Anya had never known anyone who reached that mark.

A commotion rose up around the doorway of one of the buildings that fronted the square. Anya stood on her toes to see as a pair of broad-shouldered selectmen in gray robes shoved the door open and emerged into the sunlight, dragging a ragged boy between them. She caught a glimpse of matted brown hair and a flash of wild hazel eyes, and then the selectmen and the boy were both up on a raised wooden platform at the square's heart, visible to all.

The thief was a gangly, sallow-skinned creature, all elbows

and edges, who swore and spat as the selectmen wrestled him to his knees. One of them held him steady and the other fetched a thick wooden stump, as a broad, bald man in an Arbiter's black garments came out of the courthouse doorway.

"They're not going to kill him, are they?" Anya asked breathlessly. She'd been warned by Willem that in Albion beyond the woods, people sometimes seemed immune to the sacred nature of death. That they brought it about themselves by demonstrating malice or apostasy so great, the Elect were forced to end their lives.

"No," the older woman scoffed. "Not for a failed theft. For that, they'll take his right hand off at the wrist."

Anya couldn't help the sharp gasp that escaped her. She could still see in her mind's eye the smooth stumps where Willem's hands had been, the jagged scars that ran white across her skin, the way those scars would chafe in winter, breaking out in angry sores. Anya would apply strong-smelling ointment every night to no avail. But Willem had her pride and she wore her leather-and-iron hands over the scars, come what might. Even when it hurt her. Even when the mechanical hands were no earthly use and could not replace what she had given.

With her stomach roiling, Anya began to push her way forward through the crowd.

FOUR

The Hand of a Thief

Anya had no taste for judgment or punishment—even the single exiling she'd witnessed in Weatherell, which had been a relatively peaceful affair, left her feeling bruised and brokenhearted for weeks. But this was her compulsion, and her one small courage—a refusal to turn away from pain and suffering.

"Excuse me," she said to the people ahead of her as she slipped between them, ignoring the way her palms began to sweat as she did. "Pardon me. I need to get through."

As Anya moved forward through the village square, onlookers complained until they saw her band. Then they shrank away, as if self-sacrifice were a catching thing. Only a knot of formidable-looking guards in unfamiliar blue-and-black livery stood their ground, watching Anya's passage with curious, calculating expressions.

In moments Anya had worked her way to the front of the crowd and stood a few feet from the platform. The town's

Arbiter had joined the selectmen there, and the boy accused of thievery still struggled, a torrent of curses pouring from his lips, most of which Anya had never even heard before.

Slowly, portentously, the Arbiter opened a thick book and made a show of finding his place. Though Anya could not read the Divinitas script etched across its cover, she recognized the shape of the words—it was the god's Cataclysm. The same holy book Arbiter Thorn consulted in the governing of Weatherell.

"Tieran of Stull," the Arbiter said, casting a scathing glance at the writhing thief. "*If* that be your true name, which I have reason to doubt. You have been caught in the act of theft, proved guilty, and sentenced to pay for your perfidiousness. The punishment meted out for you is as required—the loss of a hand. For the Cataclysm commands that *if thy right hand causeth thee to sin, cut it off and cast it from thyself; it is more profitable for thee that one of thy members perish, than for thine whole body to fall into judgment.* May our god smile upon the justice done this day."

The Arbiter shut his book with a bang, and one of the selectmen stretched out the thief's right arm, binding his hand to an iron ring driven into the stump. The boy redoubled his furious swearing, and struggled so hard Anya feared he'd dislocate his shoulder. She watched in numb shock as the second selectman took a hatchet from a hidden loop on his belt and ran a whetstone along its shearing edge.

None of this seemed possible. None of it seemed real. Sylvie had told her a hundred stories of the barbarous ways of the people beyond the wood, but for such acts to be carried out by emissaries of the Elect, who so strictly regulated life in Weatherell and required perfect forgiveness from those who dwelt beneath the trees? Who declared that even to harbor anger toward another person in one's heart was blasphemy? All her life, she'd been taught to strive for the sort of mercy that would sacrifice no matter the cost. To see the very Elect who'd taught her demonstrate merci-lessness was an offense so deep Anya went dizzy with it.

She might have stayed, frozen in disbelief, if the thief had not caught sight of her as he desperately searched the faces of the gathered crowd. His eyes fixed on her, and he went dead white.

Weatherell girl.

Anya saw his lips form the quiet words, for she could not hear them over the excited clamoring of the crowd. Then the thief tore his attention from her, and it was as if the glimpse of Anya and her band had lent strength to his anger. He turned to the bailiff binding his hand and began to shout with rage—a guttural, incoherent sound, with no words to it, that cut off and began again when the boy was forced to draw breath.

"Shut that mouth and take what you deserve," someone in the crowd called out.

But Anya was filled with sudden and ferocious longing. All her life, she'd lived in the shadow of women who walked willingly to their fate. Who'd given up pieces of themselves by choice. She'd never known someone who fought the way this boy fought, just to stay whole.

Without allowing herself a moment to hesitate, Anya clam-bered up the steps to the platform and stopped between the hatchet-bearing selectman and the thief. But it was the Arbiter to whom she turned her attention, fixing her eyes on him in a vain attempt to ward off her awareness of the crowd and of all the many gazes trained on her.

"Stop this," Anya said, voice shaking though she struggled to keep it strong. She forced herself to speak up, to be louder than she'd been taught was fitting. "Please, I beg you to stop. None of this is right, or natural, or just."

Though displeasure clouded the Arbiter's face at Anya's interference, he hid it swiftly after catching sight of her band. With a pitying smile, he shook his head and placed a hand on her shoulder, his touch reasonable, reassuring. Nevertheless, Anya fought back the urge to shrink away.

"We've already passed this thief's sentence," the Arbiter explained. "So there's no stopping now. I realize things are different in Weatherell, but—"

"Things *are* different in Weatherell," Anya said, desperate to make him understand. "Do you remember the second last of our girls, who walked the length of Albion eighteen years past?"

"Yes," the magistrate said tersely.

"And do you remember her sacrifice?"

Silence fell over the crowd as the Arbiter did not answer. Anya turned her back to him and faced the assembled onlookers, though her knees were like water and her stomach full of frantic wings.

"Eighteen years ago, Willem of the woods passed through this town on her way home from the god's mountain, Bane Nevis.

While she was there she'd made an offering, to keep the god quiet, and to keep all of us safe and prosperous. She came back without her hands. I can't . . . I can't let you do that to someone else, no matter his crime."

Anya turned to the Arbiter once more.

"Does the Cataclysm not say that *judgment is without mercy to one who has shown no mercy*? And that *mercy triumphs over judgment*? I'll ask for nothing but mercy in this village, then—no lodging, no bread. Just that you leave the thief whole."

"Child, you were born to a gentler place, with gentler rules," the Arbiter said, his tone infinitely kind. "In the rest of Albion, mercy is too often met with ingratitude. Out here, we must be wise as well as gentle."

The thief with his bound hand refused to look at Anya, as if her very presence shamed him. And Anya, who alone among those gathered knew her true reason for leaving the forest behind, felt entirely unworthy.

Be Ilva, if you cannot be yourself, she thought, wishing even for a glimpse of Ilva's ghost to bolster her courage. *What would she have done, if it had been her standing in this place?*

But the spirit haunting her did not appear. Instead, Anya fought back her nerves and stood a little taller.

"*You owe me this,*" she said sternly to the Arbiter. She'd never spoken in such a way to an authority before, or contradicted anyone set over her. To do so now made her dizzy and anxious, though she struggled to hide her nerves. "The Cataclysm also says *a laborer is worthy of her reward.* What am I and those who went before me but laborers on behalf of Albion? And what reward is more fitting for my mother's sacrifice than this—a hand in exchange for those she lost?"

"Let her have it," a firm voice said from the back of the crowd. The Arbiter's jaw tensed, and Anya caught sight of one of the liveried guards, a laconic smile playing across his face. Both men were obviously accustomed to being obeyed, and as she had with Ilva and Willem, Anya felt caught in the middle—a weather vane to be swayed, a pawn to be shifted at will.

"Lord Nevis has no jurisdiction here," the Arbiter snapped. "The presence of his guard this far south is not welcome by the Elect, merely tolerated. Don't mistake one for the other."

"Nevertheless," the guard replied, more easily this time. "I say you let the girl have this."

The Arbiter considered for a moment. But the guard's intervention seemed to have altered the opinions of the crowd. Whatever their thoughts on the thief, murmurs echoing the guard's sentiment rippled among the people.

"The Weatherell girl."

"Give her what she wants."

"We've no right to naysay her."

The Arbiter turned back to Anya, frustration writing itself across his face. "Very well. I can hardly deny you, of all people, can I? But if the thief ever comes this way again, we *will* exact the punishment he deserves. And I would caution you not to involve yourself in the judgments of the Elect from now on—it is not for you to decide the course of justice."

Anya could not answer other than to nod. Now that she'd won her battle, nerves rose up so strongly in her she feared she'd be sick if she opened her mouth. Instead, she gestured to the nearest selectman, who swung his hatchet and severed the rope that bound the thief. The boy flinched visibly, and Anya went to him.

The thief stayed on his knees, staring down at his hand with the rope still tied about it. Then, with a startled blink, he scrambled to his feet and let Anya herd him from the platform as the crowd broke into a muttering, indistinct commotion behind them.

Anya had every intention of carrying on into the countryside without stopping, wanting to be well out of the town that had given her so much trouble. But halfway down a narrow, abandoned lane, the thief ahead of her stumbled and Anya realized his hands were trembling like leaves in a winter gale.

"Need a moment," he mumbled, and slid down to sit with his back against a stone wall. The thief hurriedly tucked his hands under his arms, but not before Anya caught a glimpse of something she'd never seen before.

From wrist to fingertips, where he would have lost it, the thief's right hand had been *changing*. His fingers elongated and shortened, thickening with age, thinning with youth, flashing from age-spotted to freckled to clear-skinned and back again. It was bewildering, and unnatural, and like nothing Anya had heard of in any of Weatherell's stories.

She pressed her lips together and kept her counsel, waiting as the thief put his head down on his knees and drew in a few

uneven breaths. The mongrel dog, Midge, emerged from an alleyway, smelling of rubbish and looking pleased with herself, and
pushed her nose under one of the thief's arms.

"Better?" Anya asked after a minute. The thief did not look up.

"Tieran of Stull," she said, prodding him with one foot. "Come
along. I've got to be going, so you do too. You heard what the
Arbiter said—you can't stay in this place."

The boy raised his head, jaw tense, eyes bleary. Pain had written itself across his features, though Anya could see no source to
it, and the strange shifting of his hand had ceased.

"Why'd you do that?" he asked. "Why'd you meddle? Could've
just left well enough alone. Could've just let me be. Your sort are
supposed to be untouchable—you aren't supposed to interfere."

Anya bit at her lower lip. Half a day out of Weatherell and
she was already failing at passing for a proper sacrifice. But surely,
she could not be the first Weatherell girl to get herself tangled up
in the affairs of the world beyond the wood. It was impossible, to
stay untouchable throughout all of Albion.

"He's right," a cool, unfamiliar voice said from behind Anya.
Tieran the thief scrambled to his feet, fear plain in his eyes and
flight plain in his posture, but a word from the speaker stilled
him. "No. You stay."

For a moment, Anya watched the thief. The way his gaze
roamed everywhere, searching for some manner of escape. The
way his hands had begun, almost imperceptibly, to tremble again.
He reminded her of a rabbit Ilva once caught in a snare, which had
taken to eating the crops in one of Weatherell's garden clearings.

The creature had lain still beneath Anya's hands, but she'd felt such wildness in it, and such a longing for life and freedom.

Ilva had snapped its neck, in the end—its leg was broken, its prospects hopeless. When Anya cried over it, Ilva told her it was for the best. That some lives carried on at the expense of others. And Anya had felt a spark at her core even then. A hint of outrage, at the injustice of the world.

She felt it again as she looked at the thief, though she didn't yet know why he should be so afraid. When she turned to the speaker, all she saw were three robed figures—the village Arbiter, still in black with the leather-bound Cataclysm beneath one arm, and two of the Elect's devout, clad in gray habits. There were a man and a woman, both of them with ageless, unlined faces, and it was the woman who'd spoken.

"Beloved," she said with a warm smile, holding out both hands to Anya. "I'm Orielle, and this is Roger. We oversee a way station in Sarum, and came to fetch you. The high roads are safe, but an unsettling place for a lamb such as yourself, especially in a time of such grave misfortune."

Anya did not reach back in return.

"I don't—I don't need an escort," she said. "Weatherell girls are meant to travel on their own. Isn't that in the Cataclysm? Arbiter Thorn used to read it aloud to the girls—how did it go?"

She put her hands behind her back, like a child practicing recitation. It brought the words to mind more readily and kept her from having to accept the touch of the unfamiliar woman before her.

"You have tried my heart, you have visited me by night,

you have tested me, and you will find nothing;

I have purposed that my mouth will not transgress.

With regard to the works of man, by the word of your lips

alone, I have avoided the ways of the violent.

My steps have held fast to your paths;

my feet have not slipped.

As for me, I shall behold your face in righteousness;

when I arrive, I shall make my sacrifice before your likeness."

The verses came quickly to Anya, once she began. She'd always found it easy to grasp and recall what Arbiter Thorn had taught the girls—once she heard what he'd said, the words stayed within her, there to be called up at need. They seemed to serve as a comfort to most of Weatherell's occupants, though Anya had not been very old before they began to taste of bitterness and ash.

"So you see," Anya finished, nerves singing at her own audacity, in having contradicted an authority not once but twice that day, "it's part of what makes us fit for an offering, isn't it? That the girls who go to the god manage to stay unmarred along the road. I want to do things properly. I don't want what happened with Il—what happened with the last girl—to happen again."

She waited, feeling transparent and unhappy and utterly faithless, to have dredged up the memory of Ilva's failure. But the idea of having her every step watched over set her skin to crawling, not unlike the way the thief's had done. How long could her lies last, if she was so closely overseen?

Orielle glanced at the village's Arbiter, who set a reassuring hand on Anya's shoulder. She fought to keep still beneath his touch.

"I spoke of wisdom in the square," the Arbiter said. "It would behoove you to strive for wisdom yourself. As the god is already stirring, more rests on you than on most others who've worn that band. Choose your company with care, child, and submit to the discernment of your betters, rather than seeking to exercise judgment of your own. You know little of the world, and we're here to work for your protection. Don't question our fitness for that duty, and we will not question yours."

"Yes, sir," Anya murmured, fixing her gaze on the ground. She could not help the treacherous tears that swam in her eyes—even knowing what lay ahead and what she intended to do, it stung her to be corrected. Regardless of her inner contradictions, she'd always striven to be good and to meet with the approval of those who governed Weatherell. A part of her craved that approval yet, despite the path she'd set herself upon.

The Arbiter reached out, tilting her chin up with one finger so that she must look at him. There was understanding in his broad face, but Anya hated the ungranted familiarity of his skin against her own.

"I spoke of wisdom and you spoke of mercy," the Arbiter said. "The Elect are not merciless, child. And we are grateful for your sacrifice on behalf of Albion. Hold the course. Keep yourself apart from the vices of the world, and undoubtedly the god will look more favorably upon your offering than he did upon the last."

I gave him nothing, Ilva said in her hollow, lifeless voice. She swam into being in the shadow of a nearby building, the imprint of the god's terrible hand burned across her heart.

He took from me instead.

After a glance, Anya looked scrupulously away. She would not have the Elect know she was haunted. Not have them know Ilva followed her on this journey to the mountain. They did not deserve another shred of her sister.

But the Arbiter had been right in one regard. Anya *would* have to cultivate wisdom if she was to survive the pitfalls along her way and fulfill Ilva's last request. She bowed her head humbly.

"I accept the offer of escort for now," she said. "For myself and my companions."

But when she glanced back over her shoulder, both the thief and Midge were gone.

FIVE

Sanctuaries

The city of Sarum lay sprawled against the banks of the River Avon like a cluster of oak galls festering on a once-healthy branch. Where the city touched the river's edge, the water of the Avon ran dark and sludgy, and a cloud of smoke hung above the convoluted tangle of streets, which sprawled across the flat land.

A pretty picture on the outside, Sylvie had said about Sarum. *But dark at its heart.*

Apparently, in the years since she'd wandered Albion, Sarum's façade had caught up to its soul.

Anya stood on the river's far shore, surrounded by the honey-rich light of late afternoon, and stared across at Sarum in disbelief.

"I didn't know there could *be* so many people," she said to Orielle and Roger, who stood on either side of her. She tried not to think that they were flanking her like guards—they had, after all, been pleasant and polite during the several hours' walk along the high road. They'd pointed out landmarks and shared bits of history and given her a fresh oatcake flavored with herbs. "It's preposterous, that we could make such a mark upon the land."

Orielle smiled. "And Sarum is not so large, in the grand scheme of things. Londin, where no Weatherell girl has ever gone, is Albion's largest city, and a den of vice. Yew and Wintencaster hold far more people too. But you will not see one of the great cities, besides Banevale. A sacrifice must not be tempted beyond what she can endure."

"Shall we?" Roger asked courteously, gesturing to a nearby footbridge. "I think we have enough time to take our newest lamb past Sarum Cathedral, before dusk settles in."

The city did not improve at closer proximity. Buildings rose precipitously above the narrow streets, blocking out the sun and most of the sky. There were people and noises and unpleasant smells everywhere. Despite her escort, the chaos left Anya feeling laid bare, as if she'd lost her skin and were walking about with her insides exposed. In an attempt to orient herself, she kept glancing up, toward a breathtaking spire that rose skyward to pierce the heavens.

And then all at once, Orielle and Roger led her out onto a pleasant, open green along a bend in the river. Trees clung to the banks with spotted cows standing in their dappled shade, while from the center of the grassy expanse there rose a building like nothing Anya had ever seen before. It was topped by the spire she'd been looking up at, and the expanse of the structure stretched from side to side—unfathomably large, monumental enough to fit the entirety of Weatherell within its walls. Soaring windows and archways and stone carvings ornamented every bit of it, the windows glinting with colored glass. Anya's lips parted as she stared—sun shimmered off those windows, splitting into rainbows of light.

"It's quite a spectacle, isn't it?" Orielle asked. "They built it on and around the ruins of an older sanctum, that was here before the god of the mountain woke."

Anya frowned, still looking up at the brilliant windows. "If the old sanctum was built before the god of the mountain woke, who was it for?"

"The dying god," Roger said dismissively, and the disdain in his tone brought Anya's attention back to her companions.

"I've never heard of the dying god," she said, and Orielle offered her a reassuring smile. In spite of herself, Anya felt a little safer, and less uncertain. It was easy to be guided, comforting to have her life fall into old patterns. She'd been a good student—to take on that role again lent her strength. And it eased her guilt a little to feign the role that would have been hers, if Ilva had not been born with the lion's share of their courage and Anya with most of their moral scruples.

"We don't consider him a god anymore," Orielle told her. "He lived centuries ago, but made grandiose claims and died in the end, and never returned despite promising that he would. His cult was brought here by the Romans and taken away with them as well, when the god of the mountain woke to fortify Albion with his presence."

"I never knew," Anya said, struggling to keep her face expressionless as excitement stirred within her. So her vengeance might not be an impossible task—those who'd once been worshiped could be killed. Until that moment, she'd worried that the god of the mountain might prove unassailable. But if one of Albion's gods had already died and passed from knowledge, might not another?

"Of course you didn't know," Roger said, still dismissive. "You didn't need to. Come, we'll pass closer to the cathedral before taking refuge at our way station for the night. Tomorrow, you may go your own way, and our blessings will go with you. We will never be far, so long as you keep to the high roads, and if you require our care, you need only return to the fold."

At the cathedral's doorstep, a little knot of people had gathered. An animated crier in ragged clothes stood on the broad threshold, bathed by evening light and blocking the way in. He blazed with faith, fiercer than the sun itself, and Anya felt her pulse quicken. Orielle let out a small, disapproving sound, but both she and Roger stopped and Anya stood with them, rooted to the spot by the stranger's conviction.

"Our god is a consuming fire!" the crier called, his wild eyes roving across the onlookers. "Even now, his wrath burns through Banevale, and soon it will overtake every city in this blasted land. He will purify us with flame, until each one of us bears his mark. Until we are set apart for his service and cleansed of our willfulness, for the time of our renewal is at hand!"

Anya shifted anxiously and glanced at the cathedral's center window, so that the crier would not be able to pin her with his gaze. From up close, she could see that the riot of colored glass formed a picture—that of a hunched, snow-dusted mountain before a brilliant sunset, with a hidden flame burning at the peak's heart. She'd never seen it before, but what could it be besides Bane Nevis, the god's own mountain in the north?

But much smaller, hidden among the stonework that surrounded the window, she found something more familiar— the outstretched figure of Ilva's little sufferer, carved into the stone of the wall, his wounds and band of thorns still present. Unconsciously, Anya ran a finger along the soft leather of her own scarlet band.

Movement drew her attention back down to earth. The crier had reached behind himself, into the shadowy cathedral archway, and Anya kept entirely still as he pulled a child into the light. The small girl he brought forward could have been no older than eight, and her clothes were as ragged and unkempt as the crier's own. Wincing, the child ducked her head in a vain attempt to hide the vicious burn spreading across her face. The scorched marks of vast, inhuman fingers puckered the skin at the edge of her mouth, one ear fused to her skull, and patches of hair were seared away where the god's palm had stretched to the back of her head. Showing no pity for her hurts, the crier seized her chin and forced her into the full light, so that everyone might look upon her wound.

An intolerable rushing noise rose up in Anya's ears at the sight of the burned child. Ilva's death had been the product of her cowardice, so surely this must be too—surely, if she'd gone to the mountain in her sister's stead, the god would have accepted her, gentle and biddable as she'd always been, and this small girl standing with tears in her eyes would not have had to suffer.

"He isn't meant to be leaving the mountain yet," Roger muttered to Orielle, annoyance undercutting the words. "We should have had more time."

"He *hasn't*," Orielle shot back. "I had news from Banevale—there's a group of zealots in the city, who've been collecting girls to send up the mountain. None of them will be fit, of course, and we've tried to convey as much. But no, they persist in this folly."

"There are none of us worthy," the crier ranted on, his voice muffled and distant as within Anya, something dark and bitter roared. "Not from the eldest down to the newest babe. But the god favors us with his fury and honors us with his refining touch, and when the last soul in Albion has been cleansed, we will rise anew, a people united for his service and his worship."

The sound within Anya had all but drowned the crier out. A half-solid vision of Ilva wavered in the shadowy doorway's gloom, staring out at the gathered listeners, her once-glad eyes dull and milky, her loose woolen shirt slipping from one shoulder, so that the livid impression of the god's hand was clearly visible. Anya swayed as her knees threatened to buckle.

Don't go, Ilva said accusingly, in that shattered part of Anya's soul where her sister's last words lived perpetually. *Don't let anyone else go.*

A bitter taste rose at the back of Anya's throat and she

swallowed, trying to catch her breath. The rushing noise and a wave of raw panic threatened to overwhelm her, but a Weatherell girl must stay her course. Must be steadfast and immovable in the face of the world's injustices. And so, staring at the god-touched girl from Banevale, Anya rallied, though the intent that bolstered her was not one of self-sacrifice.

I will put an end to you, Anya swore silently, reaffirming the vow she'd made to herself and to the distant god on his mountain. *However terrible you may be, I will cast you down or die in the attempt. For even a god should not be above his own laws, and I learned my lessons well. Those who take a life owe their own in exchange. Those who injure or maim must pay a debt in kind. There can be no greater debtor than you in Albion, and it is time you make good on all you owe.*

"I think we've heard enough of that," Orielle said crisply. "I wouldn't fret over it, child. Such things only happen in what we call a bale year—in the natural course of things, none but a Weatherell girl must bear the god's touch. Let this be a reminder to you to hurry on the road. More rests on your swiftness and purity than on most."

"There have been other years like this?" Anya asked. "How can that be? None of the girls but Ilva have ever—"

"Of course not," Roger cut in, his impatience evident. "But occasionally, every few generations or so, an offering is too small to keep the god quiet for the full eighteen years intended. A bale year occurs then, and he makes his power known until a girl can be brought to renew his rest. Enough questions."

Roger's eyes cut to a pair of liveried guards who were pushing through the gathered crowd. Anya recognized their uniforms—only that morning, she'd seen similar jackets of black and midnight blue on the guards who'd been watching the thief's trial and who'd taken her part.

"Enough of that racket!" one of them called out. "None but the Elect are permitted to spread their doctrines publicly in these parts, by order of your own Lord Selwyn, who has the backing of Lord Nevis."

"Come," Roger muttered. "Best we reach our way station before nightfall."

Anya nodded and followed obediently as she was led away, off the green and back into the maze of the city. Within minutes she was hopelessly turned around, and reached for the rough handle of her bone knife by way of reassurance. In the absence of the high road and its markers, Ana had no way to get her bearings, so she did just as she was told, as if she were truly a good and righteous lamb.

Orielle and Roger finally stopped in a nondescript back alley, lined with windowless brick walls, that smelled of boiled cabbage and mildew. Anya glanced about them uneasily.

"This isn't what I expected," she pointed out, but Roger was already tapping on a splintered wooden door. It swung open, revealing yet another gray-robed attendant. A foolish instinct to run surged up in Anya, as she thought of her deceitfulness and the blasphemy lodged at her core, but the servants of the Elect were serene, at least, calm and composed and familiar-looking, unlike the rage-filled crier on the green.

Orielle and Roger stepped inside, and Anya hesitated on the threshold. A faint noise caught at the edges of her consciousness—a distant, rhythmic hum, coming from within the way station of the Elect. She glanced back over one shoulder uncertainly.

It was dusk now, and the streets of Sarum were a labyrinth of unsettling shadows. Somehow, it frightened Anya more, thinking of being alone among so many people after nightfall, than camping in the woods or the hills might have done. And though she must hide the truth of her journey from the Elect at every turn, they were, at least, a reminder of home, and of an order to things that she understood.

"That crier on the green . . . ," Anya began, but her voice trailed off. She wasn't sure what to say about it. All she knew was that what she'd heard and seen had hurt her, in a deep and fundamental way.

Orielle held a hand out to Anya, her eyes full of sorrow and understanding. "Oh, child. You of all people know the Elect follow a different path than that. No wholesale destruction, no wanton harm. We make one worthy sacrifice, for the good of many, rather than allow such pointless suffering and unrest. Our way is a mercy, and I'm glad you know it now."

It all sounded just and right, when Orielle put it so. Weatherell, with its long line of suffering women, its trees hung with bone charms. Willem, with her handless wrists. Ilva—

But no. Anya would never see justice or mercy in what had happened to her sister. So she stepped forward, willing to risk a night with the Elect if it kept her on the path she'd chosen.

Though the way station's exterior had been filthy and faded, beyond the door lay a web of clean, whitewashed hallways. Beeswax candles in tin sconces lined the corridors, casting off warm light and filling the air with a sweet, honeyed smell. Everything was muted—serene, even—after the clamor of the city, and from far away, Anya could hear the notes of a chanted song. Occasionally, another gray-clad individual passed them as they wove through the hallways. Anyone they met nodded to Anya's companions but bowed low to Anya herself.

They stopped before an interior doorway, marked with an unfamiliar red-painted symbol.

"These will be your quarters for the night," Orielle said. "There's a bath waiting for you. We'll put out clean clothes and wash your things. When you've finished, just step into the hall. There will be an attendant who can take you to the refectory for supper."

"Thank you," Anya said. The relief of being somewhere quiet and safe and comprehensible was so acute that tears swam in her eyes, and she blinked them back, shame heating her face as she did.

"No, my dear." Orielle bent and pressed a kiss to Anya's forehead. "Thank *you.* First days are always hard, and we understand you're carrying grief with you as you travel—you lost a sister, yes? And your mother was a Weatherell girl too?"

Anya nodded, and Orielle ran a gentle thumb along her cheek. "How brave you are, child. What a sweet and irresistible offering you will make. A selfless sacrifice, and a perfect prayer."

The shame in Anya grew to irritation. She was not brave, but hollowed out and desperate, left utterly desolate by Ilva's passing. And she was sick to death of a world in which needless suffering was seen as sweetness and virtue.

"I'll have my bath now," she said, and though it was her habit to speak softly, there was an edge to the words.

With a small bow, Orielle and Roger drifted away. The moment they'd gone, Anya slipped through the bedchamber door. She let her pack fall from her shoulders and glanced about, finding herself in a spare but comfortable room. Sheepskins littered the plank floor, and a bed sat on a raised platform. A small desk stood next to the garderobe door Orielle had mentioned, and that was everything.

When Anya opened the door to the garderobe, a waft of soft warmth and steam billowed out. A sigh escaped the girl as she caught sight of an iron tub and a folding wooden table set beside it, laden with thick towels and bath oils. There was no mirror, in deference to Anya's role, but she had not expected one. The only glass in Weatherell was broken up by the Arbiter for charms, so that the girls might not catch a glimpse of their own image and become ensnared by vanity. Windows there were oiled paper, dishes all of clay. Anya had never beheld her own face, but knew, of course, that she must look something like Ilva.

Half an hour later Anya emerged from the bath, swathed in towels and feeling, for the moment, more relaxed than she had since leaving Weatherell. She smelled satisfyingly of rosemary and mint, and her damp hair hung in short, loose waves around her face. On the bed, she found a gray robe—a match for the ones the keepers of the way station wore. Anya stared at it doubtfully before retrieving her bone knife and its makeshift sheath from the bathroom. Taking out the blade, she picked a dozen stitches loose from the right side of the robe that had been set out. Strapping the knife to its customary place on her thigh, she pulled on the robe and nodded with satisfaction. The garment's loose folds hid what she'd done, and she could easily put a hand through the opening to reach her knife.

Slipping out into the hallway, Anya caught sight of an attendant at once. The keeper glided over to her, and bowed low.

"Mistress," her keeper said. "Please follow me."

The web of corridors was even more bewildering now that Anya was warm and comfortable, and her head swam with exhaustion. She followed the keeper obediently but halfway down one hall stopped before a set of double doors that were thickly painted with red Divinitas script. The sound of singing she'd heard earlier emanated from behind the doors. It set a strange, prickling feeling spreading across the back of Anya's neck.

"What's in there?" she asked.

The keeper escorting her bowed again. "That is our sanctum, mistress. Would you like to see it?"

Anya wanted to eat hot food and sleep in a bed and be on her way, in that order and as quickly as possible. But Ilva wouldn't have passed up the opportunity to see something new and strange.

"All right," Anya said, pressing two fingers to her temple. After a morning in the sun and an unsettling afternoon, her head ached fiercely.

As the keeper swung both doors open, the sound of chanting intensified. Beyond lay a cavernous space, filled with the guttering light of a hundred beeswax candles. Robed attendants knelt here and there, singing the odd, rhythmic song Anya had heard. But all that, she registered as an afterthought. What caught her attention and held it like a vise was the sanctum's far wall. A mural had been painted on it—long generations ago, if the faded colors and chipped places were any indication. It portrayed a barren, rocky mountain—a match for the one on the cathedral window—with a great city spreading far below. A creature like nothing Anya had ever seen stood on the mountainside. It was tall and terrible, human in form but wreathed in flame, with curling horns like a ram.

At its feet knelt a girl in a red collar.

The band around the girl's neck was by far the brightest aspect of the painted scene. Crimson and slick, it gleamed in the candlelight, and Anya watched with muted horror as one of the worshipers stood and walked to a side table. The woman took up a knife that lay on the table, its blade steel, not bone, and drew the cutting edge across the ball of her thumb. Then, singing softly, she approached the mural and kissed the feet of the creature on the mountainside.

For a moment she lingered, pressing her forehead to the likeness of her god, but soon carried on to the image of the kneeling sacrifice. And as Anya watched, the worshiper drew her bloody thumb across the neck of the painted girl.

"I—I have to go," Anya stammered to the keeper at her side. It felt as if her throat were closing, as if the band she wore were tightening and within moments she'd choke. In Weatherell, the god of the mountain was not worshiped like this. He was placated as a matter of course. He was obeyed and feared, but in a distant way. This veneration was like nothing she'd ever known, and it set a sickening sense of wrongness in her bones. It was only one step removed from the ranting conviction of the crier in the city—the same brutal faith, but with a veneer of serenity and control.

Anya backed into the hallway, and the keeper followed, a curious look on her placid face.

"I'm afraid you can't go," the keeper said, though her voice sounded muffled, as if Anya heard it from underwater. "Not until our prayers go with you."

Anya's head was splitting now, and she dropped to her knees. Fumbling at her side, she tried to reach for her knife with hands grown clumsy and slow.

But then the pain in her head redoubled and everything faded away.

SIX

A Living Prayer

Before she opened her eyes, Anya noticed the smell. Sharp and astringent. Medicinal. Like the clear spirits Leech Forster would use to clean wounds back in Weatherell, when someone had cut themself badly. After that came the realization that her back and shoulders felt unaccountably cold and sensitive to the air.

Fighting her way to full consciousness, she opened her eyes and shut them again as the room spun around her. After a moment, she risked another glance, taking stock as the fear in her rose to a fever pitch.

She lay on her stomach on a soft feather bolster, but there were no covers and no pillow. Anya's hands had been bound above her head, and her robe cut to the waist, leaving her back exposed. She seemed to be in the bedchamber she'd been taken to upon first arriving, or in a room very like it. From the raised platform on which the bed sat, she could see that the room was packed with gray-robed worshipers, kneeling on the floor and softly chanting their hymns. The sheepskin rugs had been pushed away, revealing crimson words in Divinitas script that had been painted onto the floorboards themselves.

Orielle stepped into Anya's field of view, and the girl grew entirely still. Willem's warning ran through her mind, echoing in the dim space where Ilva's ghost had taken up residence.

In Weatherell or beyond the wood, folk will string you up for blasphemy if they learn the truth behind your going. The Elect will kill you, and make your very name a curse.

Had they seen the truth in her so quickly? She'd hardly spoken—how was it possible for the Elect to plumb her soul with such deftness, and see the unholy fire that burned at her heart?

But when Orielle spoke, the words put her first fear to rest, replacing it with another.

"We're so fortunate to have been blessed with your presence, sweet one," the woman said. "The third of her line to go for a sacrifice. Surely you will succeed where your own kin failed."

"Let me go," Anya said, trying to sound insistent, but her voice faltered. "It's not right for you to treat me so. I'm going to the god willingly—there's no need to bind me."

"It will be easier for you to receive our prayers this way," Orielle said, her voice gentle. "If you were to struggle overmuch, you might mar them. We intend no disrespect, but this is for the best—for you and for Albion. In a bale year, the god requires more potent pacification than in the ordinary course of things."

"I don't know what you mean," Anya protested, giving in to

panic and tugging at the ropes that bound her hands. "Just let me go and I'll bring the god anything you want. I promise."

"Beloved." Orielle ran a finger along the line of Anya's jaw. "You cannot bring our prayers. You can only *be* them."

Something stung the place between Anya's shoulders and she gasped, trying unsuccessfully to wrench herself away.

"What is that?" she choked out. "What are you doing?"

"Preparing our living petition," Orielle explained. "Setting our words and worship into your skin, so that they will be all the sweeter to the god when joined with your sacrifice. Divinitas script, scribed in ink and mingled with blood, is an offering he cannot resist. You will be comely to the god indeed, when you carry our petitions to him, my love."

The stinging intensified, until it became a maddening burn. Through a haze of fear and outrage, memory seared across Anya's mind.

Sylvie, sitting before the fire in the cottage she shared with Philomena, while Philly gently washed her. Philly had sponged water over Sylvie's hunched form, the old woman's skin so paper-thin her veins showed through. But an eerie and intricate pattern of dark ink still marked her flesh, marching in orderly and angular rows across every inch of Sylvie's back. Sylvie would never speak of where it came from, but Anya and Ilva had known—they had no such practice in Weatherell, and so the markings could only have been made during Sylvie's time beyond the wood.

The pain between Anya's shoulders returned her to the

present. But she could do nothing, bound as she was by ropes and her own deceit, besides lie still with furious tears tracking down her face. It all went on and on, for what seemed like hours—the chanting, the overwhelming scent of spirits and warm beeswax candles, the humiliating pain.

They might have asked, Anya thought wretchedly. Had they asked, she'd have submitted to the request. Not happily. Not in the spirit desired. But of her own accord, to preserve the pretense under which she traveled.

They had not asked, though. They'd given no opportunity for this to be undertaken as an act of will and so, while Anya might have felt distaste for the markings had she chosen them, she found herself filled with choking hatred for the thing being done to her.

I don't want to be an offering, she thought with a new and sharp urgency. *I never have, nor a prayer, either. I will be a knife in the dark or nothing, no matter the cost.*

And then Roger appeared at Orielle's side.

"Lord Nevis's guards are at the door," he said tersely. "They're claiming Lord Selwyn has granted them the right to an inspection. I tried to put them off, but they won't go."

A flash of anger crossed Orielle's face. "Nevis has no right to interfere in our affairs so far south! Turn them away."

"It would be unwise, given the allies he's been making across Albion, and the way he's begun solidifying his power in Londin. At the rate he's going, he'll have added the city to his holdings by midwinter. Best to placate him until the god rests again," Roger said. "We can deal with Nevis once the bale year's passed. For now, you get everyone to their posts and manage the guard. I'll see the Weatherell girl stays hidden."

The pain in Anya's back subsided a little, and Orielle snapped a few words to the gathered worshipers. Their chanting stopped, and there was a sudden shuffling of bare feet and swishing of robes as the room emptied out.

Anya fought desperately for calm as Roger knelt beside her and severed the ropes around her wrists with a short, double-bladed knife. But the moment the bonds were cut, she scrambled away to the other side of the bed, putting it between them. She wanted space, and to never feel unwanted hands on her again.

Roger sighed. "Don't have time for your nerves, we got to be on our way. The guard won't take long looking everything over."

When Anya made no move to join him, Roger gave her a long-suffering look. "One way or another, you're going to want to come with me. Don't make me drag you, is what I'm saying. You won't like it, I won't like it, it won't be good for nobody. But you'll be glad of it, in the long run."

"I won't," Anya said stubbornly, the first small rebellion she'd permitted herself since waking bound to the bed. She fixed her eyes on the floor and refused to look up.

Frustration laced Roger's voice. "Fine. Then stay here. Let those grayrobes finish with you when they get back. But best be certain you don't speak a word out of turn—they got ways of making people pay for wrongdoing, and I don't think you being high and holy will keep you safe if you get their tempers up."

"They can't possibly do anything worse than what's already been done," Anya muttered, though the words rang false even as she spoke them.

"Hey," Roger snapped. "Look at me."

With reluctance, Anya dragged her gaze up to meet his. She and Ilva had gotten muddled together in her head—hadn't it always been Ilva who behaved so stubbornly when taken to task for wrongdoing? Anya was the soft and gentle one, quick to apologize, quick to own her sins. It was her sister who met chastisement with a spark.

Anya's eyes fixed on Roger's, and it felt as if he were rummaging about in her soul.

"You think you been treated poorly," he said. "And maybe you have, a bit. But *it can always get worse.*"

He spoke with such a weight of conviction that Anya's heart sank. Nodding, she stepped out from behind the bed.

"All right," she said humbly, pushing Ilva's borrowed intransigence aside. "I'm sorry. Tell me what I need to do."

Relief wrote itself across Roger's weathered face, softening his sharp hazel eyes. Something twisted in Anya at that—a half-formed suspicion, an unfounded thought that all was not right. But nothing was right in this place, or at least not right as Anya understood the word. So she let herself be led out of the bedchamber and into the bewildering web of white corridors.

Roger kept silent as they hurried through the endless hallways. Once, he unceremoniously pushed her into a recessed doorway and stepped before her, shielding her from view. Anya frowned as she glimpsed a mixed group of liveried guards and gray-robed Elect passing them by, in the throes of a heated argument. One of the guards peered narrowly at Roger, who shifted in place and ducked his head. A minute later, as they carried on past a dozen tightly shut doors, Anya began to speak, only to have Roger round on her with a furious gesture for quiet. She resigned herself, finally, to this fraught wandering—it was certainly better than lying facedown, fighting back revulsion as the god's prayers were inked into her skin.

At last, they tumbled down a narrow back stairway and emerged in an empty storage room, the walls stacked high with crates and the air smelling faintly of turnips. Anya's pack sat in one corner, and Midge bounded joyously up from where she'd lain on top of it. With a muffled sob, Anya knelt and wrapped her arms around the dog.

"Well, wherever did you come from?" Anya asked as Midge squirmed about and attempted to lick her face.

"Get your things on," Roger ordered, pointing to a wrinkled ball of damp clothes lying next to the pack and then turning his back to Anya. "They were drying when I found them, but I wasn't about to wait till they'd finished. Don't worry, I won't steal a look. Hurry it up, though, they're bound to come after us before long."

"*Who's* going to come after us?" Anya said, voice catching as she pulled her own familiar shirt over her head and wool cloth hit the place where looping, unreadable script had been etched into her skin. "Your people or the guard? I'm not sure who you're trying to get me away from."

"Took you long enough to puzzle that out," Roger grumbled. "Ready yet?"

"Ready." Anya tugged on her sturdy boots and scrambled to her feet. "Where are we going?"

"Anywhere but here," Roger answered. Raised voices echoed from behind the door at the head of the stairs and he glanced anxiously over one shoulder. There was something strange and indistinct about his face in profile—a vision-blurring aftereffect of whatever she'd been sedated with, Anya thought. She followed close behind him as he swung open an exterior door leading to an abandoned alleyway, and Midge sprang joyously out before them.

But just as Anya was about to step over the threshold and into freedom, she risked a look back, too. And at the head of the storeroom stairs, peering down into the dim by the light of a lantern, was Roger the selectman, whom she'd spent an afternoon with on the road. He wore his Elect-granted confidence like a second skin, a haughtiness in his bearing that whomever Anya was about to follow—whoever had donned his image so perfectly—had never possessed.

Even now, as Anya's eyes widened and she glanced back and forth from one Roger to the other, she could see a feral sort of wariness in every line of the figure who waited for her. He could not be a selectman, then. No selectman ever stood so, as if the whole world had set itself against him.

"Who on the god's mountain are you?" Anya hissed, suspicion sparking fear, which sparked fury in turn.

The false Roger seized her by the hand and pulled her out

into the alley, even as the selectman at the head of the stairs caught sight of the door shutting behind her.

"Come *on*," whoever had hold of Anya's hand growled. "Just trying to do you a good turn, aren't I? Well, I won't make that mistake again."

As he pulled her down the alley and out onto a nighttime street, Anya could see his face changing. Flashing disorientingly from shape to shape.

The thief.

Tieran of Stull.

Well, that was all right. She took hold of his hand properly and picked up the pace, and then they were pelting down the dark streets, taking a dozen unexpected turns until Anya could not have found her way back to the way station if she'd tried. Still, it felt like too little distance—as if she could never run far enough to shake the lingering smell of beeswax and spirits and the sting of her back as sweat rose on her broken skin. But the thief let out a stifled groan and stumbled down a narrow, unlit side street, sliding to the ground in the deep shadows beside an enormous straw-stuffed crate.

"What is it?" Anya panted as the thief pulled his knees to his chest and buried his face in his arms, just as he'd done in the village where she'd found him. His hands trembled, shifting from shape to shape with breathtaking speed, but he said nothing—only stayed as he was, folded in on himself. And a new scent rose up to replace the remnants of Anya's betrayal by the Elect—something dark and fierce, a breath of ashes and incense and sparks.

Tieran the thief's gray hood had fallen back, showing a tangle of recognizable brown hair, and his hands had slowed a little in their frantic changing. But footsteps were ringing out along the cobblestones on the busier road only steps away, and fear bit at Anya.

"That could be them," she whispered. "Hurry up, hurry up."

"Trying to, aren't I?" Tieran's voice was barely audible. "Just need another moment."

The footsteps fell silent just shy of the side street, and Anya's stomach turned over.

"You haven't got a moment," she pressed, her skin beginning to crawl and prick with the remembered touch of the needle. "Change yourself while we go—I don't care if it looks strange. It was a shock at first, but you don't need to hide from me."

"Not hiding from you. Hiding from myself, mostly. I just need—no, there. There it is."

When he raised his head, Tieran was himself again—the boy she'd seen struggling like a demon at his trial for theft. The same bleary, pained look he'd worn after the thieves' block had etched itself across his now-familiar face.

Tieran got to his feet unsteadily, but without a sound. He held a hand out to Anya and she took it unhesitatingly. Together, they slipped away into the dark, just as a pair of gray-robed figures bearing lanterns rounded the corner from the main road.

SEVEN
First Victory

A loose stone turned under Anya's foot as Tieran urged her across a stream. She stumbled and slipped, falling to her knees in the cold, brackish water, which immediately soaked her to the waist.

"Come *on*," Tieran said sharply from the far bank, with Midge at his side. Anya couldn't understand his continued urgency. There'd been no sign of anyone following them since Sarum. All around, there lay nothing but empty, shadowed countryside.

The thief had set a punishing pace through the night, cutting across fields and hedgerows and narrow lanes in patterns that made no sense to Anya. The eastern sky was beginning to grow faintly gray, and birds sang sleepily in the hedges, but Tieran showed no sign of slowing.

Her second day on the road, Anya thought wearily as she forced herself to her feet, water and duckweed streaming from her. Her second day as a Weatherell girl, and already she'd put herself at odds with the Elect. Already she'd made her own life more difficult and marked herself out as disobedient. It had been madness to go with the thief—to flee the Elect just because she disagreed with the manner of their praying. She ought to have stayed and borne their ritual, and left with a smile.

She ought to go back and beg forgiveness and make amends. The Elect were everywhere in Albion—she hadn't a hope of avoiding them. But even the thought of returning to the way station soured her stomach. So she scrambled up the far riverbank and followed after Tieran as he led her on, through a wooded copse and out at the far side, where the distant ruins of a church were just visible, silhouetted against gray sky.

"There," Tieran said, pointing to the church. "We stop there."

Up close, there wasn't much to the building. Just a hollowed-out stone shell, but Tieran threw open the rotted trapdoor to a crypt and beckoned to Anya. Midge hurried down the crypt stairs at once, bent on examining the fascinating, musty smells wafting up from the gloom.

"Down here," Tieran said. "Get yourself in behind one of them stone coffins and keep out of sight till noon, at least."

"What about you?" Anya protested. "Where are you going?"

The thief shrugged. "Dunno. Not staying here, though. Never wanted to get caught up with you—I don't like Weatherell girls, or what they stand for, and seems to me you're worse than most. So this is where we part ways. You done a good turn for me, now I done one for you. Neither of us owe each other nothing."

"Getting me into trouble with the Elect my first day out of Weatherell is hardly a good turn," Anya protested. "I can't avoid them all the way to the mountain, and what'll I say when they catch me up?"

Tieran stared at her flatly, his hazel eyes expressionless. "You'd rather I let them finish what they were doing? Just left you there?"

"I don't know," Anya said. "I *should* wish you'd let me be, and let them do as they wanted. It's going to complicate things—that I don't, and that you didn't."

"Well, enjoy your complications," the thief said. "They're none of my business no more. Now, would you get in that hole?"

Anya only looked at him, as she used to look at Ilva when her wild twin was being especially infuriating.

Tieran let out a gusty sigh. "Would you *please* get in that hole?"

With as much dignity as she could muster, Anya got into the hole, where Midge greeted her with an enthusiastic swipe of slimy tongue across the back of her hand. Anya felt about in the shadows until she found a crypt to crouch behind. Up above, the trapdoor closed, blocking what little there was of the faint predawn light.

Anya waited. She put her head down on her knees in an agony of guilt and indecision, torn apart by warring desires. She wanted to be rid of the Elect. She wanted to pacify them. She wanted to kill a god. She wanted to vanish into the wilds of Albion. She wanted to walk the long north road to whatever end awaited her. She wanted to never move again—to sit here forever in the dark, surrounded by the familiar smells of earth and old bones.

Across from Anya, an image of Ilva wavered to life, sitting in the sole shaft of wan light drifting from above. Her sister, who had been so free and bold in life, looked like a lost soul. Smeared with grave earth, face half eaten away by decay, Ilva sat quietly, mirroring Anya's own posture. And though everything about this Ilva was grotesque—her mottled purple-and-gray skin, her jawbone showing through torn flesh, the gaping hollow where one of her sweet, bright eyes had been—Anya was overwhelmed by a surge of fierce and broken love. Of longing and grief and heartbreak so powerful they shook her to the core.

Down through the choking sea of her emotions, voices drifted.

"I hate these places," one said. It was a woman, her words sharp and quick. "Old sanctums, old ways, all tangled up with that nonsense the Elect peddle. If you ask me, we ought to raze every ruin like this—get rid of them entirely, so people forget what came before as well as the yoke they've been toiling under."

"Ruins do give me the creeping horrors," another woman answered, her voice softer, sweeter. "If there was ever a place for ghosts, it's one like this. I doubt they stopped here long, anyhow. Let me walk along the outer walls while you poke about inside. If you do see any sign of them, give a shout."

"What'll Lord Nevis do if they don't turn up?" the sharp-tongued woman asked. Anya strained to listen, needing to hear the answer. As one of the women passed by the trapdoor, she caught a glimpse not of gray robes, but of a midnight-blue-and-black guard's uniform and tall, well-kept boots.

"Oh, he'll have us wait a few days at least," the gentler-spoken of the two said. "The girl seems devout, though if we're lucky, she'll be less so than the last one. We'll keep a watchful eye for when she turns up on the road again without getting close enough to cause a fright. The Elect are bound to be on edge after our intrusion at their way station, and we don't want them spiriting the girl away entirely. They could get her from here to the mountain without anyone catching another glimpse of her if they wanted to, but they do love to uphold their traditions and make a spectacle of their sacrifices."

"Well, if Nevis is happy enough to wait, I'd rather not have gone on this goose chase at all," the sharp-tongued woman grumbled. "Let's get it over with and turn for home—I want a hot bath and breakfast."

Anya kept breathlessly still, drawing Midge close and leaning farther into the shadows behind the crypt. Taking the movement as an invitation, Midge climbed onto Anya's lap, though she was big for such things. But Anya hugged her close and waited as muffled footsteps sounded overhead.

The trapdoor hinges whined as it was swung open. The air lightened. A wooden groan from the crypt steps echoed through the dank space as one of the guards descended halfway and swung a lantern about. But the pool of warm light never reached Anya, and Midge stayed quiet.

The guard retreated.

The trapdoor slammed back in place.

Muffled voices took stock, and faded away.

Anya buried her face in Midge's tangled fur and waited for

her pulse to slow. She stayed a long time in the dark of the crypt, and when at last restlessness forced her to risk going aboveground, the sun was high overhead. Taking a moment to get her bearings, she cast about herself, looking for her pack.

And remembered with a sinking feeling that the thief had been wearing it, when they arrived at the ruined sanctum.

"It was heavy enough that there's no chance he just forgot," she said dryly to Midge. "Mercy, I hate it out here. And I'm half starved. I don't suppose you could go catch a rabbit?"

Midge cocked her head to one side and panted, a doggish grin on her mottled face.

"No, I didn't expect so," Anya said. "And I'm sure finding the high road for us is right out. We'll just have to head north, then. Can't go far wrong like that."

Squaring her shoulders, she took a moment to get her bearings before setting off, with Midge bounding along at her side.

† † † †

Hours later, it had grown fully dark once more, but Anya could not bring herself to stop walking. The raw skin across her back stung and burned as her woolspun shirt chafed it. Every muscle in her protested at the dogged trudging onward, and her eyes were gritty for want of sleep. But she was haunted by Ilva, haunted by the burned child she'd seen at Sarum's cathedral, haunted by her memories of Willem and Sylvie and Philomena and every other Weatherell girl who'd walked this way before. Ghosts drove her on, and she could not bear to stop.

She might have walked the night through, crossing over rolling hills and wooded valleys and wheat fields lying silver in the moonlight, had Midge not stopped her. At the bottom of a dell where a little stream laughed between quaking aspens and silver birches, the dog let out a short bark and hurried off. A moment later she was back, plumy tail waving like a flag, obviously eager for Anya to look at whatever it was she'd discovered.

"Oh, all right," Anya sighed. "I suppose you deserve to be humored."

With some reluctance, she followed Midge around one of the massive boulders that littered the valley—this one taller than Anya and twice as wide.

On the other side, she found herself face to face with Tieran the thief.

He sat cross-legged, a small, nearly smokeless campfire between them. Tieran wore Anya's oilskin coat—an oversized one Ilva had set out from Weatherell with, which Anya had pieced together herself and painstakingly given an inordinate number of pockets. In daylight, it was far too warm for the coat, but it was a comfort by night or in rain, and doubly so to Anya because it had been her sister's.

Next to him, Tieran had Anya's pack. From the branches of an aspen, he'd hung her traveling charm, made from the bones of a long-forgotten Weatherell girl. He held a half-eaten winter apple in one hand and a piece of waybread in the other. And when Anya rounded the boulder, he did not even have the good grace to seem ashamed. Instead, he gave her a narrow look.

"You been following me, Anya Astraea?"

Anya met his stare with the righteous indignation of someone certain that she occupied the moral high ground. "You *stole* my *things*."

Tieran shrugged. "Not my fault you don't keep your wits about you."

Anya opened and shut her mouth, then shook her head at him. "That's just—why would you rescue me, then rob me and run off half a day later? You're very inconsistent!"

Midge sat down next to the fire, halfway between the two of them. Tongue lolling out, she glanced back and forth, as if pleased to have reunited such troublesome charges, and to have her small, self-appointed flock back together again.

Tieran said nothing to Anya. Instead, he shifted himself about to lean back on his elbows and took a loud bite of winter apple.

"I have my wits in good order now," Anya continued frostily. "And I expect you to return my belongings."

Tieran squinted up at her. "You don't have anything in order. Look like you're about to fall over. Sit down, Weatherell girl. Have an apple."

Marching over to him, Anya scooped up her pack and dropped down to sit with it clutched tight. Midge, in turn, sidled over to Tieran and stared longingly at the waybread he held.

"Be good," Tieran warned as he held the waybread out. To her credit, Midge took the offering with great delicacy, before bolting it down in one piece.

For a moment, an exquisitely awkward silence fell over the small camp. The thief looked everywhere but at Anya, while Anya stared resolutely at him.

"Why did you do that?" she asked at last. "Why did you come get me clear of the Elect and those guards, whoever they are?"

Tieran shrugged again, and a wave of irritation washed over Anya. Well, if he really wanted to be unforthcoming, she'd simply treat him the way she'd done with Ilva, whenever Ilva was in the wrong.

Anya resumed her pointed and wordless staring, which obviously unnerved the thief.

"Don't like being beholden to no one," he said eventually. "That's why I done it. But now we're evened out. You done me a good turn with that village Arbiter and I got you out of the way station and clear of Lord Nevis's guards—the guard only want you to spite the Elect, Lord Nevis and them are at each other's throats these days. Since we're back on the same footing again, it's all right for me to steal from you."

He was an odd and thorny puzzle, this thief, but he knew far more of the world beyond the wood than Anya did. And if she'd learned anything over the past two days, it was that out of the forest, she was also out of her element. She could use some help.

She could use a guide.

When Ilva had sought to do wrong or to bend someone to her will, it had always been the product of impulse. Never one to waste much time on forethought, she plunged into mischief with no plan, but no malice, either, transparent in her desires despite the ease with which she lied. Anya, for all she hated deception, was more opaque. More circumspect. With her needle-sharp conscience, she'd learned to pick her battles. To save her lies for when it counted. To plot out her misdeeds with care.

She chose each of her words carefully now, weighing the balance of truth and deceit in each of them.

"We're not really even, though, are we?" she said. She let her eyes drift to the fire, giving the thief space. Let him think. Let him breathe. Let him squirm under the weight of her half-truths. "You heard me, back in that village where they wanted to take your hand. My mother was a Weatherell girl. She lost both *her* hands to the god of the mountain. My sister, Ilva, was a Weatherell girl too. She went to the mountain in spring and died for her trouble, which is why I've got to go now. My family's been torn apart for the sake of Albion—*I've* been torn apart for the sake of Albion, before ever laying eyes on the god. But I'm going to give more still to buy peace for you and everyone else on this blighted island, so we'll never be even, Tieran of Stull. Not if you spend your entire life trying to make up the debt."

Tieran shifted uncomfortably, and Anya could feel the weight of his regard as he truly saw her for the first time. Let him look. Let him take her in, small and lost and harboring perilous fire, plagued by guilt and the ghost of her broken sister and already half broken herself.

"Sorry about your family," he said, with characteristic sullenness. "Sorry about stealing your things, too. Suppose you're wanting this back."

He began to shrug out of the oilskin coat, and Anya held up a hand. "No. Keep it for now. I'm a Weatherell girl—I can ask anyone for another and they'll give it to me without a second thought. But I don't expect you've been given much, or done many favors in life."

When Anya glanced over at him, Tieran met her gaze and did not look away.

"Don't suppose I have," he muttered. There was something in his sly hazel eyes as he pulled the coat tighter about himself—a hesitance, an uncertainty—that pained Anya.

"Well, it's yours," she said. "And that's regardless of how you answer what I'm about to ask."

At once, the thief's unguarded look was replaced by suspicion.

"I want you to take me north," Anya said. "I think you'd be just the right person to help. I'd like to turn up on the high roads often enough that the Elect know I'm still on my way and still doing my duty, but keep out of their reach for the most part. And out of reach of those guards, until I know what it is they want with me. I just . . . don't want another incident like Sarum."

"Whyever not?" Tieran asked. "Should've thought any girl would love to be pulled off the street by grayrobes, tied to a bed, and stuck full of needles and ink, all without so much as a *by your leave*."

Anya let out a short laugh, but winced as her stomach twisted. "I hated that."

"Course you did," Tieran said. For a moment, an almost sympathetic expression crossed his sharp, calculating face. "Anybody would."

Anya let his admission linger between them for a moment, knowing she was a heartbeat away from winning her first victory in the world beyond the wood.

"So you'll come with me then?" she said quietly.

"Not the right sort of person for this," Tieran answered with reluctance. "For trusting, or for heading out with on the road. Don't think I'm going to do anything but let you down. Thing is, I was born leaving, Anya Astraea, and the first words out of my mouth were a lie. I'm not fit company for someone good. Someone like you."

The guilt that fueled her ate away at Anya's insides, corrosive and galling. But she could hardly tell Tieran the truth—that she was no true sacrifice. That she'd never wanted to be one. Instead, she was a heretic and a liar.

"You're wrong," she told the thief. "You're just who I need."

EIGHT
Shorn Threads

Tieran was gone.

Anya sat up groggily beside the smoking ashes of last night's fire. The sun was fully up, birds sang in the trees with aggressive good cheer, and the thief had vanished. He'd left the pack at least, and Midge sat impatiently at Anya's feet, staring down toward the stream. On instinct, Anya reached beneath her bedroll for the makeshift bone knife that was her last piece of Ilva. She'd set it aside surreptitiously the night before but wasn't sure if anything got past the thief.

That was missing too.

Fury surged through her, sweeping from head to toe. She'd rather have lost anything else. She'd have suffered the fear and indignity the Elect subjected her to a hundred times before she gave up her last bit of her sister. If she caught the thief, she'd have words for him. More than words, she'd kill him if she got a chance, she'd—

"Here," Tieran's voice said from behind Anya. "You ground the blade down all wrong."

Turning to face him, Anya froze.

"What—what did you *do* to yourself?" she managed after a moment.

Tieran stood before her, sopping wet from the waist up, his clothes damply sticking to him. With one hand, he held out her bone knife. But though he still wore the same shape, he looked entirely different—his filthy, matted brown hair had been shorn off, cut right to the scalp, and there were a dozen places where he'd accidentally nicked himself or sheared away patches of skin.

Anya's face burned and she fixed her gaze on Midge. In Weatherell, girls who might someday serve as a sacrifice were kept strictly separate from the village's boys most of the time. They saw each other in public and at community gatherings, but that was all. And a Weatherell boy would never have dreamed of appearing before a girl soaked to the skin.

Or at least, would never have dreamed of doing so in front of Anya. Ilva and some of the other girls had had their share of misadventures in the forest, with the boys and with each other, but none of it had ever appealed to Anya.

"You getting sick?" Tieran asked in his blunt way. "You look poorly."

"I'm in a hurry," Anya snapped. "We're wasting time, and every moment counts. We can't afford to stop for . . . this."

She waved a hand in his general direction, then scrambled to her feet, finding it impossible to take back the bone knife Tieran held out without actually looking at him. Clean, and with his matted hair gone, there was a new intensity about the thief—an internal edge made manifest, visible in the stubborn line of his jaw and the gleam of his eyes and the hunger-lean shape of his body.

"Fixed that for you," Tieran said, as Anya snatched her knife back with poor grace. "Sharpened it properly this time. If I get a chance, I'll show you how to look after a blade."

"How'd you even know I had it? Or get it from me?" Anya asked as she slipped the knife through her slit pocket and into the makeshift sheath she wore strapped to her thigh.

Tieran stared longingly at a half-eaten piece of waybread, lying forgotten on Anya's bedroll. "Can tell when someone's got a blade hidden on them. And I took it while you were sleeping. You sleep like someone who's been safe all her life, Anya Astraea."

Letting out an irritable sigh, Anya handed over the waybread and Tieran crammed it into his mouth. He watched as Anya meticulously packed her bedroll but made a disapproving noise when she moved to lift the pack.

"Shouldn't carry that today," he said. "Not after I had it yesterday. I'll do it."

Anya raised an eyebrow. "You've as good as said you'll disappear at some point, and last time you did, you took my things with you. So I'll be the one to carry the pack."

"Suit yourself," Tieran said with one of his habitual shrugs. "Only I did this"—he gestured to his shorn and mangled head—"on account of that cell I spent the night in before you found me. Place was full of crawlers—lice, fleas, I don't like to think what else. Since I had the pack yesterday . . ."

His silence spoke volumes, and Anya shuddered, taking a quick step back and automatically brushing at her arms.

"Why didn't you just *change* yourself to deal with it, instead of butchering your own scalp?" she asked.

Heaving the pack up and onto his shoulders, Tieran fussed over the straps. "Not that simple. I can't just pick one piece to change and not the rest, and if I do make a change, it's awfully hard to hold on to until I get used to the shape."

"Does it hurt?" Anya said curiously. "Changing, I mean?"

She thought of how he'd looked, both in the alley after his trial and when he'd gone back to his own shape after impersonating Roger. It had seemed like a hardship to him. Like something to be avoided whenever possible.

"Not the changing itself. But the stopping it, yeah. That hurts."

"I'm sorry."

Tieran sniffed. "Don't be. I'm used to it."

Anya glanced over at him. He had his eyes fixed on the ground and on his ragged boots, which were more patches than shoe leather.

"Were your parents the same?"

"No. Neither of them were much like me."

"Well, thank you for what you did back at the way station," Anya told him. "I should have said it earlier, and I know it would have been easier to just leave me with those people."

Tieran scuffed one foot against the ground and flushed, scowling to himself. "Wasn't nothing. Just don't like being beholden, that's all."

Anya couldn't help but smile at his discomfort. "Well, you'll be the least beholden person in Albion, once you get me to Bane Nevis. Are we ready?"

Midge got to her feet at the word, tail wagging cheerfully, but Tieran shook his head.

"No, we're not. You got both the Elect and Lord Nevis's guard out there looking for you. Maybe you don't know what that means, being from Weatherell, but they're at each other's throats more often than not now, Nevis and the grayrobes. He wants their power and sooner or later, I expect he'll try to take it. But the Elect won't give it up unless all of Albion lies in ruins. They're not fighting in earnest yet, just circling each other, trying to sort out weak spots.

"You're a weak spot, Weatherell girl. The Elect need you and so Nevis wants you. I dunno how far he'd go to get you on his side—the thing people like about your sort is that you choose. You decide to be a sacrifice, and so it lets everyone else feel like they haven't got blood on their hands. Nevis is no fool. He'll try to make you choose him, instead of what you're bent on, so that it seems like the righteous path. How he means to convince you, though, I couldn't say."

Anya narrowed her eyes, surprised to have heard so many words at once from the prickly thief. "You seem to know an awful lot about all this."

"I listen," Tieran said flatly. "I pay attention. That's all. But you'll be badgered from here to the god's mountain if you're wearing that red collar. With it, you're an invitation to anyone you see. Without it, you're ordinary. No one special. You ought to take it off, if you really want to escape notice."

Anya's hand flew to her throat. She'd never considered removing the crimson band—it would make life simpler, to be sure, but it was, as Tieran said, the unmistakable mark of a Weatherell girl. Ilva had worn hers all the way to Bane Nevis and back. As had Willem, and everyone else who went before.

Removing the collar would truly feel as if she had set herself on a different path than them. Between the half-finished prayer inked onto her back and a half-worn band, she would be a strange and profane thing indeed.

"It's sewn on," she said quickly, before she could change her mind. "You'll have to cut it off."

She turned her back to Tieran and he stepped closer. She could feel him behind her, the shift of his weight, the stir of air on the back of her neck, the smell of river water. His nearness put her off-center, and she fell perfectly still.

When Tieran's fingers brushed the back of her neck, Anya's eyes shut of their own accord. But the desire to shrink away that she felt with most people never came. Instead, she caught her breath with a hitch as something cold and keen slipped against her skin.

Anya felt a faint whisper of pressure as the leather collar tugged at her throat.

Tieran reached around and dropped the scarlet band into her cupped hands. Only the threads had been cut—the rest of it remained perfectly intact, its carefully crafted edges immaculately smooth. Anya realized, with a sudden pang that set her heart to pounding, that the thief still held a short, wicked-edged steel knife, a counterpart to her hidden bone blade, and that the hand he grasped it with rested on her shoulder.

He could just as easily have killed her as cut off the band. An image of the fresco she'd seen in the Elect's way station flashed before her eyes—of a girl on her knees, a line of offertory blood drawn across her throat.

"Sometimes, Weatherell girl"—Tieran's voice was low and unexpectedly earnest, his words spoken so close that Anya could feel as well as hear them, warm against her skin where the knife had been cold—"life's easier if no one knows who you really are."

When he stepped away, Anya's fear melted, leaving only an overwhelming sense of relief. She stared down at the severed band and might have been weightless, she felt so unexpectedly free.

† † † †

It was a hot, still day, muggy with the promise of eventual storms. The western horizon was gray and glowering, but the weather would not break, and Anya grew slick with sweat as she trudged along behind the thief. Blisters had sprung up on her heels, the Elect's half-finished prayer stung furiously, and it felt as if she were already, against her will, being pushed into the shape of a sacrifice.

Only the absence of the band around her neck consoled her.

She had, in this small regard—in trusting Tieran the thief, rather than the Elect—forged her own path. But the north road still seemed impossibly long, and, from the corner of her eye, she caught glimpses of Ilva, half decayed and keeping pace with her from behind the hedgerow.

Anya couldn't help but glance over whenever there was a gap in the hedge, and each time, Ilva fixed rheumy eyes on her, bones clattering within the fraying travel clothes she'd worn the day she returned from the mountain.

At last Tieran stopped in his tracks, from where he'd been carrying on a few paces ahead. Midge mirrored the action, lying down and panting in the middle of the empty country lane.

Turning, the thief fixed Anya with an inscrutable look. "You seeing ghosts, Weatherell girl?"

Too shocked to answer, Anya only stared back at him, wide-eyed.

"Can tell when somebody's seeing something what no one else can. Who is it?"

"My sister," Anya admitted. "Ilva. Who went to the god this spring and died when she ought to have lived. It should've been me who went, and not her. If I'd had the courage for it, she'd still be here, and everything would be happening the way it's meant to, instead of falling apart."

Tieran nodded. "Used to see my mum. Almost miss it now, except then I remember that sometimes it scared me half to death. But she was company, at least, while it lasted."

"How . . . how did she die?" Anya asked hesitantly. She could sense something flighty and anxious about the thief, always there, always lurking beneath the surface, even when he blustered. It made her want to be careful with him. To find a way to put him at ease.

He was silent a moment before answering.

"Died in a fire," he said at last, and turned and walked on.

They came to a small, deserted village just as the storm finally broke. The buildings were gray and wraithlike, all clustered together with the rotted ruins of a palisade wall fallen down around them. It was an old place, then—the Romans had been the ones who loved to build walls. They'd put them around their cities and towns and settlements, and in a failed attempt to hem in the god of the mountain, built two farther north that stretched the width of Albion itself. Arbiter Thorn had said that since their departure and the Elect's rise to power, Albion lived in a different way. Towns cropped up without any walls around them at all, and people led their lives freely, in the open.

Unless you're unlucky enough to be born in Weatherell, Ilva would always whisper to Anya at that point. *Then you might as well be living your life in a cell.*

Just as Tieran and Anya crossed the tumbledown palisade, lightning flashed overhead and the sky opened up, pelting them with driving rain. Midge pressed herself anxiously against Anya's legs, afraid of the thunder, and Tieran shouted something that was lost in the din of the heavy rainfall.

"What?" Anya called, shielding her eyes to keep the water

from blinding her. Tieran turned and walked back, putting both hands on her shoulders and leaning forward to speak with his face next to her own. He was better off in the downpour than she was—seeming impervious to the afternoon heat, he'd kept the oilskin coat on since they set out that morning. But rain beaded down his ridiculous shorn scalp and softened the lines of his sharp, canny profile.

"Know a place here where we can stay the night," he said, having to raise his voice even with so little space between them. "It's not much, but it'll be dry."

At the center of the deserted village lay a long stone building that might once have been a communal barn. Its moss-covered slate roof still looked sound, and the door Tieran led Anya through clung to its hinges against all odds.

Inside, it was dark as midnight without a moon. Anya unconsciously reached out and found the thief reaching for her hand too. His touch was warm despite the weather—Anya, meanwhile, was shivering, and her fingers had gone ice cold.

"That's no good," Tieran murmured, speaking low and soft now that the sound of the rain was muffled. Anya could not even make out his silhouette, but he caught her other hand and held them both between his own until the worst of the chill retreated.

"Better?" he asked, and Anya nodded, forgetting that he could not see. "Right. You wear the coat and I'll see about finding something to make a fire with."

Anya felt the weight of the oilskin settle over her shoulders, followed by the sudden emptiness that comes when someone who has stood close to you steps away.

But the thief did not get far.

"Ren," a man's gruff voice said as a lantern flared to life in the dark. "Is that you? What in the green hills are you doing here?"

NINE
Wanderers

In quick succession, a dozen more lanterns were lit. Figures appeared in the ruddy glow—thirty people at least, ringing the barn Anya and Tieran had mistaken for empty. The strangers stared at her wide-eyed, and Tieran, caught in the middle of the barn's open space, began to back toward Anya, sparking frantic energy like a cornered cat.

"Ren." The man who'd spoken stepped forward, holding out a hand. He was tall and thickset, with graying wheaten hair and a ruddy face. "Don't think I can't tell that's you. You can change all you like, but we know you well enough to see past it. What're you doing this far south? I didn't think—I thought we might not see you again."

"Not Ren," Tieran muttered, slinking to Anya's side. "Don't know who you're talking about. Don't know who you are."

The fair-haired man sighed, a gusty, world-weary sound. "I thought we'd got past this, Ren. I thought we'd earned a bit of honesty from you."

Tieran drew closer to Anya, near enough that his shoulder brushed her own. She could feel him trembling, as he'd done in the alley after the trial and when they'd run from the Elect. It was strong emotion, Anya thought, that made it harder for him to keep his shape. At the realization, a surge of protectiveness shot through her. She stepped forward, placing herself between the strangers and Tieran, chin jutting out stubbornly.

"He says he doesn't know who you're talking about," Anya said, though as always, speaking to more than a handful of people set her stomach to doing anxious things. "So you'd better leave him be. We're sorry to have intruded—we thought this place was empty. But seeing as it's occupied, and we've no interest in company at the moment, we'll be on our way."

Turning back to Tieran, she slipped her hand into his and nodded toward the door.

"Come on," she whispered. "We can leave. It's just a bit of rain, and I'm soaked through already. We'll find someplace else to stay."

But Tieran remained rooted to the spot, staring at the strangers with a haunted look that felt all too familiar to Anya.

"Ren," the fair-haired man said, wistfulness tempering his deep voice. "Don't be like this. I'm begging you—there's nothing gone wrong between us we can't fix. Nothing I wouldn't forgive. You know that."

"Not Ren," Tieran repeated. His shoulders were still hunched, everything about his posture closed off and unwelcoming, but the words came out a little softer. "I'm Tieran now."

"Tieran then," the fair-haired man said swiftly. "Good. Tieran.

You know whoever you want to be, we're happy to have you. And your friend, too—I'm Matthias, girl, and if you're a friend of Tieran's, you'll always have a place with us."

Scanning the faces of the strangers behind him, Anya wasn't so sure. She saw approval from a few of them, disapproval from others, and indecision from most. But the fair-haired man, Matthias, took an uneasy step forward, as if he was afraid drawing closer might make the thief bolt. Anya was half afraid of it herself—Tieran held on to her hand like it was a lifeline, gripping so tight to keep himself in one shape that she worried his touch might leave a bruise.

But the instinct to help, to set at ease, to make peace, was always at the forefront for her. Hadn't she been the cause of a hundred tentative resolutions between her cold, furious mother and wild, rebellious twin? They'd given her a sense for conflict and tension, a way of knowing where to push or relent if a truce was to be made.

"Tieran?" Anya murmured. "Who are these people? It's all right to say."

Tieran tore his gaze from Matthias and fixed his eyes on her. The look he gave Anya was so fraught with shame and fear and longing that she wondered how he kept his shape at all.

"Told you I'm a liar, Anya," he said, the words fraying even as he spoke them. "Told you sometimes I can't find a way to get the truth to settle on my tongue."

"I don't mind," she told him. "Just tell it to me now. I want to hear."

The thief shifted, darting a look from her to Matthias and back again.

"This is . . . my family," he admitted, though she could see the immense effort it took for him to get the words out. "As close to it as I've got, anyway."

"Could've left that last bit off," Matthias said with a sad smile. "We're your family, Tieran, full stop. You know no matter what's gone before or what comes next, to me, you're a son. Doesn't matter about the blood. Doesn't matter about the bones. Doesn't matter what you've done, either, not ever."

Anya could *feel* the thief's hand changing within her own, and then he was gone, across the space left between him and the big man with the wistful eyes. Matthias wrapped Tieran in a mountainous embrace, the slighter thief all but swallowed up by his arms, and despite his size, despite the pride with which he carried himself, the older man began to weep. He did it openly, without shame, as if it was a gift and a joy and a part of the relief evident in both him and Tieran.

Watching them, Anya struggled to fight back tears of her own. She loved Willem cautiously and had loved Ilva immoderately, but Willem was eaten up with anger, and Ilva had been filled with longing for a world beyond Weatherell. Neither of them had looked at Anya the way Matthias looked at Tieran—as if she could never do anything to sever the ties that bound them. As if she were the axis on which the world turned. She'd never known that sort of love—that required nothing but would give anything and everything in return.

Watching Matthias and Tieran, Anya felt the lack of it like a knife.

† † † †

In Weatherell, Anya had at least known her place. She was Ilva's shadow, Willem's disappointment, Philly and Sylvie's helper, Arbiter Thorn's best student. In the few days she'd been beyond the wood, Anya had also known her place. She was a living sacrifice, in every way but intent—the one thing every girl she knew was brought up for. The one thing she'd never wanted for herself or for anyone, but would have to pretend at if she hoped for even a chance to avenge Ilva. She'd played her part well enough until Tieran spirited her away from the Elect, but she had not expected to miss it.

Yet here she sat, at the edge of one of the small, clean-burning fires that dotted the interior of the barn, and an unfamiliar and restless awkwardness had settled beneath her skin. It was more than just being shy in company—without the scarlet band and her feigned purpose, she didn't know what was required of her, or who she was meant to be. So she chose a seat away from people and busied herself with untangling knots in Midge's damp fur, even as her face heated with unhappiness.

That unhappiness and discomfort were compounded when a broad, serene-looking woman in traveling clothes limped over, a pair of girls near Anya's age in her wake. The older woman leaned on a heavy and twisted buckthorn cane, and the girls were light-footed and merry. They all shared the same ebony skin and rich black hair, the same quick way of looking Anya up and down, as if she were being weighed and measured. And between the three of them, there radiated what Anya had felt from Matthias and Tieran—a well-worn and unbreakable love, of the sort that made both its giver and receiver better through the bearing of it.

"I'm Leonora Phelps. Lee, to anyone under this roof," the woman said, holding out a hand. Scrambling to her feet, Anya shook it politely. "Matthias and me oversee the wanderers here. These are my girls."

A dull pain woke inside Anya as the sisters stepped forward. They were not twins, as she and Ilva had been, but only a year or two's difference in age separated them. And they carried the same sense of closeness that had linked Anya and Ilva together.

"Pleased to meet you," Anya said, struggling to hide her anguish. The truth was, she wanted to run. Wanted to turn tail and head out into the rain, across the nighttime hills, leaving this band of strangers behind. There was no place for her here—like Weatherell, everyone appeared to know everyone else, a familiarity born of lifelong acquaintance tying them together. Anya herself was an outsider, and always would be, no matter where she went in the world beyond the wood.

"Haven't you got a name then?" one of the girls said with a smile. "Or will we have to find one for you? We had to for Ren when he first joined us, you know."

"It's Tieran now," the other sister chided. When she turned to Anya, her gaze was softer, a welcome in her dark eyes. "I'm Ella, and this is Janie, but you shouldn't mind her, she always teases. Will you stay with us awhile, do you think?"

"I'm Anya. And I'm . . . not sure."

As she hesitated, Anya glanced past the two sisters, and past the central fire where Matthias and Tieran sat side by side, talking as if they'd never run out of words. In the shadows along the far wall, Ilva's ghost waited. Her face was not the death mask it had been the last time Anya saw her, but as it was in the moments before she died. Strained. Desperate. Devoid of hope.

And for a moment, both Ella and Janie wavered before Anya. She saw them not as they were now—glad and carefree, full of life and humor, but as they might be. As Ilva had been. Irrevocably marred by the god and a breath away from leaving the world in agony.

Don't go, Ilva said, repeating her last, impossible request, and Anya's constant, impossible desire. *Don't let anyone else go.*

"No, I can't stay," Anya said abruptly. "In fact, I have to be getting along. Say goodbye to Tieran for me, won't you?"

Heart pounding in her chest, she called to Midge, took her pack from where Tieran had stowed it near the barn door, and slipped back out into the storm.

The rain had let up a little, slackening to a determined drizzle. Anya made it as far as the north end of the tumbledown palisade wall before hurrying footsteps sounded behind her.

"Could've told me we were leaving," Tieran said, falling into step at Anya's side.

She stopped and frowned at him.

"*We're* not leaving," she said. "Those are your people. Do you think I'd have asked you to come with me if I thought you had somebody? You have to stay, Tieran. They all want you."

The thief made a derisive sound. "No, they don't. Matthias might, and Lee and her girls, but the rest either don't care or would be glad enough to get clear of me. Never even planned on seeing them again—what happened back there was a mistake."

He said the last fiercely, as if he wished he could undo the moment of closeness between himself and Matthias and the admission that he viewed the group of wanderers as family. But Anya met his ferocity with stubbornness, blinking back raindrops as her frown became a scowl.

"You can't come with me," she insisted. "That's final. Do you think I don't wish I was back home where I belong? Do you think I don't wish there was just one person who'd take me as I am, the way Matthias would do for you? You're a fool, Tieran. You can't just toss that aside."

For a moment he only stared at her, chest heaving, hands balled into fists. Then:

"I already did," Tieran said, the words sharp as shattered glass. "I broke everything I had with those folk back there. They took me in when I was just a lost thing, living on the streets in Londin. Matthias raised me like his own. And half a year ago, I stole from them. They'll be lucky to make it through another winter because of what I done. I stole what little they had set by and I ran."

"But why?" Anya asked. "Why steal from them? You could've just left."

"Because that's who I am," Tieran said viciously. "I break things and I lie and I hurt people and then I leave when there's only pieces left in my wake."

Anya squinted up at him. Even in the rainy gloom, she could see the pent-up anger in his hazel eyes, and the hard-set line of his jaw.

"I don't believe you," she said. "You came and got me from the Elect, even though it cost you. You didn't have to do that."

Tieran scrubbed a hand across his shorn scalp in frustration. "Wasn't a good deed. Already told you—I don't like being beholden to nobody."

"That's another thing," Anya said. "You claim you don't like to be beholden, but nobody who hates to be indebted steals from the people who raised them. Not unless they have reason to. So you're lying about something, or you're lying about everything, and I think it's the last."

"Awfully good at spotting a lie for a girl what's supposed to be righteous," Tieran said, his temper fading to sullenness as quickly as it had sprung up.

This time, it was Anya who stepped closer to Tieran, who put her hands on his shoulders and stood on her toes to speak next to his ear in the rain. She wasn't sure what possessed her to do it—a spark of Ilva, perhaps, or of the courage her reckless sister had always wished for her to find.

"Maybe it's only this," Anya said, looking to where Ilva stood not three yards away, staring at the pair of them in the rain as skin sloughed from her bones and months of decay occurred in moments. "Maybe I can see you're a liar because I'm one too."

She drew back, just a little, and Tieran swallowed, his throat working visibly.

"Go home," Anya told him, waving a dismissive hand. "Go back to your family and make things right. I've got a mountain to climb and a god to deal with. It turns out I can't manage a wayward thief on top of that, after all."

"No," Tieran said.

Anya sighed. "Don't be difficult. I've told you, I'm busy."

"I won't go back unless you come with me," Tieran went on. "Matthias says he's keeping everyone on the road for now and they're heading north, same as you. They're private people—don't like to be noticed by the law or the Elect. And if you want to keep clear of your grayrobe friends and the Nevis guard, neither'll be looking for a girl in company with wanderers what know how to keep out of sight. They'll be looking for a lamb in a collar, alone on the high road. You couldn't do better, if you want to get to Bane Nevis on your own terms."

Despite her reluctance, Anya knew what he said to be true.

"Very well," she conceded gracelessly. "But if I change my mind, I won't give you the chance to try and follow me a second time. I'll find a way to get clear of you, and then I'll just be gone."

Tieran gave her a rueful look. "Dunno how I feel about that, Anya Astraea. I've always been the one leaving, never the one what got left."

"There's a first time for everything," she sniffed, but when Tieran reached out, she took his hand.

"Want my coat back," he said, nodding at the oilskin she wore.

"It's my coat. I'm reclaiming it on account of you being so much trouble."

"It's never yours. I stole it, fair and square."

"I'm leaving now. Enjoy your family."

". . . It's your coat."

TEN
Low Roads

If the lanes and fields Anya had journeyed across with Tieran seemed out of the way, the paths the wanderers chose were like relics from a forgotten world. They favored the low roads, which predated the Romans—ancient lanes sunk into the earth itself, with tall soil banks surrounding them on either side. In open areas, grasses overgrew the embankments, but most often, trees grew up around them and dappled the hollow ways with green light. The wanderers seemed to know instinctively where they might speak among themselves and where they ought to fall silent, if they wished to pass through the countryside entirely unnoticed.

The group had no beasts of burden—everyone, down to the smallest child, carried a pack. Midge was, in fact, the only animal among them, and she frisked along from family to family, basking in the adoration and tidbits bestowed upon her.

Even Anya was in a better frame of mind. After their conversation of the night before, Tieran seemed petrified that she'd vanish if he looked away from her for a moment, and he was clumsily attempting to make himself agreeable. He wasn't particularly good at it, but she appreciated the effort.

Matthias, too, was trying with obvious desperation to be as considerate as he could of both Tieran and Anya.

"Have you traveled with our Tieran for long?" he asked courteously as Anya and the thief walked with him at the head of the procession of wanderers.

"For a few days," Anya said.

Matthias glanced at her worriedly. "And he hasn't . . . taken anything of yours?"

"I'm right here!" Tieran protested. "I can hear you both."

Anya ignored him. "No. Yes. Well, that is, he stole my pack and left me in a churchyard crypt, but I found him in the end and took back what was mine. And before that, he got me out of some trouble in Sarum. I don't like to think what would have happened if he hadn't come for me. So all in all, one thing balances the other out."

Matthias gave the two of them a searching look, as if he were trying to solve a puzzle. "And would you say you've been traveling with him, or he's been traveling with you?"

"The last," Tieran and Anya said simultaneously.

Matthias blinked. "Really? Only I've never known my boy here to go out of his way for anyone."

"Oh, um. I suppose I'm just persuasive," Anya said. The scarlet band, tucked away safely in her pocket, felt as if it might burn clear through her skin.

Tieran, momentarily forgetting his dedication to being agreeable, caught her eye behind Matthias's back.

Liar, he mouthed.

Anya gave him a fierce look before taking a brisk step forward and smiling up at Matthias in an attempt to hide her guilt.

"I suppose you are," the big man said thoughtfully.

Not long after, Matthias called a halt, so that the littlest ones and the elders could rest and food and water could be passed around. Anya settled herself in with Midge, and Tieran wordlessly sat down on the dog's opposite side. The thief hunched himself into the oilskin coat like a brooding crow, and Anya wasn't entirely sure how he'd got it. She'd used it as a makeshift pillow the night before, but couldn't remember packing it or giving it to him either. She'd begun to think idly of chiding him for that, when a pair of bright voices rang out.

"Hello!"

Ella and Janie stood before them, arm in arm and beaming as they shot meaningful looks from Anya to Tieran and back again.

"We never really got a chance to chat last night, what with you disappearing so sudden-like," Janie said. The more outspoken of the two, she had a narrow, clever face and laughing, deep brown eyes. Ella by contrast was shorter, soft and sweet, her eyes lit with gold. "We're Tieran's cousins, so we thought we'd better come make you feel welcome."

"Not my cousins," Tieran said around an enormous mouthful of one of Anya's cakes of waybread. She wasn't sure how he'd got that, either—she hadn't even opened the pack yet.

"Well, we're as close to cousins as you're ever likely to have, unless you found some long-lost family during your latest spontaneous absence," Janie said.

"Oh, leave him be, Jane," Ella said easily. "You snipe at him too much and he'll just leave again. Then you'll be back to pestering me."

She turned to Anya with the same warm smile she'd offered the night before. "You said your name's Anya, yes?"

Anya nodded. "Anya Astraea."

A swift look passed between the sisters.

"Have you considered a name for the road?" Ella asked. "None of us go by what we were called before . . . well, before we started traveling. It's just safer that way, leaving your name and your past behind."

"Anya's common enough," Janie pointed out. "You could keep that, but Astraea's not a name you hear very often. Why not take a page out of Tieran's book, and try on something new?"

Anya blinked. "Right now?"

Ella gave her an encouraging look. "We've all done it, most of us more than once. No one changes as often as Tieran here, but among our people, it's fairly ordinary. So let's hear it. Who's the new Anya?"

"Leave her be," Tieran grumbled.

"You *know* it's for the best," Janie chided him. "And as you up and vanished half a year ago without a word, you don't get a say in what happens with the rest of us. Matthias and Mum worry when you go, there's no use any of us pretending they don't."

"Didn't ask for anyone to worry over me."

"Doesn't matter if you asked or not, we do," Ella said reproachfully.

"Anya of Stull," Anya said without thinking. No sooner had she spoken the words than she wished them back, because Tieran stared fixedly at the ground before him and went red to the tips of his ears.

Janie frowned. "Where's Stull?"

Anya shrugged, feigning casualness for Tieran's benefit as much as for anyone. "I don't know, and I don't much care. But I heard of it in passing and it's the first thing I thought of. It doesn't mean anything to me, though."

Tieran's glance at her was sharp as steel, and Anya felt entirely at sea.

"You should pick someplace else," Ella told her sensibly. "A place you've got a connection to, so you'll remember it."

Anya opened and shut her mouth. She had no connections to anywhere beyond the wood—all her roots were in Weatherell, and she'd torn them up to go to the mountain.

"If she says she's Anya of Stull, she's Anya of Stull, just leave it at that." Tieran was bristling now, though Janie and Ella seemed entirely unbothered by his ill temper. Janie laughed and bent over him, planting a kiss on the crown of his shorn head as he glared daggers.

"Love, you know we're only here to tease," she said. "You're such an easy mark. And we're trying to sort out what Anya of Stull sees in you. You're not exactly charming."

"Or attractive," Ella chimed in with an impish grin, finally switching to her sister's side of things.

"And you're much less clever than you think," Janie finished.

Salvation for Tieran arrived in the form of Lee, who came up behind the girls and gave them a warning look.

"You'd better not be bothering our new girl," Lee said. "She's not used to the two of you. Give her a few days to get adjusted, for pity's sake."

"We're not bothering her at all," Janie said airily. "We're bothering Tieran."

Lee grew easier at once, giving each of her daughters a fond smile. "Well, that's all right then, he can look after himself. Just see you're both back to help me with Nell and Finch by the time we halt this evening—they're getting up in years for the pace we've been setting, so best we make sure they get a rest while they can. Tonight we'll camp along the low road, and tomorrow we stop for work."

"What kind of work?" Janie asked, looking intrigued.

Lee shook her head. "You'll find out tomorrow, same as everyone else."

"I was just going to pry Janie away from tormenting Tieran anyhow," Ella said, slipping her arm through Lee's. "We've promised the Prynns we'll walk with them for the afternoon."

And then all three of them were gone, leaving the space around Anya and Tieran feeling empty and quiet. When she glanced at the thief, his face was drawn into an unconscious scowl.

"What's wrong?" Anya asked. But Tieran's attention was fixed on Matthias.

"Why're we stopping for work in warm weather?" he said. "Thought that was too risky. Thought we only stayed in one place and hired folk out for jobs in the cold months, when there are fewer people about."

Matthias gave no answer. He kept his eyes fixed on the next untraveled bend in the low road and took a stolid bite of cheese.

Tieran swore under his breath.

After a short while, Matthias got to his feet. For a moment, he let one of his big hands rest on Tieran's shoulder.

"I won't lie to you," Matthias said to the thief. "You know that's not my way. But I'm not blaming you, either, understand?"

This time it was Tieran who said nothing, as Matthias stumped off in the direction Lee and her girls had gone.

"It's my fault," Tieran said once Matthias was out of earshot. There was a cutting edge to his voice, and Anya knew it was meant for no one but himself. "They're taking risks they wouldn't otherwise, because they're missing what I stole from them."

"I'm sorry," Anya murmured.

Tieran shrugged, but his usual sharp look had given way to consuming regret.

"Just gonna have to fix it," he said. "Just gonna have to find a way to pay them back."

† † † †

A hushed but festive air hung over the wanderers the next morning, as Anya got up stiff and damp with dew. They all seemed to be anticipating what was to come, with the possible exception of Tieran and Matthias. The thief sat morosely on his own, and Matthias kept casting anxious glances in his direction, transparently afraid that his flighty charge would vanish.

Anya busied herself with making a pot of porridge, to hide the fact that she had no idea what her role for the day was to be.

"Well, that's just lovely. Thank you, Anya," Matthias said with a surprised smile when she brought him his shallow tin bowl, filled to the brim and steaming. He radiated a constant kindness she couldn't help but feel drawn to, and her feelings of being out of place and at loose ends began to dissipate as they ate in congenial silence.

Tieran did not touch the porridge Anya set down beside him. After a moment, Midge appeared from somewhere in their straggling, makeshift camp and bolted down Tieran's breakfast on his behalf. Absently, the thief reached out and stroked one of her silky ears.

"He gets like this, on occasion," Matthias said apologetically to Anya as he caught her eyeing the boy and the dog. "It's none of our faults, and nothing any of us can do much about. Best to just let him find his way to better spirits."

"You're right, it's his own fault," Anya said, pulling her knees up to her chest and resting her chin atop them. "He told me as much. Said he stole from you, and the rest of the wanderers, and feels awful about it all. It's weighing on him dreadfully—he means to find a way to pay you back."

Matthias gave Anya a searching look, forehead furrowing, gray eyes thoughtful. "He told you all that?"

"Yes."

"I've never known him to own up to a wrongdoing before, much less let on he was sorry for it. I think you may have had more truth from Tieran in three days than I've got in all our years together," Matthias said ruefully.

Anya's face went hot. "I'm sorry, I don't mean to—"

Matthias raised a hand. "Don't be. Every night, I pray to whatever god might be listening that my boy will find someone he can be honest with. Didn't ever think it had to be me. I'm glad he crossed paths with you, Anya Astraea."

"Oh . . . it's Anya of Stull now," she said. "Ella and Janie seemed to think I ought to call myself something different on the road."

"They're clever girls," Matthias said, an amused light in his eyes. "Don't let Janie convince you otherwise with her chatter. The pair of them see more of what goes on among our lot than anyone else, and what's more, they keep other folks' business to themselves. There's not much anyone here wouldn't do for either of them, and they're kind to Tieran, in their own way. They'd be good friends to you, if you let them."

The last was gently pointed, and Anya knew Matthias had been watching her, and the way she kept herself at a distance and felt at odds among the wanderers.

"I know," she said. "It's just, I've never been much good with people I don't know well. And I had a sister—a twin—who d—"

Anya's voice faltered, and she took a moment to steady herself before carrying on. "Who died, this past spring. We were very close. She was everything to me, and I can't seem to sort out how to be without her."

"It's not been long," Matthias said, and the reassurance behind his words made Anya want to weep. "Losses like that take time. And you don't get past them all at once—some days, you'll think you're all right, and then others it'll all come back to you. That's the way of grief. You never really lose it, you just learn to live with it better."

Anya said nothing, but Matthias could sense the question in her.

"I lost someone I loved a great deal," he said gently. "It's been a long while, and I still feel it some days. But if I could weather that, I think you're enough to weather what you're walking through. And we'll help if we can. Thing is, Anya, if you lie down with us and break bread with us, then in our eyes, you're family. Same as Tieran, same as me or Lee or her girls. Can't help unless you let us, though. That's your decision to make."

The prospect of telling Matthias everything was almost unbearably tempting. Anya's lies of commission and omission haunted her as surely as Ilva did, and it would be a relief to unburden herself to someone. But she could not bring herself to do it. Could not meet kindness and welcome with secrets that might pose a danger to their hearer or lower her in the estimation of this considerate and gentle stranger.

"Can I ask you something?" she ventured instead. "Something about . . . all of this?" Anya gestured vaguely about herself, encompassing Matthias and Tieran and the sunken lane and the wanderers scattered across a quarter mile of its length. Matthias squinted, as if he could already anticipate what she meant to ask.

"You can," he said. "Only thing is, I might not have an answer for you."

"I only wanted to know why you've all chosen this," Anya said. "Why you stay on the move, and keep to the low roads, trying to go unnoticed by the Elect and whatever guards happen to be about."

Matthias sighed. "Of course you're wondering about that. The thing is, the Elect don't like folk leaving the places they were born to, not for any reason. Traveling about, mixing with different people—it's how you get new ideas in your head, new ways of seeing the world. It's easier to keep folk under your thumb if they're in one spot and accounted for all their lives—both in body and mind, you know. When we pulled up stakes, we set ourselves at odds with the Elect. They don't like our sort, who are always on the move, and they've got a dozen ways of punishing us if they can catch us out. You can't so much as move two towns over in Albion without getting leave from both the Elect and whatever lord owns the land you were born on."

"I didn't know," Anya said. "There's a lot I don't know, it seems. We didn't get many visitors, where I'm from, so I suppose you're right. I suppose not meeting with other people does keep you in the dark."

"And where is it you said you're from?" Matthias asked mildly.

Anya fell silent, and at last the big man gave an amiable shrug.

"Makes sense that you and my boy should be finding so much in common." Matthias gestured to the empty space where Tieran had sat. The thief had vanished while they were speaking, and Anya saw no sign of him among the other wanderers spread out along the low road. "You both like to keep your truths close and your ways out wide open, don't you?"

"Yes," Anya said with a frown. "I suppose we do."

ELEVEN

Love and Fear

As the wanderers began to flit away, headed off to wherever their work might take them—some to nearby farms, some to a county fair in the closest town—Anya's impression of being out of place only intensified. Tieran had not returned, and whatever Matthias had to say about family and belonging, she felt anchorless and rudderless among the wanderers without him.

When the last of the group had gone, leaving only silver-haired elders and children too young to work, Anya made up her mind. She might as well take the opportunity to remind the Elect that she was still making progress toward the mountain. The wanderers were secretive—Matthias and Lee had both reminded their folk several times that they were to keep to themselves and draw as little attention as possible wherever they went. Anya, on the other hand, wanted to find the high road and be seen, so she doubted their paths would cross.

With some difficulty, she made it up to the top of the steep embankment on one side of the sunken lane. When she'd entered the hollow way the day before in company with the wanderers, they'd been among farms and hedgerows. Now, she came out in a wood very much like the one surrounding Weatherell, with tall, overarching beeches and oaks and sparse undergrowth starred with wildflowers.

Though the wanderers had taken care to depart the low road a few at a time, and to leave little evidence of their passage, Anya was used to trailing Ilva through the forest at home. To her, the minute signs of recent movement were as good as a road, and she followed them out of the woods and into the outskirts of a sizeable market town.

It was busy already, people milling about in the streets, carts and makeshift pens and wagons set up in any open space. A heady, buoyant air suffused the place, and the voices that rose above the din were good-natured, belonging to barkers or hagglers. Here and there, little knots of the blue-and-black-liveried guards stood about, armed with short swords or crossbows and an aura of arrogance. But most people seemed untroubled by them, or at least ignored their presence, so Anya chose to follow suit.

Ducking around a quieter corner, she fumbled in her pocket, grateful that Midge had remained behind. For a few moments, she struggled with the loose threads at the back of her band, tying the ends together as best she could. Then she tucked her hands into her pockets, one finding the hilt of her bone knife for comfort, and stepped back out into the fray.

The difference was immediate. Where before she'd been

invisible, just another insignificant element of the busy crowd, now everyone who caught sight of the band turned their head to watch her passage. Murmurs spread in her wake like ripples, and by the time she reached the town center, a small gaggle of children were trailing along behind her, using crates or wagon wheels for cover in a clumsy attempt at secrecy anytime Anya glanced back.

Still, she saw no sign of gray robes. No indication that the Elect were present and had taken notice of her. With a frustrated sigh, Anya dropped down to sit atop a small stack of wooden boxes at the edge of the central market square. A crescent of open space formed around her as market-goers instinctively gave her a wide berth.

One of the surreptitious children, a girl of no more than six, breached the emptiness between Anya and the townsfolk. Ilva materialized behind the child at once, following her closely like an eerie shepherd.

"I'm Linny," the child said abruptly, oblivious to the ghost at her back. She was a charming, unkempt little thing, with dirty hands and face, but her apron had once been made with care and had embroidery around the hems and on its pockets. "Are you a mountain girl?"

"That depends," Anya answered. "What do you mean by *mountain girl?*"

Linny's face scrunched into a frown as she glanced over her shoulder and found adult faces staring at them both. "I don't— maybe I'm not supposed to talk about them."

"Well, I can't very well tell you whether or not I am one unless you explain what you mean," Anya said reasonably.

The small girl sidled over to her, rising on her toes to whisper in Anya's ear. Her breath was warm and smelled of honeyed candy, her hand on Anya's sleeve leaving a smudge.

"You know, mountain girls. The ones who climb the mountain we live by—my mam said we had to leave our house and go south until the next mountain girl comes, but when she said it she looked sad. You look a bit sad too, so I thought maybe you was one of the girls."

"You had to leave your home?" Anya whispered back, hiding her shock.

"Yeah," Linny said. "Mam told me the Elect don't like people to go, but that we had to get farther from the mountain on account of the fire there. It's been burning every night. And there's something up there . . . I don't really know. A wolf or something? A bad creature, and it swallows the mountain girl whole. Swallows other girls instead, if the mountain one doesn't get up there fast enough."

"Nothing's going to swallow me whole, or you," Anya said quietly, patting Linny's hand. "At least, I hope not."

Tears welled in the child's eyes. "But if you *are* the mountain girl, I don't think you can help it. Not if you go up there. The bad creature even comes down at nights now. Before we left, Mam said my cousin Jessamin was sick, on account of the bad creature found her, and we had to go before it found me, too."

"Your mam is *very* clever," Anya assured Linny. "You won't

have to worry about any bad creature ever getting ahold of you, not with a mam like that."

Linny's tears spilled over, and her lower lip trembled. In her concern, she forgot to whisper.

"What about you, though?" she asked tremulously, her high, clear voice carrying on the summer air. A small knot of listeners had gathered, and though the grown folk were better at hiding their attention than the children standing about, it was still obvious who was idling because they wanted to overhear what Anya had to say. "It's not safe—the bad creature up there might hurt you. You'd better come with us instead. My mam could—"

Anya's heart sank as a pair of gray-robed Elect chose that inopportune moment to finally appear, slipping out from among the gathered market-goers. Worse yet, Anya recognized Orielle and Roger from the way station in Sarum. Orielle smiled comfortingly, holding out her hands to Anya and the child beside her.

"And where is it you'd have our lamb go, little one?" she asked warmly. "You know she has a task to complete, and there are some still in Albion who know their place. Who know where they belong, and do not stray from the role or the home they were born to."

Somewhere behind Orielle's warmth, there was a threat. She knew Linny's people had disobeyed the Elect in leaving the far-off city of Banevale. What consequence might come from that disobedience, Anya didn't know, and had no interest in learning. She leaned closer to the child.

"Go find your mam," Anya said under her breath. "Tell her

whoever you're traveling with, all of you need to leave this place. There's a wood to the east of here—if you walk into it far enough, you'll come across a sunken road. So long as no one's following you, it's a good place to hide. Do you understand? East to the wood, and the sunken lane."

Linny nodded, wide-eyed and fearful. When Anya stood, the small girl did just as she was told and bolted into the crowd. Roger started after her, but something stubborn and unyielding twisted in Anya.

"Stop," she called out. To her shock, the selectman halted in his tracks.

"Let her go," Anya said, her voice pitched to carry. "It will take more than a child to turn me aside from the path I've chosen. Whatever faithlessness exists in the world beyond the wood, you won't find it in me. Soon I'll make right what's gone wrong, and Albion will be at peace again, thanks to the care and oversight of the Elect."

Orielle's slow smile was filled with pride, and the anxiousness in the pit of Anya's stomach turned sour. Ilva had drifted to Orielle's side, looking decayed and terrible in the midmorning light. The two grayrobes drew closer, hemming Anya in, and she fought for calm, everything in her poised for flight.

"And yet despite your talk of faithfulness, you left us." Orielle's words were mild, but a reproach nevertheless. "You left before we could finish our prayers. How did that come about, child?"

Beside Orielle, Ilva was speaking, her slack mouth moving

ceaselessly though no sound came out. Fear lit her eyes, and it made Anya cautious and careful. There was, too, a strange hungriness in the way Orielle inquired about the manner of Anya's departure, which woke uneasiness in her, and a desire to hide the truth.

"It was Roger," Anya said, feigning perfect confusion and lying as if her life depended on it. "He told me you'd finished for the time being. He *said* I should go, because of the guards who'd come. He said I was to make my own way, and that you'd finish your prayers in Banevale, at the foot of the mountain. Truly, I didn't mean to do wrong. Would you have me do penance—shall I humble myself to make right my failure?"

She was wide-eyed and guileless, channeling the show of humility that had always placated Arbiter Thorn. He'd called her a perfect penitent, and though Ilva, wild-hearted and irrepressible, could not understand how Anya found it easy to abase herself, to Anya it always seemed the path of least resistance. To give way, and make herself small and contrite, rather than fighting in her own defense.

"There, child," Orielle said swiftly, clearly satisfied with Anya's innocence. "You did well to heed your elders, and yes—we'll finish our prayers in Banevale, as Roger said."

A glance passed between the two of them, swift and unreadable.

"Would you prefer for one of us to travel with you?" Roger offered. "It might make things easier on the road, and it would be our honor to undertake the task."

Anya felt an instinctive distaste and wariness at the way they continued to press her to accept an escort.

"No," she said. "The road may be difficult, but it's part of my service. I can manage."

Orielle reached out and squeezed Anya's shoulder with one hand. "Your devotion is admirable. No doubt the god will sleep long and deep after your offering."

"I pray it may be so," Anya murmured, but the false piety was beginning to stick in her throat.

At last, Orielle and Roger drew away. With a lingering glance back, they were gone, swallowed up by the shifting crowds. Ilva trailed along behind them as if to ensure they really left, and then she vanished from sight as well. Unable to restrain herself any longer, Anya shuddered.

"Did all right with them, didn't you?" a familiar voice said approvingly as Tieran materialized from behind a wagon loaded high with cabbages and crates of outraged chickens. "Maybe you were right—maybe you *are* a liar."

Anya shot him a disgruntled look. "How long have you been lurking back there?"

Tieran shrugged. "Not long. Got my own business to look after, but I caught sight of you on your way into the square and saw the grayrobes following. So I thought I'd better make sure you didn't land yourself in a fix again."

"I'm perfectly well," Anya told him. "Or as well as I can be, when there are people wandering the countryside without hearth or home until I meet with a monster on their behalf."

She folded her hands and grew very prim, unwilling to grace the thief with a smile when he'd been such poor company at camp that morning and the evening before.

Seeming not to notice, Tieran produced a broad-brimmed straw hat from where he'd been skulking and settled it atop Anya's head.

"There," he said, transparently pleased with himself. "When I got you from that way station in Sarum, your nose was all over sunburn. Thought you might need a hat."

"Did you steal it?" Anya asked solemnly.

"How about you not asking questions you won't like the answer to?" Tieran replied, equally solemn. "Found you something else, but I've only got a few minutes. Come back here with me."

"What, behind the chickens?" Anya sputtered as he drew her into the private niche created by the overloaded wagon, a make-shift pigsty, and a wall.

The uproar of the market was slightly muffled behind the wagon, and out of view, with only the thief for company, Anya's pulse began to slow. The stifling discomfort she felt in Orielle's presence faded, subsiding back into the low, constant thrum of guilt she'd felt since Ilva's passing.

"Give me your collar," Tieran said, holding out one hand. Without hesitation, Anya did, her makeshift knots giving way before a single determined tug.

The thief produced a needle and thread from his pocket, along with the two pieces of a small gold clasp. Squinting a little in concentration, he deftly stitched the pieces of the clasp to either side of Anya's scarlet band, making a neat and sturdy job of it.

"You could be a tailor," Anya said as he bit off the last length of thread and motioned to her to turn her back to him. "You did that very well."

"Could be a lot of things," Tieran said a trifle grimly, "if I could stay in one place and keep honest for more than an hour at a time."

He fixed the collar back in place, and Anya turned to face him once more. She couldn't be stern with Tieran any longer, and smiled up at the thief from under the shade of her new straw brim.

"I like my presents," Anya told him. "Especially the hat."

Tieran grinned. "Thought you would. Now, you gonna wander for a bit, or do you want to come with me? I got myself set up at a spot where none of the rest of our folk are working, so you can keep that collar on without having to answer a lot of questions later tonight."

"Oh. Well, I . . . I'd rather come with you," Anya said. "So long as you're not doing anything untoward, and I won't get in the way."

"In *my* way?" Tieran said, with an expression Anya couldn't quite parse. "Don't think so. But come on then, I been gone too long already."

TWELVE
A Moving Target

Tieran brought Anya out to the far side of the town, where a traveling fair had set themselves up in a wide green field. Anya tried to look every which way at once—at the strange games and displays and pantomimes and striped tents—but Tieran had a destination in mind and she was forced to hurry along to keep up with him.

At the edge of the field, he stopped near an open space, dotted with large wooden circles on stands. A number of people stood along a white-painted line on the grass, and the wooden stands were set up at varying distances from the line. All along the line, men and women held bows or crossbows, and at intervals would fire at the targets with differing measures of success. Each of them had a small tin pail near their lane, and after an especially good shot, onlookers would wander over and drop coins into it to show they'd been impressed by a job well done.

Tieran led Anya over to a booth, where a bored-looking man with a mustache was overseeing the proceedings. He wore the midnight-blue-and-black livery that seemed to be everywhere in Albion, and held himself with an air of vague authority.

"Thanks for keeping my lane," Tieran mumbled, dropping money into the guard's open hand.

"Would've given it up in another minute," the overseer said. "Don't think it'll be much use to you, though—it's been a slow day, and folk are holding on to their coin."

"We'll see" was all Tieran said.

The lane in question was at the end of the long white line, and the wooden target stood significantly closer to it than the rest. Anya glanced at it skeptically.

"Does that mean you're not very good?" she asked, blunt as she might have been with Ilva.

Tieran shot her a patient look as he knelt and began to lay out a number of identical copies of the wicked, short-bladed knife Anya had seen him use before. "No. Means I'm not an archer."

"And what should I do while you're busy with sharp things?" Anya asked.

"Here." Tieran fished in his pocket and pulled out a coin. "It's an exhibition, not a tournament. Means we're not competing against each other so much as against ourselves and what you think we can do. The Nevis guard have been putting them on all over Albion the past few years—if anyone shows a knack for the bow, they offer them a job. Heard the pay's all right, but I also heard they don't like being told no. So keep your wits about you, Weatherell girl."

Tieran rocked back on his heels and squinted up at Anya

for a moment. "Watchers are meant to show it when they like someone best. Go give that coin to whoever catches your eye, and don't startle nobody or walk in front of the targets, all right?"

Anya stood and considered him for a moment as he turned to his knives with a fixed concentration she hadn't yet seen in the thief. For reasons she couldn't quite sort out, it irked her to have Tieran so oblivious to her presence when she was nearby. With a decisive gesture, she reached out and dropped her coin into the pail at his side, where it landed with a small metallic sound. Tieran froze, and Anya took the opportunity to walk off at once, glancing over one shoulder only long enough to see that the thief had gone red as her band. It pleased some restless, relentless part of her, to make him flustered, and set a light and floating feeling at her core.

For a short while, Anya drifted up and down behind the white-painted line. Some of the archers seemed very capable, and there were liveried guard members watching them carefully. Though plenty of people milled about, drawn to the rest of the festival attractions, not many stopped for long, and most glanced dismissively at the exhibition before turning away. Few paid real attention, or walked the line to leave tokens in honor of particular skill.

Tieran, it seemed to Anya, was at a disadvantage, as his lane was at the line's farthest end. She watched from a comfortable distance, free to stare as much as she liked, as he finished making his meticulous preparations and palmed several knives. He handled the blades with precision, showing a self-assurance she hadn't expected. The thief had always struck her as a disaster on two legs, but here, seemingly unaware of any audience, his focus was a palpable thing, and he moved with feral grace.

Anya could not tear her attention away as, effortlessly, without appearing to choose a stance with care or focus much on the target at all, Tieran let his knives fly. One after another, they left his hand, all three of them striking hard, blades buried deep at the target's center. He repeated the act, this time with his left hand rather than his right, then fetched his knives back and began again. Presently, as if bored by demonstrating the same skill repeatedly, he adjusted focus and aimed for the outer rim of the target instead, leaving half a dozen blades quivering in a perfect circle around the target's narrow edge.

Still no one stopped, and his pail stayed empty except for Anya's offering. Though Tieran showed no outward sign of caring, Anya herself was growing increasingly frustrated. It annoyed her to see the thief working hard at something honest and gaining nothing for his efforts. Some of the showier archers had pails heavy with coin despite the thin crowds, and the guards watching them offered an occasional encouraging word.

The trouble was, Anya thought, that Tieran was all skill and no spectacle. He was unassuming and devastatingly efficient and not eye-catching in the least. He lacked the elegance of the best archers, even if he could match their accuracy. And his chosen weapons were a more visceral, brutish thing. The better archers gave an impression of righteousness, as if they were avenging angels. As if they were a defending force standing between the watcher and danger. Tieran, on the other hand, could not help giving off the air of a cutthroat. He was not a guardian, but danger itself, met in a back alley at night, and so onlookers shied away.

Well, Anya knew how that felt. They drew back from her as well, though she had one advantage Tieran did not—when she flaunted her band, all eyes fixed on her.

All eyes fixed on her.

An idea sparked in Anya. It rested within her, sharp and bright and just, and so she gave herself no time to question it, but immediately started across the green. When she'd approached the exhibition overseer with Tieran, she'd hung back, face and band hidden by the broad brim of her new hat. Now, she removed the hat, setting it aside in the shade of a nearby tent. She pushed her hair back and loosened the neck of her woolspun shirt a little, to ensure that her scarlet collar showed to full advantage. Then she strode purposefully up to the overseer's booth.

The guard's air of disinterest vanished immediately at the sight of Anya.

"Weatherell girl," he said, his voice clipped and respectful. "What can I do for you?"

"Well, I'm hoping you can help me with something," Anya answered, smiling sweetly. "I've taken an interest in your exhibition. You see, very soon—in a matter of weeks—I'm going to have to face something terribly dangerous. And I thought, standing here watching, that it might be wise to get an idea of how that feels in advance. To test my own mettle, I suppose."

A vague flash of what might have been panic crossed the guard's face. "What—what is it you're suggesting?"

"I'd like to stand in front of someone's target while they shoot," Anya told him, doing everything she could to channel Ilva's charm and confidence. "That's all. We could ask for volunteers if you like, or I could just choose someone. Of course, they should be allowed to refuse if they're not certain of their skill."

"I can't agree to that," the guard said firmly. "Neither Lord Nevis nor the Elect would approve."

"But it's what I want," Anya said stubbornly. "Everyone beyond the wood is meant to give a Weatherell girl whatever she asks for, to fit her out for her journey and her task. This is what I'm asking for. This is what I think will help."

The guard was fighting to retain his detached manner, perspiration beading on his forehead.

"I take it there's some . . . tension . . . between your ranks and the Elect," Anya said, though she had only a rudimentary understanding of the function of politics and power in the world outside of Weatherell. "I could make that tension a great deal worse, you know. I could tell the Elect you've disrespected me and my calling."

The threat came out with startling ease—Ilva's gregarious lifelong influence followed by Tieran's company were doing nothing for Anya's once-unimpeachable morals.

"We'll put it to them," the guard said reluctantly, gesturing at the white-painted line. "If no one agrees, you'll have to carry on. If anyone does agree—well, then on their head be it."

Anya nodded. "That sounds fair enough."

She followed the guard to the open green space behind the line. He took out a wooden whistle and blew a shrill blast on it, summoning the archers and Tieran from their lanes. As they came, the thief shot Anya a bewildered glance, which she pointedly ignored.

"This is our next Weatherell girl," the guard said, gesturing to Anya. "She's on her way to the mountain and wants a favor from one of you."

Every one of the exhibitors was watching Anya now, as well as any onlookers who'd been milling about. Her nerves, as always, began to sing at the attention and she tamped them down.

"You all seem very skilled," she said gently. "And you know I'm bound for somewhere dangerous, to face down our great and terrible god. I'm hoping to get a glimpse of what it might be like. An idea of the fear, I suppose."

She could feel Tieran's gaze fixed on her, and when she looked his way he was wide-eyed, imperceptibly shaking his head. Undaunted, Anya continued.

"If you're certain enough of your own skill to stand me in front of a target and shoot at it anyway, stay here," she said. "If not, take a step back."

Well over half the exhibitors hurried to back away. Half a dozen stayed, including Tieran, though he looked miserable and had his head down.

Anya made a show of looking over those who'd remained. Several were proud and overconfident, and she would not have let them loose an arrow at her for all the coin in Albion. A few were quiet and steadfast, and Anya expected they could do the job if called upon. Only Tieran, among those who'd stayed, seemed as if he'd like the earth to open and swallow him up.

"The boy with the knives," she said, after it felt as if she'd deliberated long enough.

"What, him?" one of the brashest archers protested. "He's nobody and nothing. I've been a tournament champion in eight counties. Ewan here, who's overseeing things, can vouch for me—we serve together in Nevis's guard now. Let me be the one to do what you're asking."

"The boy with the knives," Anya repeated firmly.

"Well?" the guard in command asked Tieran. "Do you agree?"

Still staring at the ground, Tieran muttered something inaudible.

"Speak up," the guard repeated impatiently.

"Said yeah, all right," Tieran answered, glancing up with a scowl.

"Good," Anya said, though her heart was racing in her chest. People had been drifting over from the fairgrounds to see what the fuss was about, and more were gathering by the minute. It was what she wanted, and yet she couldn't still her nerves. To steady herself, she held out a hand to Tieran, as if they'd never met and she expected an escort. "Shall we?"

He took it, and for all he'd looked reluctant his touch was solid and warm beneath hers, not the least bit of him shifting with pent-up emotion. Somewhere deep down, whether he'd acknowledge it to himself or not, he was certain of his skill, and that lent Anya courage.

"You sure about this?" he said under his breath as they headed for his lane, the crowd they'd gathered following after them eagerly.

"No," Anya murmured. "Not at all. But I've made a scene already and I *am* sure of you, so there's no turning back."

Tieran winced as Anya voiced her trust in him, but nevertheless walked her down the green lane to where the wooden target stood. Anya tried not to look at the way the surface had been scored and riven by the thief's blades.

"Stand like this," Tieran said, and Anya had never heard him speak so softly before. He put a hand on both of her shoulders and guided her into place, so that she stood with her back pressed against the target, arms at her sides.

"I wanted to help," Anya told him earnestly. "You needed it and I didn't know what else to do. I'm not afraid of you, Tieran, I promise."

He gave her a hangdog look. "How come your hands are shaking, then?"

"It's not on your account, it's because of *them*," she said, nodding in the direction of the waiting crowd, which had swelled alarmingly. The whole thing was so absurd Anya couldn't help but smile a bit. "I hate people watching me. Always have done."

Tieran crooked an eyebrow. "Hate it more than having knives thrown at you?"

"Well, I don't really know," Anya answered. "I've always been afraid of getting in front of people, but no one's ever thrown something sharp at me before. Give me a moment and I'll let you know how they measure up."

"Never done this before either," Tieran said honestly. "Don't like it. Don't want to do it. Want to run."

Anya shook her head. "No running. I was watching you. So long as you don't lose your nerve, we'll both be fine. I've taken more risks crossing busy lanes."

"Didn't think they had busy lanes in Weatherell," Tieran said, but he turned and walked back to where his knives waited beside the white-painted line. It suddenly seemed, to Anya, like an impossibly far distance.

Reluctantly, Tieran bent and picked up a single blade. He tested its weight carefully, as if he'd never touched the thing before. All the assurance Anya had seen in him earlier was gone, replaced by the sullen, closed-off hesitance into which he so often retreated.

Without warning, Tieran let the knife fly. Anya held her breath, but she did not shut her eyes and did not flinch as the blade sank into the wooden target with a resounding thud, fully two feet from her head.

One of the archers scoffed. "That the best you can do?"

Again, Tieran threw. Again, the knife hit the target near its edge. Half a dozen times he repeated the act, exhausting his store of blades.

The onlookers were disappointed and unhappy at how obviously he was holding back, and muttered among themselves. A few had already begun to drift away.

"Again," Anya called sharply.

Tieran came to her, and she stayed just as she was while he pulled his knives from the target.

"Stop being afraid of me," she told him. "You can do better. Don't think of me, think of your family. Think of making a start at paying them back."

"Not afraid of you," he said. "Afraid of myself."

Anya met his gaze, stubborn and immoveable. "Well, *I'm* not. Never have been. You're less of a liability than you think, Tieran of nowhere, and less of a risk than you've been told."

Tieran kept silent, and when he gave her one last look, his clever hazel eyes were haunted.

When the thief took his place on the white line once more, his attention wavered. Anya could see it, focused as she was on him. A sudden catch of the breath, a glance to the right and left, an intensifying of the hesitance in his posture. Worried, she scanned the crowd, searching for the source of Tieran's discomfort, and found Orielle and Roger standing among the onlookers, with four other grayrobes gathered around them. They watched Anya closely, a potent blend of shock and disapproval on their faces.

Her heart sank. It was evident from their expressions that it had been one thing for Anya to publicly question her betters on points of justice and the Cataclysm. But this—making a spectacle of herself, courting danger, showing an audience firsthand what it looked like for a red-collared girl to put herself in harm's way— was no longer something they could tolerate.

I could disappear, Anya realized with an awful chill. *The escort they've offered was not just a kindness but a threat. They could take me into their white halls and fit me out for the mountain and no one would question it, and I would not know a moment of freedom from here to the end of the road.*

But Tieran knew. His eyes caught hers and he nodded, and that was all they needed between them.

Palming his knives, three in each hand, the thief chose his stance carefully for the first time. A breathless and quiet moment passed, during which all that could be heard was distant music from the fairgrounds and the breeze tugging at canvas tent flaps. Anya saw the moment Tieran fully committed himself to the task at hand. Saw him sink into himself, and become not a boy, but a blade.

It was like a song, what happened next. The slight hum of the knives as they arced through the air in breathtaking succession. The percussive jolt as they hit, one after another. The calm that swept over Anya as she stepped forward and felt the hilts of Tieran's blades brush the crown of her head, the sides of her neck and arms. They'd come with an inch of her, and she had not flinched, and he had not faltered.

The crowd erupted into chaos and cheering, not for Anya but for the thief. Cautiously, she chose her moment. She waited until every hint of a gray robe had been swallowed up by the writhing mass of onlookers, and then slipped behind the nearest tent, preparing to lose herself in the tangled, bright maze of the fairgrounds. Part of her still thrilled with nerves at the prospect of the grayrobes finding and laying hands on her. But the greater part knew she'd got the best of them again, and done what she felt was right even when they disapproved.

"Weatherell girl."

The guard, Ewan, who'd been overseeing the exhibition, had noticed Anya's departure and followed. A shock of anxiety ran through her, from the crown of her head to the soles of her feet. But all he did was nod.

"That was... an education. Lord Nevis will find your conduct today interesting, to say the least."

"Why?" Anya asked. "He's not one of the Elect. Why should he care about me at all, so long as I do what I'm meant to, and placate the god?"

"Lord Nevis is always interested in the progress of Albion's sacrifices," the guard said meaningfully. "And if you ever find yourself in need of help—the sort that you can't count on the Elect for—well, he'd be willing to give it."

Anya cast a sidelong look at the guard. She didn't like his insinuations any more than she liked the Elect's interference in her progress.

"I'll bear that in mind," she said flatly, before disappearing into the crowd.

THIRTEEN
Curtains

T hat's for you," Tieran said roughly as he arrived in camp that night and dropped a heavy sack of coins down beside Matthias.

Anya had been back for several hours already and was reassured that Linny, her redoubtable mam, and their group of travelers had made it to the sunken lane, after which they were sent safely on their way. Tieran was the last of the wanderers' folk to straggle in, and at the sight of the full purse he'd brought, Matthias went pale.

"What . . . where did you get . . . Tieran, you didn't—"

The thief bridled. "Came by it honestly. They had an archers' exhibition today and there wasn't no one else throwing knives. Suppose I was a . . . what do you call it. A novelty."

Matthias did not look reassured.

"She can tell you," Tieran said, jerking his head in Anya's direction. "She was there."

Anya nodded quickly. "I can, and I was. Tieran did very

well for himself, and there was nothing underhanded involved. Promise."

"All right then," Matthias said, visibly relieved. "In that case, thank you, Tieran. This'll go far for us."

Tieran sat down a foot or so from Anya, and Midge trotted over to him, smiling her dog's smile and begging for attention. The thief threw an arm around her neck and buried his face in her ruff of long fur for a moment. When he looked up, he seemed calm and centered—more so than Anya had seen him since he'd realized the wanderers were taking new risks on his account.

"It's a start," Tieran told Matthias. "Not enough yet by half, but I'll keep at it till I pay back what I owe."

"You know it's not like that," Matthias said anxiously, breaking the corner off a hard slice of waybread and handing it to Midge, who ate it greedily and whined for more. "You don't owe me anything. Never have, never will. If this was just a matter of you and me, it'd be old history already."

"But it's not just between us," Tieran said. "And you've always had more than me to look out for. So I'll stay beholden until I've made good for everyone, not just you."

The tension between them was beginning to set Anya on edge, but she was saved by the appearance of Ella and Janie.

"Well, hello, all," Janie said breezily, settling herself in the spot between Anya and Tieran. "I was talking to Mum, and she said it would be all right if the four of us young folk took a walk this evening. At least, she said we could if you agreed too, Matthias. I've already got somewhere in mind and it'll be quiet and we won't draw any attention to ourselves. Ella suggested it, so you know it's been well thought over. Please say yes?"

Matthias looked at the four of them doubtfully. "Well, I'm not sure—"

"We want to show Anya a nice time," Janie said guilelessly, obviously well aware of just how to get her way from each member of the wanderers. Ella waited in silence, a small smile playing across her face as her more forthright sister worked to bring about their wishes, and Anya felt a fresh stab of grief and guilt at the sight.

"It's true," Ella offered quietly, when Matthias made no immediate reply. "And if we keep on north, none of us are likely to have much of a chance for fun in a week or two. Things are going to get harder, and darker, and worse, until . . ."

Her voice trailed off, but Anya knew what had gone unsaid. Things would get worse until Albion's next Weatherell girl climbed the mountain and did what she'd been raised for. Trouble was, they were all counting on Anya, and Anya's heart still burned, Ilva's last words and her own desire echoing in her ears like a shower of sparks and a second pulse.

Don't go. Don't let anyone else go.

Matthias ran a hand across his face. "I ought to tell you no. It's bad enough we've been in one place a whole night and day now, and that we had folk out for day labor. But if you promise to keep your heads down—"

Janie beamed, and leaned over a disgruntled Tieran to press a kiss to Matthias's weathered cheek. "Of course we promise. You and Mum and everyone else raised us to be cautious. We'll be next door to invisible."

Matthias raised an eyebrow and looked deeply skeptical, but relented after a moment.

"Go on then," he said.

Janie was on her feet at once, holding her hands out to both Ella and Anya.

"Come on," she said. "Let's get out of here before he can change his mind."

"Don't get into trouble," Matthias warned, staring pointedly at Tieran as the four of them started down the hollow way.

Tieran snorted. "I never get into trouble."

"Darling," Janie said with a shake of her head. "Someday I hope you become just a little more self-aware."

"Do you remember when I met you?" Anya said to Tieran, entirely unhelpfully. "How that Arbiter was going to cut your hand off with an ax?"

Janie laced her arm through Anya's. "I like this one, little cousin. I think you ought to keep her."

Frowning her sympathy, Ella fell into stride with Tieran. "Oh dear. No one on your side except me tonight, poor boy, and I don't think I'm the one you want."

"Always want you on my side," Tieran said staunchly. "On account of you're a very nice girl, and always have been, which is more than I can say for those other two."

"You wouldn't like me as much if I was nice," Anya said, with more daring that she'd have thought possible on her part. Janie and Ella's high-spirited company bore her up and lent her courage. She felt reckless and in need of distraction after an unsettling day of being watched by both the Elect and the ubiquitous Nevis guard. "I can see right through you, Tieran of Stull. You've got a taste for sharp things."

Anya had only an instant to think herself clever as Tieran flushed, because Janie pounced on her slip of the tongue at once.

"Tieran of Stull?" the older girl said, pleased as a cat with a dish of cream. "So that's where Anya of Stull found her new name. What an *interesting* night this is already turning out to be. And just where is Stull, and how did the two of you come to be traveling together?"

"No such place," Tieran muttered, and for once Anya could see he was being honest. "I made it up, on account of being from nowhere."

"And is Anya from nowhere too?" Janie pressed.

Neither Tieran nor Anya answered.

They left the low road but did not head in the direction Anya had taken that morning. Soon the forest they traveled through thinned and gave way to open land, and at the crest of a hill a city appeared, stretching out before them. It was not like Sarum, which had felt dark and forbidding and inhospitable. Instead, lights shone out from windows and down from lampposts and people on foot or horseback still filled the streets. Everywhere, spires and towers to rival that of Sarum Cathedral rose up to the night sky. The whole place seemed blanketed in a sense of expectation and excitement.

"Where are we?" Anya asked, staring as if she could take everything in and imprint the place upon her mind.

"Called Oxnaforde," Tieran said. "Folk come here for learning and such. Suppose it's all right, if that's what you fancy."

"*I'd* like it," Ella said wistfully. "If things were different, I'd study here. Lots of books and staying in one place. Knowing where you belong. I couldn't imagine anything more perfect."

Janie put an arm around her sister's shoulder and squeezed, but Anya could see a brief flash of mingled regret and fear on her face. As if it pained her to see Ella denied anything she wished for, but the thought of being parted hurt too.

Side by side, they entered the glittering expanse of Oxnaforde's cobbled streets. It was, Anya thought, the most beautiful place she'd seen outside of Weatherell. The buildings were all of stone, nestled in little enclaves behind walls and set among shadowy gardens. Light and glad voices spilled out of doors thrown open to the mild night breeze, and Anya followed her companions through a square where a domed building rose up to brush the moon, while the very air smelled like the dusty pages of Arbiter Thorn's Cataclysm. Anya took care, as she went, to avert her eyes whenever a window cast back her reflection. It was reflex to do so, more than anything. To avoid her own image, and the temptation it might offer.

Anya had just begun to settle into it all—the strange loveliness of this new place and the stranger security of being shown about by willing guides—when Ella turned down a narrow side street and stopped before an unremarkable-looking alcove door.

With a nod to Janie, Ella pushed the door open, revealing a lamp-lit stair that spiraled downward, to some unknown destination below ground. Janie in turn nodded to Tieran, who retreated to the head of the side street and glanced out at the busier road. After a moment, he returned, seeming satisfied.

"Clear enough," he said, and Ella led them down the stairs. Halfway to the bottom, a murmur of voices grew audible, as well as smells of sugar and spices and fruit.

Blinking as they reached the foot of the steps, Anya found herself in an expansive underground chamber, the walls all of stone, the open space crowded with people in fine clothes. They mingled idly, chatting and eating sweetmeats, as if waiting for something that had not yet taken place. As Anya and the wanderers stepped out into the chamber, an attendant in black-and-white livery approached them.

"For you," he said, handing each of them a paper leaflet covered in spidery Brythonic. "Admittance is four coppers apiece."

Janie was still rummaging in her pocket when Tieran handed over a fistful of coins. "That's for all of us."

"You don't have to—" Janie began, and the thief rolled his eyes.

"Don't have to, but I am. Gonna get some lemon drops, too, wait here."

"Oh, does it have to be—" Ella said, but Tieran had already melted into the crowd.

"He *always* gets lemon drops," Ella sighed. "Ever since Janie made a joke four years back about how he's too sour. You'd think we could have caramels just once, but no, not with the way these two have to badger each other."

"What's a lemon drop?" Anya said blankly, lemons in particular and sweets in general being unheard of in Weatherell. She'd forgotten, briefly, that she was meant to be acting as if Albion and all its luxuries and eccentricities were familiar to her.

Janie hid a smile. "Mercy, Anya, what rock did Tieran find you under? I suppose we can't fuss then, if you've never had them before."

Tieran came stalking back empty-handed, and Anya could see at once that something had happened to rile him, though she couldn't for the life of her sort out what.

"We got to go," he said abruptly. "Can't stay here. Come on, then."

Janie gave him a bewildered look. "What in the green hills are you talking about? Everything looks safe enough, I've been watching."

"Isn't that," Tieran muttered. "But we got to go, all the same. Did you know they're putting on a cautionary play? Is that why we're here?"

"We're not leaving," Janie said firmly. "We walked all this way out, *you* paid for the admission, we're staying. Don't ruin this with one of your moods, Tieran, we want to show Anya a nice time and there couldn't be a better way to ease her into who we are than showing her a cautionary play. Unless you don't want her to stay with us long enough to learn the truth?"

"That's not what I mean at *all*," Tieran protested, his voice loud enough that the strangers nearest to them had begun to cast frowning looks their way. Anya flushed, remembering Matthias's warning that they should keep quiet and go unnoticed while away from the wanderers' camp. "But I never would've agreed to come if I'd known this was where we were headed."

Janie threw up her hands in frustration. "Honestly, Tieran, it's just a bit of pageantry, and Anya's not made of glass. We're making an effort—what more do you want? You came back, you brought someone with you—will wonders never cease—and we're trying to show her a bit of our lives and our world. The least you could do is say thank you, especially after what you did to everyone when you left."

"Janie," Ella said reproachfully. "What's past is past, he can't undo it. Tieran's already made a start at righting his wrongs, and I'm sure he'll go on as he's been doing."

But when she turned to the thief, he said nothing, only stood red-faced and fuming.

"Please stop," Anya begged, in an agony of shame and embarrassment. "People are looking, and Matthias said we shouldn't draw attention to ourselves."

"He was right," Tieran said. "Come on, Anya, we're leaving."

"No, don't. Don't go," Janie cut in quickly. "It's awful of us to snipe at each other like this in front of you, Anya, and I'm sorry. Stay, please. El and I will look after you, and see you get safely back to camp. Tieran's no fit company when he's cross—if you go he'll only make you miserable as well as himself, *if* he stays with you at all."

Anya glanced uncertainly at Tieran. He kept silent, standing there in her oilskin coat with his face furious as a thundercloud.

"Do stay," Ella added, her smile warm and inviting. "We want your company. And it's not often any of us get a chance for a night out."

"Anya," Tieran said at last, but that was all.

"I'm staying," Anya told him. It pained her to do it, but she thought of Ilva, who had so longed to see the peculiarities and wonders of the world beyond the wood. She owed it to her sister to take any chance that came her way. There was what Matthias had said, too—he'd urged her to try to make friends among the wanderers. This seemed as good a start as any. "I'm sorry, Tieran. I'll see you later on?"

Something flashed across the thief's face so quickly Anya hardly saw it before it was gone, sealed off behind an emotionless mask. But it had been there, nevertheless. Hurt. Disappointment. Regret.

He left without another word.

"Come on," Janie said comfortably, tucking her arm through Anya's as Ella did so from the other side. "They've opened the theater doors. We can go in."

Anya let herself be led into a dimly lit room full of rows of benches, with a curtained-off platform at one end. The three girls took their seats, and Anya tried hard not to think of how Tieran had looked when she'd refused him, or how guilt over so many things sat bitter in the pit of her stomach. She was staring fixedly at the floor, trying to ignore her own discomfort, when a whisper from somewhere in the crowd ran through her like a shock.

"A Weatherell girl," someone nearby said in hushed tones, and Anya jerked her head up in dismay. The crimson band was safely hidden in her pocket—surely no one could recognize her without it.

"Look, look, it's a Weatherell girl," another watcher said.

With a sinking feeling, Anya saw that the curtains at the front of the room had been drawn back. And as she took in the stage and the scene beginning to play out upon it, she realized that Tieran's inexplicable anger had not been on his own behalf.

It had all been for her.

FOURTEEN
Emilia

The stage before Anya was set in the semblance of a wood. There was a painted backdrop of endless trees, and several tall trunks seemed to grow out of the boards. Greenery hung from the marquee, strewn with charms, and a small wooden cottage stood at the stage's center.

Seeing Weatherell again, even in pantomime, was like an arrow through Anya's heart. She pressed a hand to her chest and watched with tears dimming her eyes as a golden-haired girl stepped out of the cottage door, smiling and whole and young.

Anya watched as a story she'd never heard in Weatherell unfolded before her—watched as a sweet-natured girl named Emilia offered to go to the god of the mountain. Watched as she received her scarlet band and left home behind. As she set out along the northward road. Some of her misadventures along the way were unfamiliar, but others Anya recognized. The gray-robed Elect, the stares and whispers, the strangers who would not speak Emilia's name but would call her only by her title.

Weatherell girl.

When at last Emilia reached the mountain, Anya felt as if they'd traveled there together. She could hardly breathe and all her blood went to ice as the girl began her climb, though the mountain was only canvas spread over a makeshift tower of crates.

As Emilia entered a cave at the mountain's summit, the bright lamps around the stage were snuffed out. Anya glanced uncertainly in the direction Tieran had gone when he stormed off, but the play held her captive. A single light flared onstage as Emilia lit a lantern. Everything in Anya turned to fear and trembling as the girl made her way through a labyrinthine tunnel, expecting at each turn to meet with the god of the mountain.

And then it came. The moment that haunted Anya's darkest dreams, but that she nevertheless was walking toward, mile by mile, day by day.

Emilia turned a corner. Sudden gouts of flame roared up and cymbals clashed as she found herself before the god of the mountain himself.

Anya's mind knew it was only a man, in a clever crimson and orange and black costume made to mimic fire. But in her soul, she felt that it was *him*—the demon god who haunted her, whom she felt watching her pain and progress from the shadows, and whom she'd bent her will upon ending.

He was immensely tall, the pantomime god of the mountain, a creature of flame and shadow with curling ram's horns. Anya wanted to go. She wanted nothing more than to get to her feet and hurry after Tieran, to find him in the tangle of city streets and tell him he'd been right, she shouldn't have stayed, it had been kind to want to spare her this story.

But she remained where she was, transfixed.

Before her, Emilia knelt at the god's feet.

"What would you have of me?" the girl asked, in a voice that shook.

The god, with his hateful, merciless eyes, stared down at Emilia, kneeling before him. He considered for a moment.

"Your kindness," he said finally. "Your softness. Your light. And in exchange, I will leave the rest of you untouched."

"Is there nothing else?" Emilia asked.

Firelight flickered across the god's terrible face. "Perhaps. If you wish to bargain, we can. But I will warn you—my first offer is always easiest. Any substitution will prove harder, and hurt more."

Emilia bowed her head. Anya could see the weight of the journey, heavy on her. She could see exhaustion and home-sickness and the desire to have this moment of her long, long sacrifice at an end.

"I agree," Emilia murmured. "Take what you will from me."

Everything on the stage went dark as the curtains closed on the play's first act. Lamps were lit along the aisles and hawkers went about, selling little glasses of fruit wine or gingersnaps, two for a penny. Ripples of conversation spread across the seated audience. Some stood and walked about, or gathered up their coats and left.

Anya sat still as a stone, her eyes fixed on the stage. Dimly, she heard Ella ask if she was all right, at which she nodded. A world away, Janie and Ella spoke with each other, their voices low and thoughtful. What had Ilva been asked for, Anya wondered, when she'd knelt before the god? Had she bargained? Was that the reason she'd returned home with poison in her veins, dying for want of something missing inside her? The unknowing was a new and fresh pain, and the questions plagued Anya, keeping her in her seat when she knew she ought to get up. To walk away, before the spectacle unfolding onstage did further damage to her already battered heart.

The chatter dimmed. The curtain rose.

Emilia emerged from the tunnel into daylight, and there was something indefinably different about her. She had been changed by her encounter with the god, even if he'd left her without scars. She'd knelt before him as one girl, and come away as someone else.

The return journey was a blur to Anya, watching as Emilia made enemies everywhere she went. She snapped and swore, returning kindness with curses. But all the while, whatever words she spoke, there was heartbreak in her eyes. Emilia had been bound to cruelty, while inside, her true nature and her soul remained unchanged.

And in Weatherell again, she could not shake her sacrifice. Anya and the audience watched as one by one, Emilia broke the ties that bound her to the people she loved. Though the village understood what had happened to her, they could not help feeling the sting of her sharp temper. Little by little, they distanced themselves from their Weatherell girl, from their living sacrifice, who'd given all of her goodness to the god.

At last Emilia walked out into the woods. In the forest's far reaches, she found herself an isolated clearing. There she built a makeshift dwelling and passed season after season, set apart from others for fear of the damage she might do. The years washed over her, a living sacrifice, as she grew old alone.

Anya watched, and she could not move.

She could not blink.

She could not breathe.

The curtains closed for the last time on a silent Emilia, grown lined and gray. She sat at the center of her clearing and looked out at the watchers. Though she had remained untouched in body, there was agony in her eyes.

Anya sat too. She sat as the audience applauded, as they stood once again and stretched and chatted, as they mingled before the stage and finally, little by little, as they began to drift away. Then abruptly, Anya got to her feet. There was something building inside her—a wild sense of anguish and wrongness, which set her stomach to turning over and her heart to racing. She didn't know what to do with it, or how to calm it.

"I want a bit of air," she said distantly to Janie and Ella.

"Hang on," Ella said, pocketing her leaflet and fussing with her coat. "We can all walk together. Janie and I—well, we brought you here for a reason, and there's something you ought to be told. We might get a scolding for saying it, but you should know if you're planning to stay with the wanderers."

"That's very kind, but is it all right if I meet you back at camp?" Anya answered, using every scrap of willpower she had left to keep her voice from trembling. "I need a minute to clear my head."

And before either of the sisters could protest, she was gone. She hurried up the stairs and through the city's brilliant streets, and beneath every streetlamp, Anya saw Weatherell girls.

Emilia with her anguished eyes.

Willem with her handless wrists.

Philomena, doubled over with pain.

Sylvie, sightless and withered.

Frida with a bloody hole where her mouth had been, Gabrielle with her ruined face, Leya with one leg torn away, Florien blank-eyed and forgetful, Moriah with her thumbless hands.

Ilva, dying in the shadows.

Don't go, Ilva breathed, her voice coming from everywhere and nowhere all at once. *Don't let anyone else go.*

Abruptly, Anya stopped. She'd come out into the open square with its domed building and smell of old parchment. Though it was late, there were still people walking about, and some sat on nearby lawns in the summer night air.

Before her stood Orielle of the Elect, gray-robed and severe in the silvery moonlight.

"Anya Astraea," Orielle said sharply. "Where is your band?"

Anya's gaze skittered to the right and left. There were half a dozen more gray-robed figures, waiting in the shadows around the square. Fear and rebellion pooled in her belly as slowly, she approached Orielle. Silently, Anya took the crimson band from her pocket and held it out.

"Disappointing," Orielle said, and the single word cut Anya to the quick.

"I'm sorry," she whispered, because it was required of her. Ilva and a dozen other Weatherell girls who'd been more righteous, more faithful, shimmered at the edges of her vision. "I'm so sorry, I know I've done wrong but I swear I'll do better. I swear I'll *be* better."

Orielle was implacable, and would not meet her eyes. "All your pretty words. All your show of righteousness. And you could not be faithful even in this, the least of things."

"I can be," Anya lied desperately. "If you'll only give me another chance."

Orielle turned aside, making a small, dismissive sound. "We will find another girl. One without your family's manifold flaws."

Anya's fear turned to abject panic, even as the slight to Ilva stung. It must be her. It would break her irrevocably, to fail at her task. To see another girl go to the mountain, as Ilva had done.

Don't go. Don't let anyone else go.

The cobblestones bit hard as Anya dropped to her knees.

"I'll do penance," she pleaded. "I'll humble myself, here and now, as I've always done after straying into error. I know I've acted shamefully, *Mater*, but let me return to the path laid out for me. Let me make right my wrongs, and regain my worthiness as an offering."

Whether it was her obvious desperation, or the calculated use of the Divinitas word for a mother of the faithful that swayed Orielle, Anya could not say. But the gray-robed woman stilled and turned back to Anya, who knelt, already penitent, before her.

"The harrowing of Banevale has already begun," Orielle said pitilessly. "Those who live in the city at the foot of the mountain suffer our god's wrath because of the shortcomings of your sister. We will not tolerate another failure, and every hour you waste comes at a cost."

From where she knelt, Anya lowered herself farther still. She lay facedown on the dirty, oft-traveled cobblestones, arms outstretched like the willing offering she was meant to be. And though the posture brought shame with it, it was not the physical aspect of the penance that cut deepest. It was that Orielle saw her sister as a failure and a disgrace, and the god had found her unworthy.

How could they have been so mistaken? How could they have failed to see Ilva as Anya had seen her? As bright and wild and deserving of all good things? The wrongness and injustice of it cut Anya to the quick, even as, prostrate on the cobblestones, she prepared herself for what was to come.

A long silence fell over the square, but no retreating footsteps echoed away. And then at last:

"You see before you our newest lamb," Orielle said, her voice clear and steady, carrying well on the cool air to anyone watching and waiting, some of them Elect, some no more than curious bystanders. "She is meant for a pure and spotless offering to the god, to halt his wrath and purchase peace for Albion. It is a role the girl sought herself, after her own sister went north and failed us, bringing suffering and judgment upon those who dwell within the shadow of the god."

Dark murmurs rose up from those gathered. The longer the god went unchecked, the more any mention of Ilva stirred their anger. Anya's heart ached within her, but she did not move.

"Our current offering has faltered," Orielle said. "She has not demonstrated the modesty and self-sacrifice necessary for one who would ascend the mountain in the north. But our god is merciful, and worthy repentance is sweet to him. This new lamb has expressed contrition over her wrongs, and a desire to make them right, so we allow her the chance now. We are all instruments in her cleansing, and tools in the restoration of the humility she requires.

"I invite you all forward," the woman finished, "to remind our lamb of her failings, and that none of us are perfect, no, not one."

Anya kept very still, even as the cobblestones dug into her. From the corner of her eye she could see Ilva's ghost, wavering like an uncertain candle flame. The first of the whispers began almost at once, emanating from unseen speakers who stepped eagerly into the square to take part in her chastisement. They rose up around her, a chorus of doubts, her own internal voices made manifest.

"Unworthy."

She knew herself to be so—she'd been a coward when Ilva was brave.

"Unwise."

Had she been wise, Ilva would still live.

"Heartless."

Heartless indeed, for her sister had been her heart.

"Thoughtless."

She had not weighed the costs, and Ilva had died for it.

"Cruel."

And wicked, to stay behind when her own heart faced the god.

"Selfish."

Yes, for she'd let unspoken convictions come before the good of her kin.

"Faithless."

More than anyone present knew.

"Shameful."

So filled with shame, sometimes it hurt to draw breath.

"Your sister deserved her fate."

Never.

"You are no better than she was."

No better, no. Unfathomably worse.

On and on they went, and it seemed a very long time before the last of the accusations and chastisements faded. Even when they'd finished, Anya stayed as she was, not so much unwilling to move as unable. She could feel the dozens of eyes fixed on her, all of them unkind and unfriendly in the wake of her penance. Humiliation and grief and shame weighed her down, turning her limbs to lead.

Finally Orielle relented. She crouched before Anya and took her by the hands. Trying to get to her feet, Anya nearly stumbled, but Orielle held her up. With one finger, she tilted Anya's chin, until the girl was forced to look at her.

"Is there anything you wish to say on your own behalf?" Orielle asked.

"Nothing, *Mater*," Anya answered, her voice thin as a thread.

"Very good," said Orielle. "And you still wish to continue on your own? Without our help or support?"

"Yes," Anya managed.

"Then you may go. But we caution you not to fall into pride or to falter in your role again."

"I understand," Anya said.

Orielle gestured to her to carry on her way, and Anya did so, carefully wiping any trace of dirt from her face and shaking out her hair as she went.

Ilva kept pace beside her, an agonizing reminder of Anya's unworthiness. The ghost's lips were blue, her skin deathly pale, and hanks of her honey-brown curls sloughed off, falling to the ground like autumn leaves. A sob escaped Anya, though her eyes were dry.

Don't go, Ilva whispered, in a voice like wind over an open grave. *Don't let anyone else go.*

"I won't," Anya swore, though the words caught in her throat. "I promise you, Ilva. I promise. No one else will go."

FIFTEEN
The Touch of Wrath

Anya had become nothing in life if not a master of avoiding conversations that might sting. Even in Weatherell, isolated and cut off from the world, she'd been able to drift from clearing to clearing and cottage to cottage, nearly invisible when she didn't wish to be seen.

Now, she did not wish to be seen.

The cautionary play and her penance before Orielle and Ilva's dying were all tangled up within her, and it felt as if nothing lay beneath her skin but a network of bruises. Janie and Ella's implication that the wanderers were in some way connected with Weatherell and its girls might once have sparked curiosity in Anya, but with her heart a pained knot in her chest, any new revelation seemed like danger. Better to keep her secrets close, tucked away with the monumental weight of her guilt, and let no one past her mild and untouchable exterior.

So she made herself a ghost, still traveling with the wanderers but always where she would not be looked for, deflecting any questions or attempts to draw her out with steely self-composure. For over a week, she managed to keep herself isolated while in company, until she'd finished half her journey north. And though Matthias cast her worried, sidelong looks and Tieran seemed at a loss, though Janie and Ella attempted to draw her out with good-natured chatter when they managed to find her, she would not allow herself to bend.

After Anya's tenth night camped on the low road, followed by a day spent on foot, the wanderers left the hollow way. They stopped at a place even ghostlier than the old Roman settlement where Anya had met them—the woodland they'd been traveling through grew into a damp, hushed green forest, entirely unlike the one surrounding Weatherell.

In Anya's familiar New Forest, the trees were tall and the spaces between them relatively open, filled with shifting light and flowers. This wood was still and close, the trees' crowns clustered thickly overhead, their trunks knotted and twisted and overgrown with moss. Waist-high ferns grew close together, forming a sea of vegetation to be waded through, and everywhere there were strange noises and shadows.

A stand of small wooden huts, all gone weathered gray, dotted a section of the forest not far from the road. The wanderers moved among them with practiced ease and to Anya's surprise, the place looked as though it had been inhabited a week or so ago. Before each hut the ground had been cleared for a small cookfire, and ashes still sat there, not yet scattered, the open spaces not yet grown over. Matthias and Lee went about carefully from one hut to the next, scanning the doorframe of each and coming together to confer when they'd finished.

"The Beltayne group was here last," Lee announced shortly, her voice loud enough to reach every wanderer, yet still muffled and softened by the wood. "They've gone east, to Londin, to help with anyone fleeing from the northlands around Bane Nevis. There'll be a good deal more unhoused folk in Albion come winter, even if the god's sated soon. It'll be the job of those of us who've come before to ensure they're safe, and that they go unnoticed by the Elect or Lord Nevis."

"We've left signs for whoever camps here next," Matthias added, "letting them know we're headed north, to lend a hand to anyone who needs to find the low roads and places to stay, if they've not been on the move before."

A murmur of approval rippled among the wanderers, and Anya turned to Tieran. He was crouched nearby, rifling through her pack for reasons known only to him. His initial bewilderment over her new reserve had turned to spikiness, but Anya did not have it in her to be first to reach out. She might have, were it not for what had transpired between her and Orielle. The encounter had left her raw and aching, feeling lower than dirt and unworthy of anyone's attention or goodwill.

Anya still had no concept of who the wanderers were, or why they felt it their duty to assist those who moved across Albion without the approval of those who governed it. She shifted anxiously as Matthias and Lee continued to detail their plans, to help those fleeing for fear of the god of the mountain. It seemed to her that the whole encampment was full of secrets. The wanderers had theirs, Tieran had his, and she had hers—some of which the thief knew, but the fire of vengeance that burned low at her core, the resolve that drove her, the full weight of her grief, he'd never even be able to guess at. For the first time, Anya wondered what secrets had taken root and flourished in the soil of Weatherell besides her own. Surely every community housed its silent dissenters, its private heretics, and there had been others in Anya's acquaintance, even if she was chief among them.

Dusk turned the wanderers' camp into a constellation of gold and crimson stars, as little cookfires were lit and the soft sounds of conversation and song drifted between the ancient trees. Tieran made himself busy, and Anya felt a dull pang of surprise when he cobbled together a more-than-palatable stew out of items scrounged from her pack and Matthias's. The thief himself appeared to possess nothing, besides the array of short-bladed knives he pulled out of hidden sheaths while chopping vegetables and bits of dried meat.

Matthias was already dozing on his bedroll by the time Anya set her bowl aside, and Tieran was washing up the light tin dishes and spoons in a water bucket. Midge sat at the boy's side, happily wolfing down what was left in the cooking pot before he put that into the wash water as well.

Wrapping her arms about her knees, Anya stayed just as she was, feeling small and sad and quiet. Beyond the cast-off glow of their small fire, Ilva glimmered into being. A pale and ghastly light emanated from her, and bone showed intermittently through the fraying web of her skin as she beckoned to Anya and moved insistently back toward the wood. Ilva repeated the motion several times, and at last Anya scrambled to her feet, unsettled by the vision.

"I'll be back soon," she said to Tieran. "Don't wait up on my account."

"At least take Midge with you," he called after her, sounding more irritable than ever. "There's brigands in these parts!"

But Anya was already among the trees and did not stop. Ilva gleamed before her like a muted star, weaving through the ferns and between low-hanging branches. Anya had never yet seen her sister so. Until now, the manifestations of Ilva had been unsettling, and even gruesome. But this ethereal, urgent version of her was something else entirely. It opened up an agonizing hollowness at Anya's core, for the other visions of her sister, upsetting as they were, had at least been of Ilva decidedly in the flesh. This was her beginning to dissipate into spirit, the semblance of her physical form starting to fade.

Anya glanced over one shoulder uncertainly as Ilva led her on, to the twisting length of the hollow way. Between the muffling effect of the damp green woods and the earthen walls, no one from the wanderers' camp would be able to hear her, no matter how loudly she called.

But Ilva was insistent. She descended into the sunken lane and disappeared around a bend. After a brief hesitation, Anya let herself down onto the lane and followed. The pale, unearthly light shed by Ilva led her on until gradually, a sound of voices grew audible up ahead. Ilva continued toward them and then, quite suddenly, vanished into nothing, leaving Anya alone in shadows with strangers around the bend. Taking an anxious step forward, Anya peered around the solid curve of the low road's earthen wall.

A group of people sat huddled together around a poor, smoking fire. There were perhaps a dozen of them—less than half the wanderers' number. They had an unkempt and bone-weary look, as if they'd been traveling for days but were not accustomed to it. Where the wanderers wore muted colors, and the women practical trousers and shirts, like Anya's own, these strangers were in town dwellers' garb—heavy work boots for the men, skirts and aprons for the women, and colors or prints that might catch the eye.

All that, Anya noticed in a moment and forgot, because at the center of their dispirited group lay a makeshift litter, of canvas and sapling poles. On it rested a girl, perhaps five years younger than Anya herself—little more than a child. The girl's face was a ruin. Most of it was raw and charred with terrible burns, her hair seared away in large patches. As far as Anya could tell from her hands and arms and ankles, the damage extended to the rest of her as well.

At Anya's side, Ilva guttered back into existence, her light burning very low.

He touched me, Ilva sighed, in a voice softer than the gentlest night breeze. *He touched me, and I knew it was the beginning of the end.*

Unconsciously, Anya took a step forward, around the bend and into the firelight. Her eyes went from the girl on the stretcher to the rest of the travelers, and she found there were other girls among them. None were in as bad a way as the child on the ground, but all of them bore the terrible marks of the god's touch.

"You there," an older woman with iron-gray hair said as Anya appeared. Anguish underscored her words. "Are you from nearby? Can you help us?"

"No," Anya said numbly. "Not from nearby."

Her gaze had been drawn inexorably back to the girl on the stretcher. A slender man, with a face as gentle as Matthias's, knelt at the girl's side with a vial of clear liquid. Vainly, he tried to help the child swallow it, speaking soothing words under his breath. But the girl could not manage, and as Anya watched in horror she began to shake, just as Ilva had done.

With a ragged breath Anya fixed her eyes on the ground, unable to bring herself to watch what was to come a second time. After a few moments, a stifled cry rose up from someone in the group of travelers, followed by a ripple of shocked voices.

Anya knew, with stark and unbearable certainty, that the girl was gone. For beside Ilva's mournful ghost, another had flickered into being. A child, her face a patchwork of vicious burns, her eyes filmy and unseeing.

One, Ilva whispered.

Two, the child's apparition echoed, before both of them vanished, dissipating as if blown to pieces by a strong wind.

"Please," the gray-haired woman said. "We have others who need help. If you know of anyone—anyone at all—who might take pity on us . . ."

"Yes," Anya said. Inside her, ice was spreading, and the cold burned worse than her internal fire ever did. "I'll go and fetch them. Just wait here, won't you?"

"We have nowhere else to go," the woman said, and Anya had never heard such despair before.

Hurrying back the way she'd come, Anya pulled herself up and out of the sunken lane. She ran through the woods, losing her footing twice and tearing her knees and palms open on branches and stones, but she did not stop. Not until she was back in the wanderers' camp, Matthias and Tieran both on their feet before she'd even made it out of the trees.

"There are people on the north road," Anya gasped. "From Banevale. They're in a bad way—they have girls with them, who fell prey to the god of the mountain."

She'd not even finished speaking before the encampment burst to life, Matthias calling for Lee, Lee turning to Janie and Ella, and Tieran moving immediately to Anya's side. Anya watched in strained silence as Matthias, Lee, and half a dozen others took up packs and supplies and set off in the direction she'd come from. As they passed by, Anya started after them, but Tieran stopped her with a hand on her arm.

"All right, Anya?" he asked, his voice low and worried.

"Yes," Anya lied. There was nothing behind the word, no reassurance, no warmth. "I have to go help."

"You don't," Tieran protested. "Matthias and Lee'll look after everything. Those folk couldn't be in better care."

"Please don't touch me," Anya said quietly, and Tieran drew

his hand back at once, as if stung. She didn't want him anywhere near her—it felt as if every word spoken to her during the penance before Orielle lay trapped beneath her skin.

Unworthy

Heartless

Selfish

Cruel

She was all of these things and more, gambling the fate of every girl in Albion on the wickedness that burned inside her—on a desire for vengeance, and freedom, and a world unlike the one she'd been born into. And yet, with every girl she saw burned or maimed or killed, the heretic conviction she'd always felt grew within her.

Albion's god was *not* just. And he deserved no more of her homeland's innocent daughters.

Backing away from Tieran, Anya let the darkness swallow her up.

Down in the hollow way, the wretched travelers still huddled close around their wounded girls, and the wanderers moved among them like ministers of grace. Janie knelt before a small child, carefully cleaning burns that showed stark red against the golden-brown skin on the little one's arms and neck.

"How can I help?" Anya asked, her voice dangerously even. Anything she felt had been buried for now, though she knew there'd come a reckoning. That sooner or later, she'd pay a price for tamping down the things she'd seen and felt ever since leaving Weatherell.

"Look there." Janie nodded in the direction of a blanket that had been spread on the ground an arm's length away. Several pouches and jars sat atop it. "If you search about, you'll find a mortar. The red pouch has herbs for burns in it—hypericum and calendula and arnica. Grind them up finely in the mortar and when you've finished, add honey from the largest jar to make a paste. Then bring it to me."

Anya did as she was told, settling on the blanket and beginning to grind up the blend of dried herbs. They gave off a sweet, dusty smell and she tried to focus on it, tried to let it settle her. It did no good. Though she was able to school her hands and her body into calm, and do what she felt was her duty, on the inside she was shattering. All around her were hushed and worried voices, punctuated by the occasional sound of a ragged sob or soft, hoarse cry. It was as if all her Weatherell girls, all the ghosts she and Ilva had remembered as distant stories, were made manifest around her, and while the remembering of them had been blunted by the passage of time, seeing them in the present cut her to the heart.

"Is this right?" Anya asked in a low voice, showing Janie the poultice she'd made. Janie nodded and took the mixture, applying it little by little to clean bandages and wrapping them loosely about the young girl's burns. Janie did it all neatly and efficiently, moving with a practiced air.

"You're very good at this," Anya said.

"I should be," Janie answered, without looking away from the task at hand. "Mum was our healer before we started wandering.

She still is now, she just does more besides. But I've been apprenticed to her for ages and I'm hoping in another year or so, she'll let me take over from her entirely. She and Matthias have got enough on their hands, keeping us all sorted and safe and fed and moving from one place to the next."

"I should think you'll do well," Anya said. It made her feel more rootless and adrift and full of blasphemous intent than ever, to see Janie so capable, so sure of her place and her purpose.

"We'll see," Janie said with a smile. "I've got to work on my midwifery yet. But I'd rather this than tinsmithing, like Ella's learning from the Prynns. She sits shut up in a workshop all winter long and then does piecework if we happen to stop in one place long enough during warm weather. Not for me—I like to be with people and busy, no matter the season."

Rocking back on her heels, Janie squeezed the hand of the young girl she'd been tending. The sharp wit Anya had seen in her was softened, so that she gave off an air of comfort and confidence instead. She was the sort of person you'd instinctively trust if trouble came your way, Anya realized, and who could make things better simply by being near.

"There you are, my love," Janie said warmly to the girl. "Do you see him over there? The big man by the fire? That's Matthias, and he's got a tea steeping that'll take the edge off your hurts and help you sleep. Why don't you go get yourself a mug and find your da—you said he was watching your younger brother, yes?"

The girl answered softly in the affirmative, and though her movements were slow and careful, she was steady enough as she got to her feet and walked off. Throughout the small group of travelers, chaos was giving way to order, brought about the wanderers and their wisdom and goodwill.

Janie ran a hand across her face and looked suddenly weary, as she saw the girl she'd tended reach Matthias.

"Are you all right?" Anya asked automatically.

"Not really," Janie said with a sad smile. "This could be me or Ella or you. We're only lucky that it's not, and that we'll never have to go to the god, like Emilia in that bit of pageantry we saw."

The scarlet band in Anya's pocket felt heavy as a stone.

"I suppose," she murmured.

"Luck had nothing to do with this," the nearest of the travelers said. It was the gray-haired woman who'd first asked Anya for help. Now that the worst of things had passed, she sat by the blanket-covered body of the girl they'd lost, with a hard and unyielding look written across her face. "It was failure that started it all. The Elect should've seen the girl they sent to the god was unfit. And she should've known herself to be unworthy. Whoever they send next had best be pure and righteous, and hurry on her way."

Anya fell still as the traveler's words bit deep.

"It's easy to lay blame," Janie shot back, a bit of the customary clever sharpness returning to her voice. "But the girl who went and died for her trouble deserved it no more than I would, or any of your girls. It's a terrible thing, what they're made to do."

"They're not made to, though," the traveler retorted. "They choose to go. Our girls here never did."

Janie shook her head, disapproval evident in the set of her mouth. "Weatherell girls don't choose their path. Not really. What choice is there in being brought up for a thing from the moment you're born and told that if you don't accept it, you'll rain suffering down on all of Albion? There's no freedom in that."

"It's their lot," the traveler said, and she was angry now, bitterness dripping from the words.

"I won't argue with someone who's just suffered a loss," Janie answered, and her firmness brooked no response. "But I hope you'll feel otherwise once the edge wears off your hurt."

There was nothing left for Anya to do. The wanderers had worked a quiet magic among the unfortunates on the low road, and Janie went to join Matthias and Lee, who were speaking earnestly with the older members of the small, sad group. Every part of Anya ached intolerably—her body, her spirit, her heart. Without thinking, she carried on down the sunken lane, pulled northward. Darkness closed in around her. Ilva's ghost did not appear. There was no Midge to trot at her heels. Anya was entirely alone, but she did not freeze or crumble as she'd done at Ilva's death, and over her bones. The act of walking held her together—was *all* that held her together.

A stone turned under one of her unsteady feet and drove her to her knees.

With a blinding flash she was back before Orielle, before Arbiter Thorn, before Ilva's remains, and as she would soon be before the god.

And she was undone. The brokenness on Emilia's face as

the curtains closed had seared itself into her mind. It blurred together with the way Willem looked, when she thought no one was watching. With the way Philomena looked, when her tortured inner workings especially pained her. With the way Sylvie looked, when she spoke of things she would never see again.

With the way the travelers' girls on the low road had looked, marked by the hand of the god.

With the way Ilva had looked, in the moment death stole her.

With the way Anya felt, constantly, beneath the thin and fragile armor of her skin.

With a frantic burst of movement, she pulled herself out of the low road and up into the forest, where she dropped down among the sea of ferns. The wood smelled of green things and soil, of Weatherell, of everything that would never truly be hers again, because even if she *did* go back, home was an unfamiliar place without her sister.

The full weight of Ilva's death and of the burden she'd taken on was enough to shatter Anya. She'd grieved before, but there'd been a vain shred of hope. That somehow, if she walked the same road Ilva walked, if she climbed the mountain Ilva climbed, if she vanquished the god that ended Ilva's life, she might undo everything that had gone before.

Walking the north road had made one thing starkly clear, though—no matter how badly Anya wished for it, there was no going back. A sacrifice, once given, could not be reclaimed. Ilva was gone. Other girls had suffered and died since, and the line of offerings would go unbroken if she could not manage the impossible and withstand the wrath of a god. But if she failed—if she failed she would not die a martyr, but a traitor and a heretic, her hands stained with the blood of all the girls who'd suffered since Ilva and all the girls who'd suffer after she herself burned.

Anya shook, and as heat spread across the back of her neck, she was sick among the undergrowth. Tears stole her vision, but even as they did, she felt a steadying hand on her shoulder.

"Here now, Anya Astraea," Tieran's voice said. "You're a disaster, aren't you?"

When there was nothing left inside her but overwhelming shame, Anya sat back. She was still sobbing and shaking and it was the funeral clearing all over again, with Weatherell's villagers watching as Anya lost hold of herself over breaking up Ilva's bones.

But Tieran the thief was nothing like Weatherell's self-contained, righteous forest-dwellers. He knelt in front of Anya, so close that their knees touched, and took both her hands in his own. There was no quiet embarrassment on his face. No discomfort. He did not shy away from any part of her relentless sorrow.

"This is my life," Anya said between sobs. "All of it, that people out here see as a curiosity to watch on a stage, or a frightening story to tell their children, or a terrible misfortune that comes upon them because someone else failed in their duty. It's everything I know. Everyone I love. Everyone I've lost. Do you understand? It's not a story or a mistake to me. It's what I'm *meant* for."

"I know," Tieran told her, with unrestrained fury in his voice. "I know, and I'm sorry, Anya. I'm so sorry."

Anya leaned toward him, every part of her aching with the desire to be understood. "I have been afraid every day, for as long as I can remember. Afraid of what happened to the girls who went before me. Afraid of becoming one of them, or not becoming one of them. Afraid of Ilva going in my place, and something unspeakable happening to her. Sometimes it feels like there's not a bit of bravery in me—like all I am is fear and broken pieces, and every nightmare I've ever had has come true."

When Tieran spoke, his words were the last thing Anya expected to hear.

"I met your sister," he said, and Anya's eyes went wide.

Tieran looked down at their joined hands. "Didn't know if I should tell you or not. Still not sure. I saw her twice—once in a place called Longmorrow on her journey out, and then again in that town where you found me, when she was headed back home. The first time it was by chance, at a market. I came round a corner, and there she stood. Bartering with a shopkeeper like it was a game. I didn't think Weatherell girls were supposed to be like that—sharp as tacks, and fierce."

"Ilva was always that way," Anya told him tearfully. "Fearless. Ready to take on the wide world and everything in it."

"Well, I kept clear of her," Tieran said. "Not keen on people who're too bold to be afraid. Never liked the idea of a stranger giving something up on my behalf, either. I didn't ask for that. Don't deserve it. It made me feel like less than nothing, seeing her so confident in what she was doing. Still lit up from the inside, when she knew where she was headed."

Anya put a hand to her mouth as fresh tears pooled in her eyes. But she nodded, because that had been her Ilva. Fierce and flawed and bright.

"Don't think I should say anything about the second time I saw her," Tieran said as he glanced uneasily at Anya.

"Oh, please," Anya begged. "No matter what it is, I want to hear."

Tieran ran a hand over his shorn head and let out a reluctant sigh. "I'd gone south. Wasn't far from your wood, and she was nearly home. I'd camped out in a cheap inn—the sort of place with more bedbugs than bed—and she stopped for the night. She was sitting across the common room, and as soon as I laid eyes on her, I could see it. She was dying. And not just that, but she knew she was dying, too. So I went and sat with her."

Anya looked at him in shock. "Why would you do that? You don't even like Weatherell girls, or anything we stand for."

Acute embarrassment flitted across Tieran's face. "Dunno. What do you want me to say? Sometimes I get lonely. Sometimes I'm a soft touch. Don't want to be, but there it is. I got a heart in my chest and some days I can't stop it bleeding, no matter how hard I try."

"Did you talk?" Anya asked. "What did Ilva say? Did she—did she mention me?"

"Mostly we just sat. But we talked a bit. She said she wanted to get home, before . . . well, you know. Said she had family she wanted to see. And she told me she felt like a failure and that hurt worse than anything, because even though she'd suffered, they'd send another girl once she'd gone. Said she knew who it would be, too—that she had a sister who always looked after her, and fixed everything she'd ever broken."

A thought struck Anya and she gave Tieran a reproachful look through her tears. "You're not lying? You wouldn't say all this just to make me feel better, would you?"

"I would, but I'm not," he said. "Swear it on my dead mum's ashes. It wasn't a good night for me, Anya. Didn't do me no favors. I lost myself for a long time after that—got downcast, and stuck, not wanting to go anywhere or see anyone. It's the only reason I was still in that town where you found me—I'd been there since your sister, living off what I stole from my own people and wondering what in the nine hells I'd been doing with my life. Because no one would ever say that about me—that if they failed, I'd fix things. I don't fix things, I break them.

"And then after a while, I thought I'd have a go at making something right. So I tried to steal back what I owe Matthias and the wanderers and got caught like a fool. Everything went wrong, and they were going to take my hand, and you turned up. Now we're here and I haven't fixed nothing, hardly, and it's all more of a muddle than it ever was before."

"Why did you steal from the wanderers in the first place?" Anya asked gently. All the time they spoke, they'd been sitting with their hands clasped, and she couldn't help glancing down at Tieran's strange, changeling skin against her own. In spite of everything, his touch sent warmth tingling through her fingers and running up her wrists. One of his thumbs moved, slow and soft, tracing circles on the back of her hand.

He shrugged. "I just—I know what you mean, about being afraid. I'm afraid of things too. Of getting close to people. Of them hating who I am once they know me. Of losing anyone, if I start to care about them. So I leave, before anything I'm afraid of can happen. I make them hate me, before they can get there on their own."

The last of Anya's tears had been spent, and she shivered now, not with grief but with cold. The night was cool and damp, and mist was gathering in the forest hollows.

Tieran got to his feet, keeping one of Anya's hands in his own. When he'd stood, he helped her up and led her through the ferns, away from the mess she'd made. Shrugging out of the oilskin coat, he draped it around her shoulders, ears turning red as he did.

"You know, this would be a lot more gallant if it wasn't my coat in the first place," Anya sniffed.

Tieran gave her a look. "Don't bother me when I'm being nice—I haven't had much practice. Anyhow, it's all I've got."

They walked southward, back toward the wanderers' camp, and Anya put her hands into the pockets of Tieran's coat.

"There's an awful lot in here," she said groggily, exhausted by her own grief and by the troubles of the road. "What is this? Is this a bone?"

"One of your good-luck bones," Tieran said, looking assiduously away from her and out at the moonlit wood. "Took it from the pack. You've got five more, and why should you have all the luck?"

For a moment, Anya thought about chiding him for taking the charm without asking. But she was finally growing warmer inside the oilskin coat, and there was something wistful on the boy's sharp face, as he stared at the looming trees.

"Tieran?" Anya said.

"Hm?"

"You can have anything that's mine. You don't have to ask to take it. Or feel bad if you do."

"Don't like that," Tieran said with a shake of his head. "Don't like having you trust me. Anya, I'm—I'm not the right sort of person for that. I'm never going to do anything but let you down. So don't do this. Don't act like I'm someone to put your faith in, just because I've been all right to people a time or two."

"You've come after me three times now," she told him. "Do you know what we say in Weatherell? *Once for chance, twice for luck, thrice tells the heart of a thing.*"

"Doesn't mean nothing. Doesn't mean I won't leave in the end." But Tieran looked at her and they were caught, gazes tangled together in the moonlight. For one shining moment, Anya felt a pull between them—something perfect and fragile and infinitely precious. She took a halting step closer, wanting to obey that pull, to lay hold of what stretched like gossamer between her own heart and his. To strengthen it and lend it force and light.

The thief faltered, and glanced away.

"Don't like this, either," Tieran muttered. "You looking at me like I'm worth something when we both know I'm not. Think you could hurt me, Anya Astraea. Think you could break my heart, and no one's ever come near it before."

Anya watched him, half poised for flight, like a rabbit crouching in the underbrush or a fox caught out on the trail. And a new fear woke in her—that perhaps he was right. Perhaps she was a danger, with unquenchable grief and unholy vengeance mingling like water and fire at her center. With her dark desire to end a thing that had always been worshiped before.

Vengeance is mine; I will repay, said the still small voice that had taken up residence in Anya's soul.

"Then you break my heart first," she offered, to hide her fear and to silence the voice. "I've already told you what's mine is yours, and that I'm in pieces. How much can a little more really hurt?"

Tieran only shook his head wordlessly. For a long while, quiet stretched between them. Night insects sang among the sea of ferns, and wind sighed overhead. They were nearly to the encampment now, and a distant sound of voices drifted to them, along with the faint smell of woodsmoke.

"Don't go," Tieran said at last. "Don't climb that mountain. Don't offer yourself to no god. I told you before—you've given enough. It's not fair. I don't want to watch you give something more."

"Life's not fair," Anya said, though her stomach was in knots and guilt slicked her palms. "And you don't have to watch, you can always leave. I can't, though, Tieran. I have to go—this is my road and my lot and my ending. If you'd come down and seen those girls from Banevale—I can't let that go on a moment longer than necessary."

Tieran was still pale and unhappy in the moonlight, but something else had written itself across his face—a grudging respect. In spite of her lies it buoyed Anya up, and patched the hole left in her by the penance she'd made before Orielle.

"And you told me you're not brave," the thief said.

SIXTEEN
Sharp Things

Anya was unaccountably restless. In less time than she'd thought possible, the wanderers had entirely reorganized themselves, galvanized by their encounter with the unfortunate party from Banevale. They'd left the travelers in the care of their own elders and families with small children, and Matthias and Lee had been up well before dawn, settling all those who could not risk the journey north on an expansive and out-of-the-way farm in the vicinity, whose caretakers were sympathetic to their plight.

Since then, they'd moved fast, heading north at a brisk pace, stopping seldom, and then only for a few minutes at a time. Anya was anxious on Lee's behalf, but though the older woman's limp seemed more pronounced and there was a grim set to her mouth, she was as matter-of-fact and good-humored as ever, never letting out a complaint. Ella and Janie kept close to her too, and Anya noticed Matthias and Janie in quiet conversation in the early afternoon, after which the stops grew more frequent, though no lengthier.

Anya herself drifted between the wanderers, but as the day wore on, impatience and anxiety rose up in her. The sense of being on edge only intensified when she fell in with Matthias and Tieran, so she walked aimlessly along the sunken lane, moving from group to group, pretending to be checking on the ever-gregarious Midge.

But Anya had no taste for the idle conversation others attempted to draw her into, and by the evening halt, she found herself reluctantly returning to Matthias at the head of the band. To her annoyance, Tieran was gone. She'd seen him walking with Matthias not half an hour ago, and now there was no sign of him. It wasn't that she particularly wanted to see him—in fact, she'd rather avoid him after the embarrassing way she'd bared her soul the night before—but it irritated her that he'd disappeared.

"He went up top," Matthias said long-sufferingly, after Anya sighed for the third time in as many minutes. They were making a cold camp along the low road—no fires, dried rations, bedrolls spread along the packed earth of the lane. "I'll boost you up."

"Oh no, I—" Anya began to protest, but Matthias raised a hand.

"You're not staying here with me, not when you're all nervous edges."

Anya frowned.

"You know, you're much nicer to Tieran sometimes than you are to me," she complained, though there was no bitterness behind the words. Matthias was unfailingly kind to everyone, even if he did fuss a little more over the thief he'd raised.

In answer, Matthias only got to his feet and held out a hand.

"This *is* me being nice to you. You'll figure that out eventually. Go on, then."

Putting a foot into his cupped hands, Anya let herself be helped out of the hollow way and into the tangled woods above. As soon as she scrambled upright, a rhythmic sound that had been muffled by the earthen walls of the sunken lane caught her attention. It was not unlike the familiar noise of wood being split for the hearth, but softer, and more even. With a glance back at the wanderers, Anya headed in the direction of the sound.

It led her to a small clearing a quarter mile from the low road. At the center of the open space, Tieran paced back and forth. The same uneasiness rising to a fever pitch in Anya seemed to have afflicted him as well, the only difference being he'd found himself an outlet of sorts. In each hand, the thief held one of his throwing knives. All his restless energy had been honed to a point, and as he paced he would occasionally stop or turn, and launch one of the blades at a distant tree, or both blades in quick succession. That was the sound Anya had heard—the dull impact of a cutting edge striking wood—and as she stood watching Tieran, her lips parted.

Anya thought, suddenly, of her intention in traveling to the mountain and of the bone knife she carried. Seeing Tieran work so capably set despair uncurling in her belly. What was her intent, after all, but idle fancy? However powerful her wish for vengeance, she'd been brought up in peace and bred for one thing—sacrifice. She was made to shatter and made to suffer, and it was foolishness to grasp for anything else.

"Show me how to do that," she said, before she could wish the words back.

Tieran did not startle at the sound of her voice, but he glanced over swiftly, uncertainty written across his face.

"Don't think Weatherell girls are supposed to know how to throw knives," he said, crossing the clearing to pull his blades out of an unoffending tree trunk.

"They're not supposed to fall in with thieves, either," Anya pointed out. "Or cut off their collars, or vanish on the high road, or wander about with half-finished prayers inked into their skin. I'm not a very good Weatherell girl, as it turns out."

"Seem all right to me," Tieran said.

Anya stepped out from among the trees and went to him.

"Please," she said. "The world's harder than I thought it would be. I want... I want to feel less helpless, while walking through it."

It wasn't entirely a lie, but nevertheless, the half-truth sat heavy in the pit of her stomach. Tieran was already wavering, though.

"I dunno, I—"

"Tieran." Anya fixed her eyes on his, refusing to give way. "Don't make me beg."

Scrubbing his free hand across his face, the thief nodded. "You ever done this before?"

Anya laughed nervously. "No. I've skinned rabbits and butchered goats, but nothing like this."

It was not Ilva's ghost that looked out at her from the trees as she answered him and tried to collect her focus. It was a bastard version of the god of the mountain—an amalgamation of the effigy she'd seen at the Elect's way station, and the creature the cautionary play had brought to life, and the demon that haunted Anya's own imagining. Tall and shadowy and broad, he stalked the edges of the clearing, never fully visible through the trees, smoke trailing in his wake.

"I've never done this before either," Tieran confessed. "Taught somebody, I mean. Maybe come over here?"

Anya took a step closer.

Tieran shook his head. "No. Closer yet. Like this."

Reaching out, he pulled Anya nearer still, and turned her gently so her back was to him. It was the night he cut the band from her neck all over again, only this time, Anya knew that the way her heart thundered in her ears had nothing to do with the knives in his hand.

"You're all tied up in knots, Weatherell girl," Tieran said quietly. "Can't throw nothing like that. Shut your eyes and let it go."

Anya did as she was told, taking several deep breaths. Though her blood still sang in her veins and her pulse ran like a river in spring flood, a bit of the tension drained from her shoulders.

"Better," Tieran said. "Now stand just so."

His hands went from Anya's shoulders to her hips and she did as she was told, shifting her feet, fighting to maintain the slight calm she'd settled into.

"Which hand?" Tieran asked.

"Um. Right."

He pressed the hilt of a knife to her palm, and she glanced

down at it. It was an unappealing, keen-edged thing, fit for violence and not much else. But Tieran arranged Anya's grip around it as if he had gifted her something precious and fine. He showed her how to draw her arm back and where in the arc of her throw she ought to loosen her grip.

"Think you can manage?"

Anya blinked at the tree towering before them and envisioned the god of the mountain in its place. "We're awfully close. Shouldn't we back up a bit?"

She could hear the smile in Tieran's voice when he answered. "This is plenty far enough for now. Gonna be surprised if you stick it, to be honest."

Anya scowled and did as she'd been told, staying loose on her feet as Tieran stepped away.

"Don't forget—keep that wrist locked up," he cautioned.

The god of the mountain. The god of the mountain before her, wreathed in flame, with Ilva's name on his monstrous tongue.

Anya threw the knife, and it stuck fast.

She turned on her heel immediately, cutting Tieran off as he began to say something congratulatory.

"Would that kill someone?" she asked.

The thief frowned. "Depends. On what you threw, and who it was, and where you hit them. I don't do this to kill nobody, just so we're clear, Anya. You were right—I like sharp things and it's a trick that earns me a bit of coin if I show it off in market towns. But that's all."

Anya pulled her bone knife from its hidden sheath. "Could

I kill someone with this? It's sharper, now you looked after it."

Tieran gave her a pained look. "Dunno? Expect you could kill somebody with anything, if you wanted it badly enough. That's not gonna do much if you throw it, though. With that, maybe you could cut someone's throat? But you'd have to go in from the side and really get your arm into it."

"Show me," Anya said, and Tieran pantomimed how it might be done—the thrust of the bone blade in through the side of the throat, the jerk of the arm forward to sever the artery and the windpipe.

When he handed the knife back, Tieran hesitated. "You got someone what wants killing? Because if somebody hurt you, you can just say."

"No," Anya lied. "It's nothing like that. I'm just tired of being afraid, that's all. Will you show me how to throw again? I want to be sure I remember."

There was something uneasy in Tieran's eyes, but he came to her at once and positioned himself behind her. Anya busied herself with finding the right stance, and it wasn't until she felt the brush of his fingers against the base of her neck that she realized Tieran's attention had settled on her in a new and entirely different way. When she turned, he drew his hand back quickly, guilt plain on his face.

"What were you—" she began.

Then she remembered the unreadable prayer, etched into the skin of her back. For a moment, she and Tieran only stared at each other, wide-eyed.

"You can read Divinitas," Anya breathed, and Tieran, to his credit, did not lie. He only nodded miserably.

"Can read it on account of my father, from back before I joined the wanderers."

"Will you tell me what the words say?" Anya asked, unable to hide her eagerness. "I can't even read them, we're only taught Brythonic."

Tieran shook his head, fierce in his denial. "No. Not gonna do it."

"Please," Anya said. "I don't want to ask the Elect. Not ever. But I don't want to just live with not knowing, either."

Fixing his eyes on the ground, Tieran flushed. "You're wanting a lot from me today, you know that?"

In answer, Anya turned her back to him. She slipped out of her braces and pulled the shirt up over her shoulders, leaving her back laid bare. She could hear Tieran draw in a quavering breath, and then he was closer again, his fingers trailing across her skin.

"It's from the Cataclysm," he said. "But I don't like it. You're not gonna like it. And it isn't finished, but I can tell you what the rest would say if it was."

"Just read."

Slowly, Tieran spoke the words.

"A garden enclosed is my lamb, my offering;
A spring shut up, a fountain sealed.
Awake, O north wind; and come, thou south;
Blow upon my garden, that the sacrifices thereof may flow out.

Let me come into my garden, and feast upon the offered fruits.

As the lily among thorns, so is my love among the daughters.

My beloved is mine, and I shall feed upon her: I feedeth among

the lilies.

Open to me, my lamb,

My love,

My sacrifice,

My undefiled."

For a long moment, nothing was audible in the clearing but the wind and the night insects, already shrilling as the last dim remnants of daylight faded.

With infinite care, Tieran smoothed Anya's shirt back into place. She stood as she was, and the tension that had plagued her all day came rising up with a vengeance. It blazed through her like fire, even as she cast her eyes on the woods and saw the shadowy form of the god, dogging her footsteps, haunting her path. This time he had Ilva at his side, one of his ponderous hands on her narrow shoulder, and her face was a mask of agony.

"Anya?" Tieran said. "You all right?"

When she turned to him, all she could feel was flame, searing everything that lay beneath her skin.

"I'm not his," Anya said adamantly, even as Tieran nodded in agreement. "Whatever they say, whatever they make of me, I'm going to choose what I give or don't give, and it won't be all of me, and I'll *never* be his. You know that, don't you?"

"I know," Tieran said, and he made the words a prayer for her, to rival the injunction written across her back. "You're your own, and nobody else's."

"My own, and nobody else's," Anya repeated. "I choose what happens to me until I get to the mountain, and afterward, if I come back down."

"*When* you come back down," Tieran said stubbornly.

Anya reached up and cupped the side of his sharp, clever face with one hand, running her thumb from the corner of his mouth to the line of his jaw.

"I choose what happens to me," she whispered.

"You do," Tieran answered, his voice a raw and wanting thing.

And Anya chose. She rose up and kissed Tieran the thief the way a dying girl kisses a boy—with hunger and regret and desperation. She kissed him like a sacrifice, holding nothing of herself back, her hands on his shoulders and on the stubble of his shorn hair. And Tieran, despite his sharpness and his lies and his leaving, kissed her like a worshiper, as if he would lay all of himself out at her request, and count it glory just to be looked upon by his god. They came together and did not part for a long while, and when at last they did, it was Tieran who moved back first. His hands were trembling, shifting from shape to shape, and Anya took them in her own and pressed them to her lips.

"I want to be a knife," she told him.

"You are," Tieran swore.

"Make me believe it."

"Anya Astraea, you could cut me open with a look."

"With a touch?"

Anya glanced up at her thief. She put a fingertip to his chin and ran it down his neck, his chest, the travel-lean stretch of his abdomen, and before she could go further, Tieran let out a sound that set every part of her alight. He took her by the wrist and pulled her closer and they were kissing again, a wildfire between them, but the burn of it did not feel like blasphemy or vengeance or anger. It felt, to Anya, like shackles cast off. Like the first bright day of a journey that could lead only to joy.

So Anya knew as she kissed Tieran that her heart was a worse liar than the rest of her, and selfish as well. There could be no joyous ending for them, and if she were righteous and fair, she'd pull back now, for the journey she'd set herself upon would only lead to devastation. But Anya could not bear to think of that or to pull away. Instead, she carried on, tangling herself and the thief together, and it was a mystery to her how she could all at once feel so tainted by guilt and radiant with glory.

† † † †

Something was burning.

Down in the hollow way, smoke hung everywhere, oily and choking, filling the air with a thick gray pall until Anya could not see her hands stretched out before her.

"Tieran?" she called, starting upright from where she lay on her bedroll. "Matthias?"

A fit of coughing seized Anya, bending her double. There was no sign of the camp she'd dozed off at the heart of—everyone was gone. Her eyes smarted and panic clawed at her insides, but the wanderers kept to the low road whenever possible. She could not risk climbing up to clearer air and losing them in the smoke.

"Tieran? Midge?"

Reaching out, Anya felt for one of the sunken lane's earth walls. Her fingertips hit gritty soil and gnarled tree roots and she stumbled forward, still calling for the wanderers.

"Janie? Ella? Anyone?"

Through the smoke, a noise grew audible over the hammer strikes of Anya's own heartbeat. Hot and arid, a hiss and snap—the sound of flames eating away at dry fuel. She pushed forward in spite of it, desperate to find the wanderers. But as she rounded a bend in the lane, she stopped short, feet striking something heavy and yielding.

Her eyes shut, and she took a sudden breath, which ended in another fit of coughing. When it had calmed, Anya knelt.

There was a body, propped up against the wall of the sunken lane. As Anya knelt beside it, a gust of wind tore down the hollow way, clearing the shroud of smoke for the first time.

Matthias lay before her, his plain clothes singed and scorched through in places, his face a ruin of crimson and ashen burns. Even in death, he'd found no rest, for his eyes were open, staring farther down the low road to where the remainder of the wanderers lay scattered. Every one of them was utterly still, the sunken road turned to a graveyard.

"Tieran," Anya whispered, and struggled to her feet, moving unsteadily forward.

At the center of the carnage she found the thief, facedown in the earthen lane. She knew him by the fraying, charred oilskin coat he wore, and by the way he had one arm thrown over Midge's lifeless body. A piece of Anya knew she shouldn't look. That she should spare herself the sight of Tieran's sharp, familiar face.

Instead, she reached out.

As she did, the dim hiss and snap of flames intensified. A new billow of smoke wafted through the hollow way, pouring not from some unseen source, but from Anya herself. Her hand, reaching for Tieran, was a twisted and inhuman thing, wreathed in fire that emanated from her, and yet she did not burn.

It was only those around her who had.

With a sickening jolt and an intake of breath, Anya woke. In the quiet dark of the lane, surrounded by sleeping wanderers, she pressed both hands to her mouth, fighting to keep silent, to stay still, to stop shaking with leftover panic and despair. Everything around her was as it should be—night insects singing in the woods overhead, the camp at perfect peace.

Or almost perfect. Before Anya, in the few feet between her and the wall of the sunken lane, Ilva wavered to life. A trio of girls flickered into being too—strangers this time, the marks of the god's dread touch unmistakable on each of them.

One, Ilva whispered. *Two.*

Three, the first of the girls said.

Four, added the next.

Five, said the last.

And after numbering themselves among the dead, they faded

entirely, leaving only Ilva to linger a moment longer, her filmy gaze a reproach.

Then Ilva vanished too.

Anya curled in on herself, alone in the dark with the unbearable weight of the guilt she'd carried for as long, it seemed, as she could remember.

Soft noises drifted through the night. Anya stayed just as she was. A blurry, mottled gray-and-black shape appeared before her, and Midge settled down, warm and real and comforting, fitting herself into the curve of Anya's body with the uncanny and perfect geometry of dogs. As Anya's arms went around Midge, she felt an equally stolid presence behind her.

"Just gonna sleep here for now if that's all right?" Tieran murmured, quiet enough not to wake his people. "On account of maybe you could use someone close by."

Anya nodded. Carefully, Tieran shifted until his back was to hers, and draped the oilskin coat over them both. Little by little, the fear and creeping darkness that had taken hold of Anya subsided, driven back by the sounds of Midge gently snoring, and of her thief humming tunelessly under his breath.

When sleep found her again, she did not dream.

SEVENTEEN
Banevale

The following weeks passed in a haze of walking from dawn till dusk. Of cold camps, made in haste and broken before sunrise. Of dreams of burning, and ghosts numbering themselves before they disappeared.

Seven.

Nine.

Fifteen.

Twenty.

Twenty-eight.

Of slipping away with Tieran, any night the moon was out. Though Anya had begun to hit a target reliably with a thrown blade, it still felt like too little from too close. It worried her, as Tieran explained how to drive a knife through the ribs to pierce the lungs or the liver, to think that perhaps the creature she intended to kill did not have lungs or a liver, or flesh that could be damaged at all.

But she said nothing of her pervasive fears, or her true reason for wanting to learn to do violence. And if Tieran ever seemed troubled by her determination and the relentlessness of her focus, well—with a look or a word she could ignite the spark between them, kissing him until his hands trembled and flashed like quicksilver and any doubt slipped from his mind. He'd proved an easy mark, this changeling thief, and Anya tried to ignore the soul-deep unease that ate away at her when she surreptitiously held his hand, or when he looked at her and she caught sadness in his eyes. Perhaps she had not been entirely honest, but he knew she was going to the mountain. What more was needed? That much was enough to warn him they'd never have a happy ending. She wasn't keeping him entirely in the dark.

And then one day, after a fortnight of unforgiving travel, it was simply there.

The wanderers had carried on walking under cover of darkness for hours the previous night, eager to reach the city of Banevale and the god's mountain beyond, knowing their goal was close at hand. When Anya woke in the cold gray light before dawn, sore from weeks of travel, she could see it on the horizon.

The mountain. Bane Nevis. Her beginning and her end.

A few of the wanderers were stirring already, but most kept to their scant bedrolls. It was cold at night in the northlands, which were wild, barren places. The roads they traveled now were not sunken lanes and hollow ways but faint footpaths across wind-torn and heather-clad moors. Matthias and Lee traded off leading the group, picking their way forward carefully at the head of the straggling procession, and more than once Anya had been struck by the thought that even without her crimson band, she'd found as much support on the road as any Weatherell girl had ever been given. The realization made it worse, to know that she would soon leave the wanderers without a word or a thank-you and attempt the unthinkable. The unholy.

Shivering, she made her way to the edge of the haphazard, open encampment. Morning was coming on clear and fine, and rosy light already softened the distant mountain's face. It was no young and jagged peak, but an ancient thing, worn down by weather and time. It sat amid a range of lesser precipices, and something in Anya splintered as she looked at it. She felt herself fragment, breaking down into yet smaller pieces, and it had been a lie when she told Tieran that a little more damage couldn't possibly hurt. It took her breath away—the sight of that gray, weathered mountain, the knowledge of what waited on its heights, the fire that seared everything within her, burning her up from the inside out. Anya wrapped her arms about her middle and stood utterly still, wishing that she, too, could be impervious stone.

"It cuts at you, seeing it for the first time. Don't you think?"

When Anya turned, it was not Tieran standing an arm's length away, but Ella.

"First I saw it was in winter," the other girl went on, soft and wistful as she fixed her eyes on the peak. "All that gray was covered up with snow, white and fair against a far blue sky. It was beautiful. And it hurt to look at."

Anya stole a glance at her, quiet and gentle, yet radiating a sort of confidence. Ella was certain of her people and her place in the world, in a way Anya herself had never been. And at last, she found it in her to ask what truth Ella and Janie had meant to tell her the night of the cautionary play.

"Ella?" Anya said. "Who are all of you? Why do you choose to stay hidden?"

"It's not much of a choice," the girl said with a slight smile. "Or at least, Mum and Matthias say it didn't feel like one when we first set out."

Anya waited and Ella gave her a searching look. "We don't . . . tell many folk the truth of this, you know. There are wanderers like us across Albion, and not all of them have our reasons for it. Some fell on hard times, some like the freedom, some were born to the life and can't imagine any other way of being. It's not easy—the Elect and Albion's lords never approve, but they're more at odds with us than with others. Or at least, the Elect are."

"Whatever the truth is, you can trust me with it," Anya said. "I'm certainly carrying secrets of my own."

"Aren't we all?" Ella said. Letting out a breath, she nodded. "Well then, Anya. Welcome to Weatherell. Or what's left of our version of it."

Ice lanced through Anya. "What? I don't understand."

Ella's expression grew pained. "No. Mum and Matthias didn't either, when we first took to the low roads. They'd thought we were the only ones. But we weren't, and we aren't. The Elect have copies of Weatherell all across Albion—villages cut off to raise spotless lambs for the sacrifice. Best we can tell, a girl goes out to the god every year—some years more than one is sent, if the monster on that mountain is restless."

Anya could not look away from the distant gray shape of Bane Nevis, and it felt as if all the world were shifting beneath her.

"Mum was one of the girls who went from our village," Ella continued. "The god twisted her spine, and that's what gives her trouble walking. She's stubborn and never complains, but I know it's been worse than ever this year. When Janie and I were still little things, she told Matthias she was leaving with us, so we'd never be pushed into what she did. Matthias was our Arbiter back then—can you even imagine him as an Arbiter?—and he'd never yet had to send a girl out. The Elect kept him in the dark about a great many things, because despite his position, they didn't trust him. I suppose they were right not to. He says the job didn't fit him, on account of him and one of the selectmen carrying a flame for each other. They could never say anything, or even let on how they felt. And when Mum told Matthias she was going, he knew she was doing the brave and right thing, and that if the rest of the village didn't have the courage to follow, they'd be worse than cowards."

Anya shivered and wrapped her arms about herself. She could not even imagine such a thing happening in her own Weatherell. Arbiter Thorn was unfalteringly strict and stringent in his application of the Cataclysm's requirements, and Willem—well. Willem was who she was.

"So those of us who were willing left," Ella said. "In the dead of night one spring, we disappeared. Matthias's selectman wouldn't come, and Mum said if our father hadn't died of flux a few years back, she doubted he would have left either. Mum and Matthias cut our village in half to do what they knew to be right. I was little yet, but I remember creeping away, and those first days on the road. None of us are who we were then—we've all taken new names, and been changed by the traveling and by living out here at the edges. But Mum and Matthias still say we'd have lost ourselves if we'd stayed and kept on watching our girls suffer to keep us safe. This way, we chose who we became. I think they're right in that. Always have done."

Anya hesitated. She glanced back at the encampment and saw that while many of the wanderers were up and ready, none were within earshot of herself and Ella. The girl's quiet thoughtfulness made her brave, and she decided to risk speaking of something she'd never so much as hinted at since leaving Weatherell.

"Has no one tried to end the god?" she asked, her voice low, fire burning hot and bitter in her belly. "Has no one ever decided to cut this trouble off at the root?"

"Five times, that I know of," Ella said without hesitation. "I've asked Matthias the same thing. The Romans tried, when they first woke the god. Sent a *centuria* of men—eighty souls, all told—up that mountain. Every one of them died in torment. Those were bad days, and the Elect don't speak of them. For years after, the god ravaged the north country, killing countless folk. So the Romans built walls clear across the countryside, which did little to stop him, and finally they declared this land cursed, and left it altogether. There was no peace until the Elect had already risen and begun to worship the god and sent out the first offering."

With the sun warming it, Bane Nevis looked serene and untouchable, as if it could not possibly have weathered so much trouble, and seen so much bloodshed on its vast gray slopes.

"And the others?" Anya asked.

"Two more groups made it up the mountain," Ella said. "Both failed and died and brought about a year of terror afterward, as the god refused to rest. Another two were found out by the Elect before they ever reached Bane Nevis and put to death in ways crueler than even the god could manage, to spare the north the devastation another failure would bring. The last attempt was over a hundred years back. No one tries anymore."

Nearby, Ilva took shape like a will o' the wisp, and stared at Anya with mournful corpse eyes.

Has one of us ever tried? Anya wanted to ask. *A Weatherell girl, I mean?*

But it felt too close to the heart, and she could not bear to speak her truth within sight of the mountain, so she kept silent.

"Lee says we'd best get moving," Tieran said from behind them, and both Anya and Ella turned. The thief stood hunched into the oilskin coat like a disgruntled crow, all spines and discontentment. His eyes shifted from Anya to the mountain, and without another word Tieran strode back to camp.

"Don't think I've ever seen him so anxious before, and not light out for elsewhere," Ella said. "You've worked wonders with the boy."

But it was not enough for Anya. She found herself hungry, here within sight of the end. Starving for life and contact and gladness and a certain future. For more of a chance than she in her collar, or Janie and Ella with their ceaseless wandering, had been given.

If this was how it had felt to be Ilva, always yearning for more and better, she wondered how her wild sister hadn't flown apart.

† † † †

The first sign that things would be different in Banevale came when Matthias and Lee called a halt in the afternoon, before the city had even come into view. They broke the wanderers up into little groups—no more than three or four together at most. Everyone was given instructions as to where to enter the city, what names to give, which guards to bribe and which to avoid altogether. A map was passed around, with entire sections of Banevale engulfed in alarming red-painted circles.

"Anya, you're with Tieran," Matthias said gruffly when the wanderers had already begun to scatter, and in spite of the mountain, Anya felt a small lightening of her soul, followed by an immediate stab of remorse and dread.

Not long now. Not long until she did the leaving.

Banevale was not at all like Sarum, which had been busy and dirty and loud, nor like Oxnaforde with its glistening streets and glittering lights and crowds of happy people. The mountain towered over the city, a constant and undeniable presence, and the entire place was surrounded by an old Roman wall, kept in immaculate condition.

Through the nearest gate, Anya could see a line of people waiting to exit, but she and Tieran were the only ones on their way in.

"Just keep quiet and let me talk," he said, taking her hand, and she anchored herself with that—with the touch of his skin, warm against her own.

At the gate, a pair of bored guards in blue-and-black uniforms were looking over travel papers or openly accepting bribes. They glanced quickly at Tieran and Anya, and then one held out a hand. She was an older woman, perhaps Willem's age, with a self-assured way about her.

Tieran passed the guard a heavy gold coin, his half of the exchange moving so swiftly it was as if the coin had appeared on the guard's palm by magic.

"Names and purpose of travel?" the guard asked.

"Tieran and Anya of Stull, brother and sister, here to see about bringing our cousin Esme out to Essex with us till the city's safe again," Tieran said without hesitation. "Just her, though, the rest of her family stays, and she'll be coming back—don't want too many people shifting about, and we'll get papers sorted for her before going. To be honest I think my uncle and aunt'll be glad to see the last of our Esme for a while—she's a bit of a lazy one, she is."

The words tumbled out of him, jovial and assured, as if, just as he claimed, he'd been born with lies on his tongue instead of truth. But when Anya gripped his hand tighter, he gave hers a reassuring squeeze in return.

"And you?" the guard said, turning to Anya. Her gaze was intent, searching up and down, though Anya couldn't sort out what she was looking for. "What do you think about your shiftless cousin Esme coming to stay?"

"No use asking her nothing," Tieran cut in before Anya could speak. "She's mute, see. Not much luck in my family when it comes to the girls."

Anya shot Tieran a glowering look and he returned it with a bland and innocent stare.

"Well, I don't envy you your journey home, with a mute sister and a lazy cousin," the guard said with a smile. Her gaze cut again to Anya, who fixed her eyes instinctively on the ground. "Here're your entry papers. You're to present them if a guard ever asks, so we know you came in properly and were accounted for at the gates. Move on then, boy."

Nodding, Tieran drew Anya through the gate and on into the city.

"Look, it was either I make you mute or a liar too," the thief muttered as they passed out of earshot of the guards. "And much as you like to pretend to be the last, I *know* telling falsehoods doesn't sit right with you—can see it in your eyes every time you twist the truth. Maybe you lie, Anya, but that doesn't make you a liar. You don't lie about what matters, either—think if I could see through to the heart of you, there'd be only true things."

Anya slipped her hand out of his, suddenly unable to bear the touch. She feared she'd burn him, with the fire beneath her skin, the force and scope of the lies even he hadn't been able to see.

They hadn't got far from the gate when a sound of booted feet came hurrying along behind them. Tieran glanced anxiously about, but the road they traveled on was busy, the buildings on either side pressed up against each other with no convenient alleyways to bolt down.

"You there," the Nevis guard who'd questioned them at the gate called out. "I need a word."

Tieran squared his shoulders staunchly and stepped in front of Anya, but the guard shook her head.

"Not with you, boy. With the girl."

"It's all right, Tieran," Anya assured him under her breath, before approaching the guard.

"Anya Astraea," the woman said bluntly, "it's no good pretending you're anyone else. We've been keeping an eye on you since you first appeared on the road."

"Well, who hasn't?" Anya said with some irritation. It seemed every shadowy power in Albion was following her progress, and she hated the idea of being watched, whether she could see her audience or not. "I don't see what business my journey is of yours, though. I'm here on behalf of the Elect."

"Everything that happens in Banevale is Lord Nevis's business," the guard said, taking no notice of Anya's frustration. "And most of what happens in Albion, besides. If he has his way, the Elect will hold less power before long."

Anya stayed stubborn. She could not falter this close to the mountain—could not let on that she was anything less than holy, and a perfect offering. "All of that may be your Lord Nevis's business, but it isn't mine. I'm meant for climbing a mountain and placating the god. No more, no less."

The woman fixed Anya with an incisive stare. "You wouldn't want more if you could have it?"

Anya swallowed. "No."

Still unconvinced, the guard held something out. A small, unremarkable coin, one face stamped with the god's mountain and the other a smooth blank.

"If you ever change your mind, just leave this sitting out. It doesn't matter where you are—we have people everywhere. Once you do, Lord Nevis will ensure your safety."

Reluctantly, Anya reached out and took the coin. "I won't be needing this. But thank you for your concern, I suppose."

The guard nodded. "I'll relay your thanks to Lord Nevis. Good day to you."

And with that she was gone. Anya turned back to Tieran, who'd been watching all along.

"They're uncommon interested in you," he said. "Nevis is always making trouble, and I think someday he'll have it out with the Elect, but I've never known him try so hard to push a Weatherell girl off her path."

"They haven't succeeded, and they won't," Anya said, entirely truthfully. She couldn't be pushed off a Weatherell girl's true path, not when she'd never really been on it.

"Well, if you mean to do what you set out for, you got a plan from this point on?" Tieran asked as they walked side by side through Banevale's too-quiet streets. There were not enough people about, and everywhere, doors were closed tight and windows shuttered. The air smelled vaguely of ashes, too, and in some places gaps showed between buildings, filled with charred and smoking rubble.

"Wait till tomorrow morning," Anya said. "Then put my collar on, find the Elect, and finish what I started."

She chose her words with care, adding layers to her lies, so that he might not see all the way to the truth. Sure enough, Tieran gave her a disbelieving look.

"You dodged the Elect all the way here only to have them see you off at the end? Not likely."

Anya gave the appearance of relenting. "Well, all right. I'm not going to do what I ought to. I'll go quietly at first light, on my own, and get things done without a fuss."

"I'll see you off," Tieran said. "Don't care what I told you, or what anyone else did. I can be here for that, Anya. I can stay for you."

"Thank you," Anya murmured. What she did not say was that it was the wanderers she intended to slip, and not the Elect. It would not be tomorrow that she went, but tonight, as soon as she was able to get away unnoticed. And Tieran the thief would certainly not be given an opportunity to see her off. It would break her yet again to have him do so, and she could not endure it—not here, with her task and her vengeance scant miles away.

As they walked on, the streets grew not just quiet, but abandoned. The city turned into a dwelling fit for ghosts, and Ilva peered around every corner. Then, quite suddenly, they reached a place of utter devastation.

A square opened up before them, and beyond it lay the city's northern wall, right up against the lowest slopes of Bane Nevis itself. The wall, so well maintained elsewhere, had been blown to pieces. A vast, rubble-strewn hole gaped in it, the edges blackened with scorch marks. Trails of burned and broken cobbles led off into unknown sections of the lifeless city, and here and there immense, charred handprints blossomed upon the walls of buildings, cracks radiating out from the god's destructive touch.

"Don't look," Tieran said under his breath, "don't look, it's all right, you don't have to look," and Anya could not be sure if he was speaking to himself or to her.

For her part, she looked. She fixed her gaze on the scale of the devastation the god had wrought and let it sink down into the very deepest parts of her soul. She let her fire answer his until it seemed as if the word *vengeance* rang from the empty housetops and echoed from the sides of the mountain itself.

Vengeance is mine

I will repay

And Ilva's words, whispered back from every alleyway and shadowed corner, tangled together with that louder refrain.

Don't go. Don't let anyone else—

Vengeance is mine

I will repay

"Come on," Anya said fiercely to Tieran. "Let's not stand about, I want to get this over with."

The wanderers had already begun to gather in a disused mill

at the center of a near-abandoned section of Banevale. Pigeons roosted among the rafters, making soft, frowsy sounds, and the whole place smelled of dust and bird droppings. A few doors led off the mill floor to small storerooms, but after looking them over, the wanderers kept to the expansive open space at the mill's center. The mood among them was hushed and expectant, and Anya sat restlessly at Tieran's side as Matthias and Lee got up to speak.

"I've put out word that we're in Banevale, with the intention of assisting anyone who wants to leave without the permission of the guard or the Elect," Lee said without preamble. Her voice was strong and even, but she looked tired and a little sad. Anya couldn't even imagine Philomena or Sylvie braving the road north a second time, as Lee had done. Willem, perhaps, might manage it if necessary, but it would be wrath that carried her, not the resolute compassion that fueled the wanderers.

"We'll let a few good people know where we can be found, so the news will spread," Lee went on. "By day some of us'll go into the city, looking for anyone who seems like they might want help. The rest will stay here, to sort out whoever turns up. Matthias and me will buy spare packs and travel rations, so we don't have to send folk away with nothing—you all know better than most what a blow it is to leave everything behind, even if it's just for a while. We'll outfit those we give a hand to until our money runs out. If you've got a bit set aside and want to chip in, that's kind of you. If you can't, there's no shame in it."

Anya watched as a number of the wanderers, spread across

the dim, echoing space of the mill floor, began to search through their packs and pockets.

"We won't pretend to you that what we're doing isn't a risk," Matthias said, straightforward as always. "But it's something we all agreed to before heading north. Should anyone turn up here who seems like other than what they say, you turn them away without a second thought. If they so much as look at you strangely, or give you an odd feeling in the pit of your stomach, you heed that warning. We've all been on the road too long and been through too much not to trust ourselves and each other. Better we turn aside one or two on a faulty suspicion than have all of us fall into the hands of the Elect, or even the guard. We'll be using the old tunnels under Brewer's Square to get folk out this time, but if you end up in a tight spot, a guard named Wicks at the northeast gate is a friend too."

A thought struck Anya as she glanced over at Janie and Ella. The sisters sat side by side, Ella's head resting on Janie's shoulder.

"Tieran," she said under her breath. "The Elect always want the girl who goes to the god to choose it for herself. So why do they bother making life difficult for all of you? Why do the wanderers have to hide, just because they preferred not to be another Weatherell?"

"Someone told you who they all are, then?" Tieran asked, and Anya nodded.

"Ella did."

The thief shrugged. "Trouble is, you think if anyone else knew they could leave—like this Weatherell done—they'd stay and watch their girls suffer? They'd all try to get out from under the Elect, and there'd be no one left, and it wouldn't be just Banevale that ended in flames."

Tieran spoke the words tersely, as if it hurt to dredge them up and speak them.

"It's cruel," Anya whispered, drawing her knees up and resting her chin on her arms. "All of it."

"Think I don't know that, sitting here next to you?" Tieran said.

As darkness gathered over Banevale, deep-voiced bells tolled throughout the city, the sound echoing back from the slopes of Bane Nevis.

"They're curfew bells," Janie explained. She'd drafted her sister, Tieran, and Anya to help her fill packs with rations and blankets for anyone taking to the low roads, and they all sat together in a circle, working quickly by firelight.

"The god only comes down from Nevis after dark, so folk are supposed to be locked up indoors. Some can't, though, on account of working late in the woolen mills, or running messages, or being corner girls. Others don't care—they think themselves righteous enough, and that the god wouldn't visit his wrath on them if they crossed his path."

"So he'll be here tonight?" Anya asked. She felt dizzy with the knowledge, but forced herself to stay placid, to keep on with the work at hand.

"Maybe," Janie said. "Some nights he comes, some he doesn't. They say he walks the city more nights than not, though. That it's getting worse, and he's roaming farther. If he's not checked, eventually he'll move past Banevale and start preying on the villages beyond."

Anya scrambled to her feet.

"Going to bed," she murmured. "I'm worn out."

Halfway to where she'd left her bedroll, Tieran caught her up. "Anya?"

"Yes?"

He sighed. "Nothing. Just... don't leave without saying goodbye."

Stepping forward, Tieran bent and pressed a kiss to her forehead, gentle and delicate in the way of a wild thing. Anya fought a ferocious urge to cling to him—to tell him all of her truths, and to warn him that she was likely on her way to her own end, and that he ought not to break his heart over her.

But the words stuck in her throat. She wanted to leave with him still thinking she was good and righteous, rather than this creature she'd become. A bitter soul, half alive and haunted, unable to shake her ghosts or her fate or her guilt.

So Anya lied to Tieran. She lied to him more cruelly than she'd ever done before, and she did it with a smile on her face.

"I'd never," she said. "I want you to know when I go, so you can watch for when I come back."

For an interminable stretch of time Anya lay on her side on her bedroll, eyes shut tight, feigning sleep. Finally the hum of the wanderers' quiet, purposeful activity subsided. Fires were doused, blankets laid out, and silence fell over the mill.

Anya sat up.

Halfway across the mill floor, Ilva stood beside the embers of the encampment's central fire. So close to the mountain, she was hardly a ghost—more a wraith, the suggestion of someone who had once been human. Her once-lovely eyes were preternaturally large, turned to vast wells of grief, and her mouth, as she counted the dead, worked in a stomach-churning, unnatural way.

One, Ilva wept, her voice like wind over old bones. *Two. Three.*

On and on she counted, numbering the girls Anya had seen die and vanish, until more spirits glimmered to life before her.

Forty-eight.

Forty-nine.

Fifty.

Each counted herself and vanished, leaving only Anya, among all the living, to number the sorrowful dead.

Staring at the final shreds of her sister's tormented spirit, Anya could not bear the thought of bringing still more of her up the mountain. The god had been tearing Ilva to pieces since before she and Anya were born—they'd inherited a legacy of injustice and brokenness. Anya would not bring even a shattered fragment of Ilva into his presence again.

Soundlessly, she crept between the wanderers to where Tieran slept. Slipping her hand beneath the bundled blanket that served him for a pillow, she drew out two of his short, sharp-edged blades. In its place, she left the bone knife crafted from the last remnant of her sister.

It was as much of an apology and as much of her heart as Anya could spare, this side of the mountain.

From there it was only a few steps out of the mill and into the night air, and it all but killed Anya not to look back. She felt utterly low—only a shade less bleak than in the moments after Ilva died. But she did not look back, and she did not give in. She let the fire in her grow to an unrelenting heat, and left the wanderers and her thief behind.

EIGHTEEN

The Shadow of the Mountain

When Anya reached the broken gap in the city wall closest to Bane Nevis, the stones that had been charred and cold hours before were crimson and smoking. She stared at them, and everything in her quailed. She glanced back toward Banevale, where a path of little fires still burned in the god's wake, flames licking at the cobblestones and at places on the walls he'd touched.

It was, in a way, a good sign. She'd wanted to know the god was off his mountain and out in the city. She had little enough working in her favor—she could at least claim the element of surprise.

A waxing moon lit the slopes of Bane Nevis. Anya was glad of it. She hadn't thought to bring a light, and the path, although well-worn and marked with occasional red arrows, was treacherous in places and choked with loose stones.

She climbed as quickly as she could, in a panic that the god would return and catch her on the trail. Everything passed in a blur until she came out, quite suddenly, on a plateau. At its center a long, narrow lake glinted in the moonlight, and Anya's path ran past it. She slowed a little to catch her breath, and at the lake's far side, stopped short.

Banevale lay spread out far below her, most of the city in shadow, but one glittering quarter of it shining with light and life. Buttoning up her oilskin, Anya pushed her hair back from her face and frowned. The city was under curfew—it did not seem right that part of it should glow so brightly she could see it from the mountain itself. As she peered down, she could make out a thin, fiery trail on the city's darkened side, which ended in something that burned like an ember.

Swallowing, Anya hurried on. The next leg of her climb was a precipitous scramble, so steep in some places that her stomach dropped out from inside her. At last, she reached a broad, rock-strewn plateau. Casting about herself in the clear night air, she saw there were no further heights to climb.

She'd reached the summit of Bane Nevis.

Tall cairns, rising above Anya's head, led across the plateau in an eerie procession. Each one was painted with red runes for protection, and as Anya drew closer to the first, she found that they were not built of stone, as she'd initially thought.

They were made of bone. Of hundreds of human skulls, bleached white by rain and sun.

Anya took in a sharp breath, thrown back to the day she'd broken up Ilva's bones. It had been Arbiter Thorn she'd given her sister's skull to. Tradition dictated that the Arbiter received it, and for all Weatherell's many bone charms, she'd never seen that particular piece of a girl anywhere about the village.

Because they were brought back here, to the mountain.

Anya's hands formed involuntary fists at her sides. It was unfair, and intolerable, that after being indelibly marked by their journeys to Bane Nevis in life, the Weatherell girls should have this part of themselves brought back in death. Enshrined on the mountain, watching with blank eye sockets every time another girl walked by, every time the god broke his vows and his infinitely costly bonds and went burning down the slope.

Though Anya burned too, there was a cold pit of fear at her center, behind that fire. Every cairn was a testament to the centuries the god had spent on his ruthless predations. A reminder of his unchecked power and of the history Anya was about to set herself apart from. Squaring her jaw, she walked on. There could be no true life for her while she remained burdened by her guilt over Ilva and by the weight of her own unfulfilled conviction, summed up in her sister's last impossible wish.

Don't go. Don't let anyone else go.

Anya would be a blasphemous flame all the way into death if need be, even if it left her name forever cursed. She only prayed, to the sky and the mountain and whoever might be listening, that she'd be able to drag Albion's vicious god along with her.

Ghosting between the shadows of the cairns, Anya couldn't help but search for Ilva, uncertain whether she hoped to find her or wished for her to stay far from the god and his lair. There was no sign of Ilva, though, not peering out from behind the stone monuments nor materializing between shreds of the fog that had begun to gather.

Ice pooled in Anya's stomach as she found herself utterly alone, and she forced it back by fanning the embers of her internal fire.

Ilva.

Willem.

Philomena.

Sylvie.

All the ones who went. She was here for their sake as much as for her own anger. She would not allow herself to be turned aside.

At the end of the cairn-marked trail, an edifice rose from the plateau at Bane Nevis's summit. A hollow beehive of stone, forming the yawning entrance to a stair that led down into the bowels of the mountain itself.

For a moment, Anya fought back fear on the threshold. Her heart began to race, her breath to come hard and fast, but with a monumental effort, she forced herself into calm, or numbness—it didn't particularly matter which. So long as she did what was required, one foot set in front of the other as she descended the winding steps going down into the pitiless earth.

It was not lightless, the god's lair on Bane Nevis. Torches guttered along the circling stair and then the tunnel at its base. They'd burst into flame as the god passed, Anya imagined, though who replaced them when they burned down, she could only guess. The Elect, presumably. Gray-robed sycophants, so filled with faith that they were willing to risk the mountain, to keep the crimson-painted trail well marked and the god's resting place lit for the girls who would placate him. The thought made Anya bitter and furious, until she rounded a bend in the tunnel and stopped short, her anger melting away.

She'd come out into a vast cavern, filled with shadows and torchlight. At its far end, a stone altar stood, but Anya could not bear to look at it just yet. Her gaze drifted to the cavern walls instead, one side lined with skull-filled alcoves, the other painted with faded frescoes. Removing a torch from its bracket, Anya walked.

She skirted the painted side of the cavern, taking in the frescoes as she went. They told a story—of the Romans arriving in Albion and building their towns and their walls. Of the uprisings that had occurred, the eventual hideous and bloody pacification of the Brythonic tribes, who gave up the fight and resigned themselves to life on the margins. And then, something Anya had never seen or heard before. An eventual alliance, between the Romans and the Brytons, as they mingled and dwelt together over centuries. A melding of their story and their history and their faiths, as those who hungered for power rose to it, regardless of their origins. Gray-robed figures appeared among the people and set themselves apart, and held themselves above reproach.

A trio of gray-robed figures climbed Bane Nevis, intent on determining whether the source of an old legend might yield them more power. They entered the god's cavern, where it was not a girl who'd been bound to the altar but the god himself. The devout broke the god's bonds and set him free, and he visited devastation on Albion, until the few Romans who still clung to their old ways and old citizenship fled, and the Elect forbade departure from the island, for fear of an exodus in the face of the god's wrath.

The god of the mountain could not be contained—not in the same manner as before. The Elect struggled to subdue the demon they'd wakened, and lives were lost until at last a first girl, of her own choice, went up to Bane Nevis and met the god in the heart of his fiery lair. There, she lulled him into temporary peace and satisfaction with the sweetness of an offering—of a piece of herself, willingly given—and bound him to the altar once more.

Anya walked along, the frescoes unfolding before her. The god quieted and rose, quieted and rose, and every time, a girl went out to him. Some of them died, for reasons she couldn't discern, but most of them lived, and the god rested, and on and on the offertory girls went, until whole villages were made to house them, to bring them up gentle and pure, and they were sent out in crimson collars, assuming the fate that had wavered before them from birth.

Abruptly, Anya stopped. She'd come to the end of the frescoes, and the altar stood before her, as tall as she was at the shoulder. Setting her torch in an empty bracket and reaching out with a trembling hand, she brushed her fingertips against the ancient stone. Several of the jagged rocks jutting out from the altar's side had been worn smooth, used for footholds by Weatherell girls to ascend to the place that once held a god and to make an exchange that would subdue him for such a brief span of time.

So much given, in exchange for so little.

A muffled sob rose up in the back of Anya's throat as she thought of Ilva climbing that altar and arranging herself for a sacrifice. She reached instinctively for the bone blade she'd carried since Weatherell, but the hidden sheath was empty. Anya was, for the first time since leaving home, truly on her own.

Slipping into the lightless gap between the altar and the cavern wall, Anya gripped a stolen knife in each hand and waited, the minutes and hours passing by in an agony of anticipation. She felt utterly alone, a thing meant to be preyed upon made a hunter by necessity. But violence was not in her nature and neither had it been nurtured into her. She could not help the hot tears that burned at her eyes and tempered the fierceness of the fire at her core.

And into the blur of Anya's grief and fear and hatred stepped the god of the mountain.

She heard him before she saw him—a terrible grating whine of stone against stone in the tunnel, and footsteps so heavy the cavern floor shook. A scorching smell of burning things wafted into the chamber, and the light intensified, growing bright as day, though the color of it was wrong—all scarlet and crimson and flame.

Anya stayed motionless as a low growl rumbled out, thunderous in its pitch.

"I know you're here," the god of the mountain said, in a voice like grinding rock and hissing flame. It was a loathsome, unnatural

sound that turned Anya's skin clammy at once and sent a deep shudder through her as her stomach went sour. *"Do you think I cannot tell when someone has hidden away in my home? Who are you, little coward? One of the grayrobes' waymarkers? An assassin, come to die for your troubles? Or the next of my lambs, made shy by the glory of my presence?"*

Anya said nothing. She wrapped her arms about her knees and wished that she had never been born, that she was back in Weatherell, that she was only dreaming. It was madness that had led her here. Madness and pride and folly. The hot, ashen smell of the god was everywhere, making her sick and dizzy.

Summoning the tattered shreds of her resolve, Anya stole a look around the altar.

There he stood, the god of the mountain, the very incarnation of her own dread and despair. Twice a man's height, with curling horns and an inhuman face, he was a creature of flame and malice, wrought from shadows and fire and hunger. She had not expected him to be so vast, his presence so all-consuming. Ilva had tried to warn her, and yet Anya had not fully understood. The sight and awareness of him hurt some deep, indefinable piece of her, as if just to see him were to sacrifice.

"Come to me," the god said, a curious note in his awful voice, and to her horror, Anya went. She hadn't been prepared, and so she could not help herself. At his bidding, her feet moved of their own accord. All she could do was tuck her hands into her pockets, to hide the knives she held.

"You smell of sacrifice," the god said quizzically as Anya approached, her eyes darting to him and down again because she could not

look at him for long. *"But why hide yourself, little lamb? And why do I think I have tasted someone close to you before?"*

"My sister," Anya said, unable to lie. "She came this spring. But she made no offering—you stole from her instead."

"I am no thief," the god scoffed. With her eyes fixed on the ground, Anya could see the way the loose pebbles moved, dancing across the cavern floor, stirred by nothing more than the raw power of his voice. *"If a lamb is unworthy, she does not survive. Those who are strong and pure are the ones who live."*

"My sister was strong," Anya managed to get out. Not even a god would malign Ilva to her. "She was pure. She was *perfect*. And you murdered her. You killed her when she would have given whatever you required."

Drawing her eyes up, Anya met the god's fiery gaze. She could feel his attention like something physical, weighing her down, scorching her skin. But she would not continue to look away. Not while this monster spoke ill of her sacred dead.

"Are you so certain?" the god asked. *"That she would give whatever I required?"*

"Yes."

The god of the mountain shifted, and Anya nearly stumbled as the ground beneath her shook.

"I remember your mother," he said. *"I asked her for something at first, and she refused. Do you know what it was I bade her give?"*

Anya shook her head and clenched her jaw. His words were like decay working in her, weakening her bones, stealing her breath.

"I bade her give the children, that she had not even known were quickening

in her belly," the god said. "*And when she refused, I demanded something of equal value to her. A hand. One for each of her bastard girls.*"

Anger blazed through Anya, but for the first time, it was on Willem's behalf, not Ilva's.

"*A family trait, that refusal,*" the god went on. "*I asked your sister for something too, only to have her beg for a substitution. I grow weary of your bloodline's denials, Weatherell girl.*"

"What was it?" Anya whispered. "What did Ilva refuse to give?"

The god drew closer, until he was only an arm's length from Anya, and she grew faint with the overwhelming heat of him.

"*You would like very much to know, wouldn't you?*"

Anya could hardly breathe at all now. Black spots swam across her vision and she knew herself to be the worst of fools, to think she could stand against this creature.

"*Kneel,*" he commanded, and, unable to do otherwise, she knelt.

The god stooped, and Anya's whole narrowing field of vision filled with him. All was fire, all was fury, all was hunger and cruelty and rancor. When he spoke again, his voice was low and uneasy, like the sound of an approaching storm.

"*I asked the girl before you for one thing only. I asked for the memory of her sister, and when she refused, she had nothing of equal value to give.*"

With a wrenching gasp, Anya caught her breath.

"I will see you suffer," she said through tears. "I will see you hurt as I hurt. I will make a ruin of you, as you have made a ruin of me."

The god's brutal laughter brought stones falling from the

cavern ceiling, which shattered on the floor around them. Anya fought the urge to duck—she must be in control, must not waver, must hold her wits together as it was so near impossible to do in the presence of this vicious thing.

"Empty threats, little lamb," the god said, bending closer still. *"Empty as your arms in the absence of your unworthy sister. None can stand against me."*

"I can try," Anya breathed, and with one swift motion she forced herself to her feet and drove her steel knives into the god of the mountain's heart.

NINETEEN

Born Leaving

The nearness of the god swept over Anya like heat from an oven. He gripped her by the forearms and she was burning, burning, the sleeves of her oilskin coat and the roughspun wool shirt beneath disintegrating into ash at his touch. A smell of charred skin filled the air, and devastating pain surged through her. If the awareness of his presence had been overwhelming before, it was maddening now, under her skin and within her, tainting her entire perception of the world.

Through the fog of it all, Anya saw that her efforts had been meaningless. The knives she'd wielded lay broken on the cavern floor, their blades shattered, and though she'd marred the god of the mountain, the wounds she'd left knit together before her eyes. The god let Anya go the moment she fell back to her knees, but the pain in her arms and the enormity of his presence within her mind were unbearable. She gasped and choked, even as the god stood over her and pronounced her doom.

"You dare to stand against me?" he raged, the entire cavern

shuddering at the force of his fury. *"A lamb meant for sacrifice, whose own kin was insufficient? I will make a reckoning of you, foolish girl. I will tear you into four pieces and fix one to each of Banevale's gates and make every child I burn curse your name as she suffers."*

Intolerable heat rolled off the god and Anya's vision blurred, black spots threatening to swallow up everything as his nearness and the pain of the marks he'd left swept over her. But for a moment, her head cleared and her focus snapped back to the cavern, from where it had been drifting into other realms.

A softer, gentler light flickered behind the god. Ilva beamed with the clear cold glow of stars reflected in still water. Here on the mountain, she did not look gruesome or decaying. She was whole, her honey-brown curls stirred by an invisible wind. A stern expression settled on her face—the sort she reserved for moments of frustration, in the aftermath of confrontations with Willem or the Arbiter.

Don't go, she told Anya insistently. *Don't let anyone else go.*

Anya tried, once more, to push herself into action. She reached for the broken hilt of one of her stolen knives and found the strength sapped from her hands by the god of the mountain's touch. It was agony even to move her arms, let alone grip something. And when Anya attempted to rise to her feet, the demon looming over her lashed out with a single word.

"Stay."

Lent hideous strength by her internal awareness of the god's presence, the order bound Anya irrevocably—it set what felt like the weight of the entire mountain atop her. She could not stir, not even to save her own life. Not even to fulfill her sister's dying wish. She was powerless in the wake of the god's touch, and while Anya had shed bitter tears before, they were nothing to those that rose in her eyes as she knew herself to be a failure on every front.

"Please," she whispered to the god, and at first, that was all she could manage.

The god of the mountain bent closer still to listen.

Anya clasped her hands and knit her fingers together, even as the motion set fresh pain searing through her arms. She had never prayed to this terrible god before, not truly, but here and now she did, putting every last shred of conviction she possessed into the petition.

"Make an end of me, if I cannot stand against you," Anya pleaded. "I have never wanted to be an offering, or to watch others go in my stead. I can't live in your world—where I must either tear myself apart or watch someone else be damaged on my behalf. I've neither the courage nor the conviction for it."

Ilva's words were everywhere. She muttered them over and over from her place behind the god, an incantation and a demand, a requirement that Anya had felt for as long as she could remember, but was unable to fulfill.

Don't go, don't go, don't go

Don't let anyone else go

The god of the mountain calmed suddenly, his monstrous face overcome by wicked cleverness.

"*You wish to be made a martyr,*" he said. "*If you cannot do the impossible and put an end to me, you desire an end yourself. Well, I have thought better of my anger, little lamb. I will not give you the satisfaction. You will live with your failure and with knowing there was nothing you could do to stand against me. You will watch as I scorch the earth of this island and make prey of whomever I wish. And if another lamb rises up, pure enough to sate me, you will live with the knowledge that you could not forestall her sacrifice."*

"No," Anya said, and the heat of the god was so great that the tears she shed dried on her face at once, as if they'd never been. "I *can't.* I'll give you my life, do you understand? My still-beating heart. However you wish to bring about my end, you can take what you desire. Only grant me this one small mercy. I may not be a fit sacrifice, but I can't watch anyone else go. I can't bear that I watched her go."

The god fixed his fiery gaze upon Anya, and she faltered, looking to Ilva instead.

I'm sorry, Anya said, the words coming out soundless. *I'm so sorry. It should have been me. I was the one fit for an offering. But I never wanted it, and I let you go instead.*

The god of the mountain stood and considered, extending a monstrous hand to Anya as he did so. She could not help but think of how his touch had scorched and scarred so many girls. How it had already done so to her. But when she slipped her own small hand into his, the contact no longer burned. She'd become willing, and her own intent shielded her now.

The god, however, did not lead her to his martyr's altar, where so many Weatherell girls had made their offerings. Instead, he brought her to the corridor that led out of his sanctuary. He escorted her, footfall by heavy footfall, up the winding staircase and through the beehive cairn at its head, into the cold, gray light of morning.

Out on the plateau at Bane Nevis's summit, the god's fire dimmed. He seemed smaller somehow, but no less dreadful—a twisted thing of embers and death now, rather than a demon of fire. Wind whipped the oilskin coat around Anya's legs as her teeth began to chatter uncontrollably and her breath came in high, thin whines.

"*Leave,*" the god of the mountain gritted out in his stony voice. "*May your failure lead you to a bitter end.*"

His power and strength and the insidious nature of his touch compelled Anya. To hear, now, was to obey.

If Anya had felt despair at Ilva's death, it was nothing compared to this. For her sister had at least failed in faith—Ilva had tried, for Albion's sake, and been cruelly rejected. Anya had not even managed that. She had profaned herself, and her sacred calling, and sentenced still more girls to a terrible end. Within her, the awareness of the god's brutal presence twisted and grew cold, crumbling in on itself, leaving only ashes and ruined hope where flame had been.

But the force of his order dragged Anya to her feet and set her stumbling down the mountain trail.

† † † †

Somehow, Anya made it down the breakneck slopes of Bane Nevis and back to the city at its base. It was all a blur to her—she did not even realize she'd returned to the wanderers' encampment until Tieran began to shout for Matthias, his frantic voice echoing from the rafters of the empty mill.

Anya felt more than saw Matthias's steadfast presence. She was lowered to the ground and surrounded by a hum of worried voices. All the while, Tieran stayed at her side, and she fixed her eyes on his face as it swam in and out of focus.

She was made to swallow something bitter, and at last, the world faded away.

† † † †

When Anya woke again, she could see through one of the mill's grimy windows that night had fallen. The pain in her arms was a constant distraction, but not as all-consuming as it had been before. Glancing down, she saw that her coat had been removed and the sleeves cut from her loose shirt at the elbows. Her forearms were neatly bandaged, and a clean herbal smell rose from the dressings. All was as right with her as it could be, under the circumstances.

And yet she had never felt more wrong, with leftover awareness of the god still lodged inside her. It was not flame as her vengeance had been, but lifeless ash, strength-sapping and insidious, like a slow poison in the blood.

Anya was not out on the mill floor, where the wanderers had made their camp, but rather in a small storeroom opening off it. Through the door, which had been left ajar, she could catch a glimpse of the wanderers' small, carefully built fires, and several of them passing restlessly from group to group.

Sitting up, Anya let out a quiet hiss as pain lanced through her. Bit by bit, it subsided until she could bear it again, and she cast about herself only to find Tieran, fast asleep on her opposite side. He seemed subtly different, with the god's internal presence marring her view. A thin line of sparks limned the thief, but she blinked hard and the vision dissipated.

Tieran had his head pillowed on the smoky, tattered remains of Anya's oilskin coat. He looked worn to a thread, a worried frown tugging at the corners of his mouth. The hair he'd shorn off had begun to grow back in a downy brown fuzz, and Anya reached out, running a hand over it. Tieran tensed visibly beneath her touch and then relaxed at once.

"Gonna live then?" he asked without opening his eyes, voice still hoarse with sleep.

"For now," Anya answered dully.

"What did you give?"

There was no use lying to him any longer. He'd see the result of her blasphemy soon enough, when darkness fell and the god once more came rampaging down his mountain. When more girls suffered, because Ilva and Anya had failed. "I didn't."

Tieran sat up with a single fluid motion, his full attention fixed on her. "What do you mean?"

Hot tears pooled in Anya's eyes and she ducked her head. "I mean I didn't give anything. I've never been faithful. I've never been an offering. I've always meant to kill the god of the mountain, and I tried last night and failed."

Tieran gave her an agonized look. "Anya, you could've said.

Could've told me that's what you were bent on. I'd have warned you then, that there was no point to it. I'd have tried to convince you not to go."

"I wouldn't have listened," she said, striving to sound uncaring, though the words came out fraying at the edges. "Because it doesn't matter to me if I die, so long as I take that monster with me."

"It matters to me," Tieran shot back. "Matters an awful lot. More than anything, I think."

Anya dragged her gaze up to meet his and they regarded each other for a moment, both anxious and acutely unhappy.

"Trying to say something," Tieran said, running a hand over his hair in a compulsive nervous gesture. His fingers were changing, slipping from shape to shape, and even after all that had happened on the mountain, a part of Anya wanted desperately to reassure him—to twine those fingers through her own or press them against her skin. "Trying to tell you . . . I love you, Anya Astraea."

A thrill of shock sang through her. *"What?"*

"I'd give the heart out of my chest if it'd keep you safe and well," Tieran admitted. "Didn't ask to end up like this, but here I am. Can't change it. Wouldn't change it—not for nothing."

"You're lying," Anya whispered, wiping at her eyes with the back of one hand. "You told me yourself, you always lie."

"Do I, though?" Tieran said. "Or is that just another one of the lies I can't help telling?"

Anya's voice came out barely audible, a small and broken thing. "I wish this hadn't happened. I wish we hadn't met. It would make things easier. Because I'm never going to be happy or whole so long as the god of the mountain exists. I'll become something twisted up and bitter—a monster in my own right, and I won't be with you while that happens."

Hurt flashed across Tieran's face.

"Oh, don't," Anya said hurriedly. "Don't look so. In any other world, you'd be the sun in the sky to me. It's not our fault this one's broken."

"It's all right." Tieran scrambled to his feet, and the hurt Anya had seen was already shut away, locked up tight behind his usual spines and sharpness. "Every fool in Albion except me knows there's no happy ending if you fall for a Weatherell girl, even if you aren't one properly. Not your problem that I haven't got any sense."

But with his hand on the door, Tieran stopped.

"You hear something?" he asked warily.

Anya listened. "No, I—wait. Is that someone shouting?"

From outside the mill, a distant raised voice could be heard. Anya joined Tieran and he motioned to her to keep quiet and to stay unseen within the shadows of the storeroom. Together, they peered out as the wanderers got to their feet in dismay.

One of the mill doors flew open, revealing a dozen gray-robed Elect, in company with as many liveried city guards. Matthias was being dragged along by them, his hands bound behind his back, and he shouted protests as they went.

Tieran took in a quick, ragged breath, and when Anya glanced at him, he'd gone dead pale.

"There's nobody here you want," Matthias was still ranting. "We're only travelers, trying to make our way. Don't you—"

One of the Elect struck him across the mouth, and he fell silent. Anya saw, with a sinking feeling, that it was Roger, whom she'd met in Sarum, and that Orielle was with them too. Several women in gray robes had split from the group and were spreading out across the room, looking over each of the wanderers, taking their faces in their hands, sorting through their things.

"Everyone stay just where you are," Orielle said, her voice clear and assured. "Understand that we know where you've come from and how you've profaned your calling. Furthermore, your village was under the jurisdiction of Lord Nevis, and we are in accord for once—you had no right to leave your place or your land."

Anya's eyes cut to Janie and Ella, who stood with their arms about each other, wearing matching expressions of horrified dismay.

Matthias spat blood. Anya had only ever seen him gentle before, but he was radiating outrage now, his face a mask of anger. "We haven't done anything wrong. There's no *law* in Albion that says you can't pick up and move from a place if you choose."

"We are the law in Albion," Orielle answered coolly. "Together, the Nevis guard and the Elect represent both the moral and civil rule of this island. But we would be willing to overlook your faithlessness for the moment, Arbiter, in exchange for information regarding the company you've been keeping."

Beside Anya, Tieran had gone rigid with the effort of keeping himself from shifting. Sweat stood out on his forehead, and his breath came in shallow gasps.

"We want the Weatherell girl, and the thief she travels with," Roger said. He was tense and impatient, pacing about before the gathered Elect and the guards. "Don't bother pretending you've no idea what I mean, we know they've been with you. Like calls to like, and sooner or later, heretics fall in together."

Matthias made a great show of scanning the gathered wanderers before shrugging expansively.

"No sign of anyone here," he said, his voice pitched to carry. "Suppose you'll just have to keep on looking."

"Anya," Tieran breathed. "We got to go."

He reached for her hand, but she stayed rooted to the spot, listening.

"What of this?" Orielle said to Matthias. "A trade in kind. You give us our straying lamb and her escort, and we'll let every single one of your people go free. You'd be getting the better end of that bargain."

Lee stepped forward, staunch and unyielding. "We don't play that game any longer. No more trading a life in exchange for more lives. Think we'd do it now, when it's everything we walked away from? That's not who we are at all."

Orielle rolled her eyes. Snapping her fingers, she recalled the women prowling among the wanderers.

"Anya Astraea," Orielle called. "This is your decision. We're offering you a chance to make all your wrongs right. You've strayed yet again, but you can still choose the upward path. You can save these people, and perhaps be the saving of us all. The only thing we require is for you to come forward."

In the corner of the storeroom, Ilva stepped out of the shadows, her eyes beseeching, flames burning beneath the translucent net of her skin. Tieran, by contrast, had shrunk away. He stood by the storeroom's window, one hand already on the latch. Anya turned to him and could see what Janie and Ella and Matthias had warned her of. What Tieran himself had been trying to tell her, from the beginning. It cut at her worse because she'd grown to rely on him. Because she'd thought better of him, and now he would not so much as risk his freedom for the family who'd loved him longest and best.

"They'll only hurt you, if they find out what you've done. But you can come with me." Tieran's words were dark and ashamed, and he spoke them as if he could not help it. As if he was compelled to. "We'll go together. Wherever the Elect are, we'll be elsewhere. Wherever the god is, we'll be a hundred miles away. Don't care if you get angry or hard-hearted on account of the god and what he's done. Doesn't matter to me if you end up monstrous, like you said, not when I've always been that way too."

But Anya knew, with a dull certainty, that she could not let others suffer in her stead again. Perhaps she'd failed on the mountain, but she could at least succeed in this—in saving the people who'd helped her along the road, even if she could not save a single Weatherell girl who was to come and had not saved Ilva when she might have done so.

"I can't leave them," Anya said. Everything in her went numb as the thief refused to meet her gaze. "It's not in me, Tieran. Not yet, at least."

He nodded miserably.

"You could stay," Anya went on. "Do what no one thinks you can. Maybe . . . maybe if I'm penitent, and become a proper sacrifice, like I was always meant for—the Elect will let you and Matthias and everyone else be. If I asked them to, they'd hardly say no. Not if I put an end to all this, and give what's needed. I'd have to go back to Weatherell, and take my place as one of the ones who went, but we'd both be alive."

Even as Anya spoke of willing sacrifice, her skin crawled and her stomach turned over. The god's ashen presence still lived within her, along with her memories of Willem and Philomena and Sylvie, and Ilva dying with the god's hand imprinted above her heart.

"I'd never have been able to make myself an offering for Albion," Anya said quietly. "But I could do it for your family. I could do it for you. I could've done it for Ilva, though I didn't know it at the time."

Tieran was shivering, minuscule changes running like ripples across his skin.

"It's not in you to go, and it's not in me to stay," he told her after a moment. "I never lied to you about who I am, not really, but I've always been worse than you thought. Have to say good-bye now, Weatherell girl."

Something deep within Anya's chest ached unbearably.

"Did you mean *any* of what you said?" she asked. "About me, and about your heart?"

Tieran paused, already half out the window, half on his way to wherever else he was going. Somewhere safe, far from Weatherell girls and their troubles. An open road where he could outrun any memory of Anya, or of the wanderers who'd given him everything a family could.

"Suppose we'll never find out," Tieran said.

And then he was gone.

Anya took a moment. She wiped the tears from her eyes. Smoothed her hair. Set her shoulders. Last but not least, she took the red collar from her pocket and clasped it around her neck.

Letting out a breath, she stepped onto the mill floor. It was no work at all to assume a chastened and grief-stricken look, but only the outworking of what she felt, and unlike Ilva, Anya Astraea wore repentance well. Unlike her wild twin, her face was made for penitence.

She had been born for sacrifice, one way or another.

"There she is," Orielle said with a satisfied smile. "I never doubted you, my love. Today we rejoice, for we have found our lamb who was lost. But where is your companion?"

"Gone," Anya said. "I'm sure he's out of the city by now—there's no point looking for him, he knows how to hide well enough. He left me, once he found out who I am. Or rather, who I ought to be, and will become."

A murmur spread through the wanderers. Anya could not bear to look at them, not after all her lies and what had happened on the mountain. Instead, she lowered her head in deference to Orielle as the gray-robed Elect and the guards closed in around her and shepherded her out into the street. But as she went, Anya tucked her hand into her pocket. She pulled out the summoning coin she'd been given at the city gates by the Nevis guard and let it slip quietly through her fingers to the ground.

TWENTY
Wolves and Lambs

White halls.

Distant chanting.

The pervasive smells of honey and astringent herbs and blood.

It was as if the last few weeks had never been—as if Tieran, a thief and a trickster to his core, had never arrived in Sarum to steal Anya out from under the very noses of the Elect. As if she'd never met the wanderers and learned her Weatherell was not alone in Albion. As if she'd never stood before the god and failed at the vengeance she'd laid out for herself—failed even to convince him to put an end to her wretched and haunted existence. Numb to the core, Anya let herself be led into another chamber painted with a dizzying array of crimson runes, another bed on a dais.

This time, they did not bind her hands.

Orielle fussed over the bandages on Anya's arms, and Anya said nothing about where they'd come from. Not because any sense of self-preservation kept her from speaking, but because immobilizing ashes had settled within her, and they bound her to silence.

Meek and with no shame, Anya removed her shirt and laid herself down, and she did not flinch at the first prick of the needle, finishing the prayer that spread across her back. She kept still as a stone through it all, and the silent tears that tracked down her face had nothing to do with bodily pain—that, she hardly felt. The hopelessness unfurling like a poisoned blossom beneath her skin was far worse.

In time, the prick of the needle stopped, and Anya knew she had been made a living prayer. Something cool and slick was spread across her aching and inflamed skin, and the Elect who had gathered filed out, leaving only Orielle behind.

The woman briefly left Anya's field of vision. There came a sound of water being poured into a basin, and then Orielle returned, kneeling at Anya's bedside.

"Sit up and dress yourself," she said, firm but kind, and blankly, Anya did as she was told. She thought, as she looked down at Orielle, that the woman bore a strong resemblance to Philomena. They had the same reassuring lines etched around their eyes and mouths, the same unshakeable serenity shining out from within.

"The road has not been kind to you, has it?" Orielle asked, and her warmth was near irresistible. "I'm sorry for that, my lamb. We would have eased your way, if we could. Why not at least let me change those bandages for you?"

Instinctively, Anya crossed her arms in front of herself and held them pressed against her body. She knew what lay beneath the dressings—the livid red imprints of the god of the mountain's implacable grip, stretching from her wrists to her elbows. Her own rebellion, etched into her skin for all to see.

"I'll be gentle," Orielle soothed. "You needn't be afraid."

Anya shook her head fiercely, panic welling up in the pit of her stomach. She knew her fear must be showing, that without fire to temper it she was transparent as glass.

Orielle rocked back on her heels.

"Child," she said slowly. "Is there something you ought to confess to me?"

Anya said nothing. She hadn't spoken a word since entering the way station. To break her silence felt impossibly difficult, and also dangerous—as if every blasphemous truth she harbored would spill out of her if she gave them the slightest chance.

Rising, Orielle settled herself on the bed. She put an arm around Anya's shoulder and, starved for absolution, for encouragement, for stability in any form, Anya did not pull away. Tears pooled in her eyes and she hated them, hated her own weakness, hated how small and useless and frail she had always been.

Ashes. Ashes at her core.

"There is nothing that will shock me," Orielle said. "Do you think the rest of our beloved girls have not also found themselves in the path of trouble and temptation? We'll learn of whatever it was sooner or later—best to tell the truth and let yourself be cleansed and fasted and made pure once more."

Anya no longer had it in her to resist. Everything about the Elect felt so achingly familiar. It would be a relief to finally let them have their way. To return to the path they'd set out for her, to a world where she knew and understood what was expected. Where she might be seen as good and dutiful, once she'd atoned for her grievous sins. And yet Anya knew that even if she made the required offering and spent the rest of her days as a living sacrifice, she would never shake her nagging guilt over Ilva and the girls who went before, and those who were to come.

What else could she do, though, here in the web the Elect had spun for her?

Carefully, Anya unraveled the bandage around her left arm, revealing the mark of the god's hand seared into her pale skin.

The look that crossed Orielle's face was nothing like what Anya had felt when confronted with god-touched girls. For her, it had been all shock and futile rage. But Orielle reached out tentatively with worship in her eyes, awe in the set of her mouth.

"I went to the god last night," Anya said, her own voice sounding strange and hoarse. "I climbed the mountain, and I . . . I tried to kill him. It's been my intention since leaving Weatherell. My sister . . ."

Ilva appeared as if summoned, sitting in a corner with her head leaned back against the wall. She looked just as she had in the final clearing, during the moments before she died.

Don't go

Her voice was wind over an open grave, ice in the bones.

Don't let anyone else go

"No one is beyond our god's grace," Orielle said. "Does the Cataclysm not say he rejoices more over one straying lamb than all those who stayed their course? If you turn from your wickedness and become a true sacrifice, you will be pleasing indeed, child. His sleep will be long and dreamless, and many lives will be spared through your courage and benevolence."

Be brave, little moon, Ilva said.

I know you'll find your courage without me.

"I want to do right," Anya confessed, and it was the beat of her heart and the cry of her soul. "I want to do right so badly. But this"—she touched the scarlet band that rested around her neck once more—"doesn't feel like the good I've always been taught it was. There must be more. There must be a better way."

Orielle shook her head, all sadness and sympathy. "Sweet girl. What you want is an impossibility. There *is* nothing more. There is the world we live in, and the rules of it, and the path set before you. You will be a saint and an icon—isn't that enough?"

Anya fixed her eyes on Ilva, who had once been living and vibrant and was now no more than a bone knife and a figment of her grief. Ilva had chosen this, and tried for this, and seen it as enough. Had Anya possessed the courage and conviction to do so before, her sister would be living now.

"I don't—I don't know," Anya said, and she had not wavered so since the day she broke up her sister's bones.

Orielle reached out and cupped Anya's face with one hand. "Understand this. We've never sent a girl to the god who was unwilling. If you can't face him again, we will send someone else in your place. But we cannot let you go home unrepentant, having failed to complete your task. If you choose not to go, you will join the ranks of the Elect and be kept safe and watched over."

A prisoner, Anya realized. She would be little better than a prisoner.

"And if I go, and finish what I started?"

Orielle smiled. "Repentance is a blessing. If you offer yourself properly after such grievous error, it will usher in a lifetime of peace and prosperity for Albion. A reprieve. You will accomplish so much of the good that you desire."

Anya dried her eyes with the back of one hand. "How do you know? How can you be sure?"

Orielle's smile grew sad. "Do you think yourself the only girl who's ever shown steel to the terror and glory that is our god? Others have tried what you did and failed. But to their credit, they all returned to the path of righteousness. They all sought holiness, and the pure light of abnegation once more."

Anya shut her eyes, mired in darkness and ashes within and without.

"You saved your wanderers," Orielle said. "You can save others, too. Sometimes, Anya, the greatest good is the one within your grasp. Sometimes right means surrendering to those who know best, rather than striving for the unattainable."

And Anya realized she'd always been a fool in her hope—in believing that she might undo the crushing pain and guilt of

Ilva's death, might put an end to a god, might save every girl born after her.

Might be enough to make a boy born for leaving stay.

Anya slipped from her place on the bed and knelt before Orielle. She clasped her hands, and bowed her head, but even now a piece of her rebelled. Even now, she did not desire to become an offering except as a very last resort.

"Will you make me a sacrifice?" she said. The words felt wrong, spun out of jagged edges and shame. She was meant to have a choice, but if one truly existed, she would take any path before this one.

"Beloved," Orielle said, drawing Anya to her feet. "We've been waiting for you to ask."

† † † †

After turning herself over to the Elect, Anya sought the dark. She curled inward, withdrawing every tender and vital part so that she was small as a stone and felt nothing besides the ashes the god's presence had left within her. Outwardly, she was biddable, doing just as she was told with perfect grace. Orielle led her through the rites and rituals meant to transform a tempting lamb into an irresistible offering—she was bathed, scented with the essence of a dozen sacred blooms, and dressed in a plain frock of perfect white. More flowers were twined through her hair, after which Anya was left entirely alone, locked into the way station's sanctum. Another ceiling-high fresco of an offering served as the center point of the room, and this time, it wasn't Ilva that Anya saw in the face of the sacrificial girl, but herself.

After a quick glance she fixed her eyes on the floor and did as she'd been told, though there was no one to see. She dropped to her knees, then prostrated herself before the likeness of the god, lying flat on the sanctum floor as she had done on the cobbles during her penitence. There she waited, flawless in her obedience, for hours. Dimly, her body registered that her legs and back and arms ached and her belly was an empty pit and thirst burned at her throat. The essential part of her—soul, spirit, heart—felt none of it. If it were up to Anya, they would never feel again.

The multitude of beeswax candles lit throughout the sanctum burned down and guttered and died. Their cloying honey scent was replaced, little by little, with the odor of smoke and ash, and at last Anya was left in darkness without as well as within. Behind her, a key scraped in the sanctum's lock. A shaft of light cut across her, streaming from Anya to the figure of the god.

"Anya Astraea," a soft voice said. "It's time."

Automatically, Anya got to her feet, though the hours spent in one attitude had made her unsteady. She joined the figure waiting at the door—a sweet-faced girl with gentle brown eyes. Orielle, it seemed, considered her job done now that Anya had reentered the fold.

And then, even as she was, even closed off to the world, Anya felt a flash of remembering. A lance of desperate hope. She turned to the girl and searched her face intently, bent on finding some hint of rescue, some trace of sharpness in her posture, or a shimmer of clever hazel in her eyes.

There was nothing. As Anya gripped the girl's arms, she remained steadfast and mild, undeniably one shape, no piece of her capable of or tempted to change.

The moment of hope burst like a soap bubble, and Anya drew into herself once more.

"This way," the girl said. "We've arranged an escort."

Anya followed in her wake, and just the act of walking felt unspeakably wearisome. How she'd summit Bane Nevis again and manage the downward journey, she couldn't imagine.

"Here we are," the gray-robed girl said with a tentative smile, gesturing to an unmarked door. There were sadness and regret behind her eyes, and no matter how Anya withdrew, she could not help but feel stung by such things. Not knowing the source of that sorrow or how she might lessen it, she instinctively reached out and took both the strange girl's hands.

"Thank you for your help," Anya offered, putting as much warmth as she could into the words.

For a moment, the girl clung to her, tears shimmering in her eyes.

"It was nothing," she said, voice wavering. "I know you meant to do the same for me, and all the rest of us."

Then she fumbled with the lock of the unmarked door and pulled it open. Anya took in a breath of chill, smoky night air and had a confused impression of an alley filled with liveried guards. It lasted only an instant before her vision was cut off by the smothering closeness of a burlap sack, and her hands were wrenched around behind her and roughly bound. But even as Anya was made a prisoner, the girl slipped something familiar into Anya's pinioned hands.

The cold disc shape of her token.

"We're not lambs, not really," the girl in the gray robe said. "And we never should have been made to become so. I hope you find your courage again, Weatherell girl."

TWENTY-ONE
Astraea

Anya knew the place she'd been brought to wasn't the god's mountain, at least. There'd been a jolting wagon ride along cobbled streets, intermittent stops and muffled voices, and then she'd been chivvied out and along on foot for what felt like an age.

Now she stood ... somewhere. In what was an open indoor space, judging by the movement of air and the echo of booted steps as the guards retreated, leaving her alone.

Anya simply waited, just where she'd been left. She couldn't find it in her to want anything—not the return of her vision, nor to be loosed from her bonds. The choking ash at her core kept her still. From some dim, unseen distance, muffled strains of music drifted, followed by the hum of voices. But it all seemed so far removed. As if there were Anya, and the world, and they moved on parallel but eternally separate planes.

A light, swift tread came toward her and she remained as she was. Remote. Untouchable. Cold.

From behind, a blade severed the ropes around her wrists, and again that treacherous arrow of hope shot through Anya, leaving a wound. It could not be Tieran, though, not even in another form. She knew his scent, his feel, what nearness to him was like.

Anya retreated further into herself.

Be vengeance. Be a flame.

But though she sifted through those internal ashes, she could not find a single spark among them.

The burlap sack was drawn away, leaving her blinking, eyes smarting in a sudden flood of full light.

She stood in a place like nothing she'd ever seen before—a vast, glittering room of glass, filled with an array of verdant green plants entirely foreign to her. The nearest of them were trees in heavy pots, all hung with orange and yellow fruits. The floor was a sweep of some manner of stone in alternating black and white, and without the suffocating burlap, the air proved sweet and floral.

A stranger stepped into Anya's field of view, and she took him in emotionlessly. He was a trim-figured older man, immaculately dressed in breeches, snow-white shirt, and embroidered waistcoat. A touch of gray softened his black hair around the temples, and though he stood only a little taller than Anya herself, there was something flinty about his knowing gaze.

"I'm terribly sorry about the journey here," he said courteously, with a small bow of the head. "But the Elect wouldn't have let you go without a fuss, and it needed to be done at speed.

Still. I apologize about the manner of your"—he waved a hand—"removal. I'm Lord Nevis, of course."

He spoke as if their meeting and his name were a gift he'd presented to Anya. She said nothing, but only looked at the stranger with the silent regard she employed when discomfited or unsure.

"Keep your own counsel, don't you?" the gentleman mused. "Well, your mother was like that, too, until you'd found a way in."

Anya blinked.

"Yes," he said. "I knew Willem. Rather well, actually. She spent some time here at my family's estate before heading on to the mountain. I would have had her stay indefinitely but she was dead set on going. Is it true, what they say about her offering?"

"What do they say?" Anya asked tonelessly.

"That she gave her hands."

Anya nodded, and the stranger went pale.

"God on the mountain," he muttered. But almost immediately, he composed himself. "May I show you something?"

With scrupulous politeness, he offered his arm. Anya only looked at him again, level and intractable, and he sighed. "Yes, you're Willem's daughter all right. Follow me, then."

Anya trailed along behind Lord Nevis, through a dizzyingly high-ceilinged foyer and equally impressive hallway, lined with paintings nearly the size of the hut she and Willem occupied back in Weatherell. She was ushered through a door halfway down the hall and found herself in an office, with dark wood paneling and shelf after shelf of books, some in Brythonic, some in Divinitas, others in scripts or languages she didn't even recognize. But it wasn't the books that caught and held Anya's attention—it was the pictures. The walls were hung with framed charcoal sketches, all done with breathtaking fineness and care. And as Anya stepped closer to one, an eerie chill ran down her spine.

They were of Weatherell. And not any Weatherell—these were of *her* village.

Here was the final clearing with its golden beech, here the cluster of huts and cottages built around spreading trees. Here an elder's bones lying at peace under the pines, here a set of portraits—Philomena, looking younger but still bearing pain in the set of her mouth. Sylvie, sightless and knowing and already old. Arbiter Thorn, stern-faced and reading from the Cataclysm.

There were more. Studies of plants, of woodland creatures, of a small rill of water near the village, the laughing rapids drawn so skillfully it seemed the froth might dance off the page. Of bone charms, the weave of the twine that bound them wrought in minute detail. Of the very hut in which Anya had always lived, and of the hearth, where each morning she had bound on Willem's useless iron-and-leather hands.

Anya fought to maintain her distance. To keep herself closed off and unfeeling. But she could not help the tears that started in her eyes.

"She did those," the gentleman said, from where he'd taken a seat behind an ornately carved oak desk. "Your mother, I mean. She had a gift. A way of seeing beauty in everything around her and making it immortal. Is she . . ."

He hesitated, and a sad, eager light sprang to life within him. "Is she still that way?"

He loved her, Anya realized dully. *He loves her yet.*

Ilva got to her feet, materializing from behind the stranger's desk. She stood there, just at his back, and light from a tall window made a halo of her honey-brown curls, though her face was a fleshless skull like the staring bones that had watched Anya's failure on the mountain.

Trying to tell you I love you, Anya Astraea, Ilva said, but it was Tieran's hoarse whisper and not her own voice that came out. *Wouldn't change it—not for nothing.*

"I think," Anya said, choosing her words carefully for the stranger's benefit, "that life has not been as kind as my mother hoped it would be."

A shadow crossed the gentleman's face. "I'm sorry for that. I'd have made it a constant wonder for her, if I could. Do you know who I am, Anya?"

She nodded slowly. "I believe I can guess, sir."

"My title may be Lord Nevis, but my name is Jonus Astraea. The Astraeas hold ancestral claim to all of Banevale, to the mountain the god sleeps upon, and to most of the land within a hundred miles of here. I myself have added to our holdings tenfold."

Again, he spoke the words with an air of entitlement—as if everything he mentioned were only his due. Anya, who'd never owned more than her traveling pack and its contents, grew cautious.

"The people of these parts know me as Lord Nevis," Jonus

went on. "As they knew my father before me, and his father before him, and back for generations. That is your family and your legacy, as much as Weatherell is. You're my daughter, Anya."

Anya pressed a hand to her forehead. She'd never been particularly curious about her father—the troubles of Weatherell and its women had occupied her time and thoughts. To be confronted with him now seemed an unwanted distraction. All she'd needed was a moment to draw breath. A chance to regroup and sort out what she ought to do next. This was no more than a complication.

But that was unfair, and unkind. Jonus Astraea had taken great pains to watch over her on the road, and to spirit her away from the Elect once she wished it. Perhaps he deserved Anya's goodwill.

"What I'm trying to say," Jonus went on, "is that I'm a powerful man. Should you wish for something other than the path the Elect have laid out, I can protect you. In fact, it is my fervent wish that you *would* choose another path. I have no one in this world, Anya. No one to take up the name of Astraea after I die or to fulfill the responsibilities a position such as our family's comes with. I understand the north road has been hard for you and that we've only just met. But my desire is to claim you publicly and to make you my heir. Everything I have would pass into your hands, and rather than a sacrifice, you would become a power, beyond the reach of those who would use you for their own ends."

Anya stayed rooted to the spot, unsure what to think or feel or do.

Give the heart out of my chest if it'd keep you safe and well, Ilva said in Tieran's voice, and Anya couldn't help but flinch.

"You needn't make a decision now," Jonus said swiftly. "Why not wait a day or two? It'll give you a chance to look over the house and the grounds."

"I don't have time," Anya said, the words coming out like an answer she'd learned from the Cataclysm, automatic and remote. "The god—"

"Will be kept at bay by my guard," Jonus reassured her. "We can manage to ensure he does no real damage for a few nights. I can *give* you time, Anya. I can give you anything you want, as I would have done for your mother. All I ask for in return is a chance to win your regard."

I've always been worse than you thought, Ilva said. *Have to say goodbye now, Weatherell girl.*

"Did you speak to my sister, Ilva, when she came this way in spring?" Anya asked.

Jonus shook his head regretfully. "I was never able. She arrived already in company with the Elect, and left with them as well. I hadn't yet made up my mind to stand against them then—it's not a thing to be undertaken lightly. They have a great deal of influence in Albion, and no one who might serve as a rival has yet been brazen enough to do so. But I would, for you. Please stay."

"I suppose another day or two can't hurt," Anya conceded. But it was not a desire to please that fueled her surrender, or a flicker of curiosity. It was only that she could no longer see a clear path before her, or fathom how to live in a world where she'd failed at the task she'd set herself.

† † † †

A uniformed maid brought Anya to a bedroom that would have fit both her own hut and Sylvie and Philomena's within its walls. Presumably the room was stuffed with luxuries and wonders— Anya did not know. She went to the bed and curled up on her side. But after a few minutes, the softness of it and the strong lavender-and-rose scent of the bedding grew too overwhelming. Slipping off the bed, Anya laid herself down on the floor.

She missed the wanderers. She hadn't expected to, and yet she did. Despite how often she had felt awkward and ill at ease among them, she wished desperately to hear the comforting sounds of camp being made for the night; of Matthias and Tieran in conversation over what scraps they could magic into a passable dinner; of Janie and Ella's bright laughter. She kept entirely still, a bottomless well of longing, and Ilva's ghost lay opposite her, so close Anya could smell little wafts of decay. They fixed their eyes on each other, and alone in a strange countryside, in a stranger's house, with only her sister's unquiet spirit for company, Anya felt herself cease to be a Weatherell girl, though who and what she was in the absence of it she did not know.

Her burned arms hurt, where the god had touched her.

Her back stung, where the Elect had made her a living prayer.

Her spirit ached, where she carried the moment of Ilva's dying.

Her heart—

But she had only herself to blame for her heart. She ought never to have given it away, and should have known better than to place it in such untrustworthy hands.

† † † †

Voices filtered in through the fog that had descended over Anya.

I'm meant to ask if you want a tour of the grounds, miss.

I'm to take you through the house so you're able to see what could be yours, miss.

I've been asked to bring up the rest of your mother's drawings, miss.

Lord Astraea, swimming into focus as he knelt at Anya's side.

Whatever it is that happened to you, I can make it right. Just tell me, and I'll do what's needed. It pains me to see you so, child.

Somewhere, in that separate, parallel world, it grew dark and light and dark again.

Across from Anya, Ilva wavered out as a figure replaced her. Fathomless brown eyes. Gray robes. It was the girl who'd smuggled her away from the Elect this last time, though Anya could not understand how such a thing was possible.

The girl laid herself down in Ilva's place, and met Anya's gaze just as her sister had done.

Do you know what I risked, to free you from that way station? the stranger murmured. *Do you know what it cost? All because I could see you were drowning and hoped you'd have the strength to finish what you started so long as someone dragged you to shore.*

Anya said nothing. She was no longer flesh and blood but a

failed idea—the charred remains of an unrealized vengeance, the foolish and broken dream of a better world.

I gave everything for you, the girl pressed, insistent when at the way station she'd been kind. *I made an offering of myself for you, not to the god, but to the Elect. Because I heard you confess what you'd done on the mountain and thought you were more than this.*

Before Anya, the girl's eyes rolled back, going entirely white. She convulsed, as Ilva had done, and then blood was seeping from her mouth, her eyes, her nose, her ears. Wavering, she grew transparent, but the blood stayed, the aura of death stayed, and Anya could not stand to look at her any longer.

Pushing herself upward to sit, Anya winced as ghosts flickered into existence throughout the room. Dozens of them—girls in red collars or gray robes or plain clothes, all holding their rotting hands out to her.

Don't go, they whispered, with one voice and many all at once. *Don't let anyone else go.*

Scrambling to her feet, Anya fled the room. In the hallway, she nearly collided with Jonus. He was dressed immaculately in a black broadcloth suit and looked pleased at the sight of his daughter.

"You're up! I was hoping if we gave you time, you'd come back to yourself. I'd stay with you if I could, but I'm hosting a banquet tonight—it's our duty to raise spirits in hard times."

"By having a party, while the god is out there destroying whatever he touches?" Anya asked flatly.

"Ah." Jonus smiled, but his eyes remained unchanged. "He's

not destroying anything important now, though. You asked me to keep him contained, and I've done so."

"I asked you to make sure he didn't hurt anyone else," Anya said. Something was twisting in her stomach that had nothing to do with a roomful of ghosts and everything to do with an instinct for danger that gnawed at her in Jonus Astraea's presence.

"And he won't," Jonus answered, quick and courteous. "He won't do any damage that matters."

Anya fixed her eyes on the floor, because she didn't trust the man who was her father and couldn't say so outright.

"I'm off," Jonus said. "I don't suppose—would you care to join everyone? Now that you've got out from under whatever cloud it was that came over you?"

"What happened to the girl who helped you get me away from the Elect?" Anya asked. "When I was leaving, she seemed unhappy and afraid."

Jonus waved a hand. "That's nothing to trouble yourself over tonight. In your room you'll find—"

"Tell me what happened," Anya insisted. She planted her feet and met his eyes and oh, it felt like coming back to life, to resist again after falling into despair.

A repentant look crossed Jonus's face. "I'm afraid she was killed for her betrayal. When the Elect are turned against by one of their own and it's discovered, they force whoever it is to take poison. But Romana knew the risk when she reached out to me and said she'd help get you clear of that way station. She *wanted* to do it."

"I see," Anya said, even as new guilt knifed through her. That, too, was familiar, though, and enlivening, and she held it close. "And you're sure you didn't use any . . . undue influence . . . to secure her help?"

"She came to us." Jonus spread his hands wide in an innocent gesture.

Gnawing at her lower lip, Anya thought quickly. She'd been trapped and overawed by the Elect, and while Jonus Astraea certainly did not seem safe, Romana must have believed Anya would be safer with him than she had been with the grayrobes.

We're not lambs, not really. And we never should have been made to become so. I hope you find your courage again, Weatherell girl.

Anya let out a breath. *I hope so too.*

"What should I wear to this banquet of yours?" she asked Jonus.

TWENTY-TWO
Sparks Fly Upward

Anya sat at the center of the unnaturally soft bed in the room she'd been given. Ghosts lined the walls like silent sentinels, and she kept her eyes fixed on the satin coverlet so as not to see the way their haunting gazes followed her every move.

I love you, Anya Astraea, they whispered, dozens of voices joined as one. *Give the heart out of my chest for you. Why didn't you go? Why did you let us go?*

Vainly, Anya pressed her hands to her ears in an attempt to drown out the sound. It wormed between her fingers, though, insidious and all-encompassing, until her numbness gave way to guilt and her own heart answered back.

Unworthy
Heartless
Selfish
Cruel
I'd rather it had been you

It should have been you

Don't go

Don't let anyone else go

He touched me, and I know it is the beginning of the end

"Miss."

A living voice cut through the choir of phantoms, raised so that Anya would hear it. Jerking her head upright and dropping her hands from her ears, she found herself staring into the face of a bewildered maid, the girl's face flushed with life and warmth and confusion.

"Miss, your father asked me to bring you this. He said to tell you it was your mother's while she stayed here, and that he thought you might like to wear it."

The maid set down a slim cedar box on the bed next to Anya before retreating to the door. She paused on the threshold and glanced back. "Are you all right, miss?"

"No," Anya said honestly. "But I haven't been for a very long time, and there's nothing you can do."

Seeming at a loss, the maid vanished. Anya's dead girls all stood motionless as she pushed open the box, revealing a drift of fabric so light and airy it seemed doubtful human hands could have woven it at all. Still dressed in the offertory robe the Elect had given her, Anya was not sorry to strip down to her skin and pull on the garment her mother had worn. It fell over her softly, loose sleeves hiding her bandaged arms, the waist tucking in near the bottom of her ribs, the back dipping low to reveal most of the prayer inked into her skin.

Anya felt strange and ghostly herself, in the garment that had been her mother's. It still smelled faintly of Willem—a lingering breath of grass and pine and warm earth. Philomena's words upon Anya's departure ran through her mind: *There's more of your mother in you than you think. And whatever Willem's faults, she was made for living.*

Anya did not think of herself as made for living. If anything, she was made for confusion and turmoil and heartache. But she found herself wishing that she'd striven to see more in her mother than anger. If she had, perhaps she'd feel less broken in the wake of her own failure. Less lost and directionless, like a faulty compass that could not find true north.

On impulse, Anya stepped into the garderobe that adjoined her borrowed bedchamber. It was a tall, expansive room, white-and-gold-tiled, with long windows obscured by gauzy curtains. Dying light filtered in, and standing in one corner, something had been draped in thin black fabric.

A mirror.

The way it had been covered spoke of Jonus Astraea's familiarity with Weatherell girls and the righteousness required of them. Until now, Anya had scrupulously avoided her own reflection, cast back at her in windows throughout the world beyond the wood. But this time, she moved toward the mirror.

Though she'd never seen her own face, Anya always knew it must be like Ilva's. There were differences between them, to be sure—her hair was black to Ilva's honey-brown, and her sister stood inches taller. The essential aspects must be the same, though. They'd shared a womb and Anya was certain that if she were to look at herself, she'd find a version of her twin—an Ilva with her edges filed off, her wildness tamed. Her heart saw her as Ilva's double, no matter what her head knew.

Taking a breath, Anya pulled the shroud from the mirror.

A stranger stared back. Behind her own, unfamiliar reflection, Ilva's ghost flickered to life, no longer shocking in its decay.

Little moon, Ilva murmured, her cold words stirring the hair at the nape of Anya's neck. *Little moon. Won't you rekindle your courage without me?*

The stranger in the mirror, all wide solemn blue eyes and pale skin and night-black hair, lived up to the nickname she'd been given. Willem's gown clung to her, once white, now faintly golden with age. Small chips of clear gemstones had been stitched to the fabric like glints of starlight or moonbeams, and for the first time ever, Anya saw sense in the endearment she'd always thought foolish.

She did not look like Willem or Ilva with their restless self-assurance. Nor did she resemble Jonus Astraea, polished and ambitious and contained. She looked, standing here in a gilded room at the base of the god's mountain, like the moon itself. Chill and serene, unmarred except for the clean bandages around her forearms and the shocking crimson of the band the Elect had placed, once more, about her neck.

Her father, Anya thought suddenly, would approve, for there was power in the way she appeared. She was no longer a Weatherell girl or an offering, but something legendary. Someone who had transcended her purpose, becoming not a lamb to prey upon, but a force in her own right, fit to match wits with the gray-robed legions who served a cruel god. A god Anya had withstood—threatened, even—and walked away from, without giving an offering. Without losing her life.

No wonder Jonus had followed her progress across Albion with such interest. No wonder he had worked to gain her attention and taken the risk of spiriting her away from the Elect. For the first time, standing and seeing herself in the flesh, Anya realized that there was not only sacrifice bound up within Albion's Weatherell girls. There was power, too. The power to prevent or enable disaster and suffering, and to become a figure of veneration or an anathema, for centuries after death had claimed them. They were Albion's icons, all cast in the same sufferer's mold. Anya herself had broken that mold and was in the process of becoming something strange and new.

Where it would end—how *she* would end—remained uncertain.

"You look beautiful," Jonus murmured, and Anya turned to find him standing in the bedchamber doorway, hemmed in by her honor guard of unseen spirits.

Beautiful was not the right word, she knew. She was potent and remote, the cold ash at her center resting as uneasily as her blasphemous flames always had. But when Jonus held out a hand, Anya went to him and took the arm he offered.

"I tried to kill him, you know," Anya said quietly. "The god of the mountain, I mean. I stood before him and drove two knives into his heart, and yet he did not die."

"Yes," Jonus answered. "Romana told my people you'd confessed to that. What a child to claim, I thought. What a worthy heir."

An expectant silence fell between them, as if he were waiting for thanks. When Anya did not give it, Jonus frowned slightly. But he said nothing more and led her into the hallway, where the sound of music and many voices could be heard drifting up the staircase.

"Half of Banevale is waiting to meet you," Jonus said, his tone light, his manner easy. "My daughter, who had the courage to pit herself against a god. Though perhaps you'd like to remove that collar, and set yourself apart from who you were?"

Anya hesitated. Everything with Jonus seemed like a struggle for power in some way—a war of attrition, played out on a personal scale. She had a sense that every debt he felt was owed to him, no matter how small, would be collected upon eventually.

"No, thank you," Anya said, fixing her eyes on the wide stair they were approaching. "I prefer to wear my band."

"You don't need it," Jonus said dismissively. "The Elect I rescued you from aren't here to enforce their backward rules. There's no reason to keep it on."

"I've already said I prefer to," Anya repeated. "Isn't that reason enough?"

"I'd prefer that you didn't," Jonus pressed, an edge to his voice. "Isn't that reason enough *not* to?"

Anya knew she ought to feel compelled to oblige him. She would have, only weeks ago. But the road had changed her and her great failure had already come and gone—she'd stood before the god of the mountain and had not made an end of him. She'd branded herself a heretic forever and doomed herself to carry the blame for every girl the god touched from the day of her transgression on. The only absolution for her rested in death, or in resuming and fulfilling her impossible purpose—in putting an end to Albion's vast game of gods and girls and penitents.

The faintest spark of anger flared into life at Anya's center, and this time it was not for Ilva or any of the girls who'd gone before. It was on her own behalf.

"No," she said. "That's not reason enough for me."

In answer, Jonus reached out. He hooked two fingers around the front of Anya's band and tore it from her throat, the clasp Tieran had so carefully sewn on giving way. Jonus dropped the collar onto the carpeted floor in a single, dismissive motion, as if it were rubbish to be tossed aside.

"There," he said. "That's better. Let's go down."

Anya's longing for the wanderers lanced through her once more, so sharp it felt like a physical pain. Perhaps she had never fully learned her place in their world, but none of them had tried to tell her what that place ought to be. She had not been pushed or molded into a prescribed role, and half her discomfort when among them, she realized too late, had stemmed from the simple fact that she'd never acquired a taste for freedom. She'd always been overshadowed and overawed, her own possible futures laid out for her as if they were already decided upon. A life at the side of Lord Nevis, it seemed, would be no different.

Stooping, Anya retrieved her band without a word, and tucked it into her pocket.

Jonus led her down the stairs and into a room so large all of Weatherell would have fit within it. There were people everywhere, dressed in flamboyantly colored gowns and suits, frothing with lace and laughter and gossip. The music was overwhelming, so loud that it was necessary to raise your voice if you wished to be heard. Dancers swirled about at the center of the room, tables piled high with food lined its sides, and liveried attendants moved swiftly about at the margins, waiting upon those who'd been born more fortunate than them. Everywhere Anya looked, she found only wealth and safety, and after what she'd seen elsewhere in Banevale, the sight was utterly disorienting.

At her side, Jonus gestured to one of the musicians. Within moments, the entire room was still. Every eye fixed on them, and though Anya tried to will herself into calm, her stomach turned over. Her palms slicked. Her hands began, ever so slightly, to tremble.

Jonus gave her a quick, disapproving glance.

"Compose yourself," he muttered, before gracing the revelers with a calculated smile.

"My friends," Jonus said with expansive goodwill. "I'm glad to see you all safe and well tonight, despite the trouble visiting our city. It is my pleasure and privilege to keep you so, and I'm certain we will weather this particular outburst of the creature on the mountain as well as we've done every other."

Sustained applause rose up from the crowd, and Jonus bowed

his head, accepting them magnanimously, as if he had not expected and courted them with his words. Anya stole glances at the gathered revelers and tried to quell the anxiety in the pit of her stomach. Her ghosts were scattered among the crowd, staring at her fixedly with glassy eyes, and she did not let her gaze rest on them for long. Instead she looked from face to face, restlessness growing within.

"It is also my pleasure," Jonus went on, reaching out to take Anya's hand as he spoke, "to present my daughter to you. You will have heard by now how she set herself against the Elect, and against the god of the mountain himself. Truly, I could not have a more worthy heir to someday take my place and serve as your protector here and throughout Albion."

More applause. Contrarily, Anya's nerves did not grow worse, knowing attention was now on her. She did not like Jonus Astraea's familiar manner, or how he spoke for her and claimed her future when she'd not yet made up her own mind. It was no wonder Willem had left him, trading the prison of this glittering estate for the simpler one she'd grown up within.

"Enjoy your safety tonight," Jonus said, letting go of Anya and taking a glass from a nearby attendant. "Enjoy your time with us. Before long, the god will have quieted and you will all return to your own homes. But I hope you remember, when you do, where help lay in time of trouble. That it is the Astraeas who protect you when the Elect cannot. That we are the ones who stand before gods, rather than cowering or offering up the weak."

TWENTY-THREE

Bones Are for Protection

Anya quelled the urge to roll her eyes as the banquet-goers applauded Lord Nevis yet again. Jonus raised his glass and, on cue, music resumed.

With a dismissive gesture to his audience, Jonus dispersed the gathered crowd and drew Anya aside.

"I've business to attend to tonight and can't be with you much," he said. "Soon you'll be able to help me with such things, but for now, I've found you an agreeable escort."

A young man appeared, stepping over from where he'd been waiting for his lord's command. He wore a dark broadcloth suit not unlike Jonus's own, save for the addition of a lavishly embroidered waistcoat. Though he was towheaded and broad-faced and arrogant in his bearing, Anya could not help giving him a searching look.

But there was nothing, not the vaguest hint of her thief about him. Catching Anya looking at him, the stranger offered her a self-satisfied smile.

"This is Delaford," Jonus said. "He'll keep an eye on you."

And with that, Anya's father vanished into the crowd. It was as if he assumed Anya's allegiance was already within his possession. As if he'd won her, in taking her from the Elect, and decided her path by speaking of it.

"An easy task, overseeing Lord Nevis's daughter," Delaford said smoothly, "when what I'm meant to be watching is a pleasure to look at."

Anya met his flattery with the blank stare she'd always employed against Tieran and Ilva, but her escort seemed unflappable. With a smile that had little of humor in it, he offered one arm, and unsure what else to do, Anya took it.

"Do you know, His Lordship has spoken of nothing but you since word came that you were in Banevale?" Delaford tried again, speaking low and leaning close to Anya as if imparting a confidence. "I've the honor of serving as one of his personal aides, and it's been all praise of Anya Astraea since your arrival."

"How nice," Anya said tersely. She didn't like the boy's over-familiar air or way of speaking as if there were a secret between them.

"He's not easily impressed, either." Delaford drew Anya over to one of the delicacy-laden tables and made a great show of their closeness as half the room covertly watched their progress. Anya's face burned, and she ducked her head. "Of course, we would have loved to meet your sister, too, but she wasn't suitable—only kept company with the Elect after arriving in the city, and your father's always been at odds with them. Whatever happened to her? Your sister, I mean? So many girls come and go from the mountain, I can't keep track of what happens to them afterward."

"Her name was Ilva, and she died," Anya said, voice toneless, eyes hard as flint. Deep within, her spark was gathering more heat, illuminating the ashes. "That's why I'm here. I'd never have left home if she hadn't been killed."

"Pity," Delaford said, waving a dismissive hand. "All's well that ends well, though, and Lord Nevis is terribly proud to have you with us."

"Is he?" Anya's gaze cut to her father. He was deep in another intent discussion, and it did not seem to her that there was anyone in the room to equal him—anyone who could hold their own against the Lord of Banevale, or to whom he would acquiesce. It gnawed at her. She could see already that he was not the sort who could be easily denied, and that so long as he lived, she would be just another piece of property. A thing to show off, like this glittering estate or the god's mountain.

Anya Astraea, my daughter who was meant for a Weatherell girl. Whom I stole from the Elect themselves.

From somewhere out in the city, there came a distant crash and rumble, and the ground shook. Crystal trembled on the laden tables, but at a sharp word from Jonus, the music swelled louder.

"What was that?" Anya asked.

"Nothing for you to worry about," Delaford said with a forced smile. "We're safe here, you know, behind your father's walls, though we all pay for that safety one way or another."

"Tell me what you mean by that," Anya pressed. "How is it Lord Nevis is keeping Banevale safe, and what sort of payment does he require?"

Delaford shifted anxiously. "I'm not sure I'm allowed to say."

"Then don't," Anya said. "Show me instead."

When Delaford hesitated, she smiled up at him, acutely aware of her unaccustomed finery and the confidence she wore like a borrowed glove. "You said you're my father's personal aide?"

Delaford nodded.

"I suppose that's a coveted position," Anya went on, toying with one of the crystal chips gleaming on her sleeve. "One which comes with any number of privileges. One any number of people would jump at, should you need to be replaced."

She had no idea whether her influence on such matters would carry any weight with Jonus. But Delaford clearly seemed to think it would. He paled and nodded.

"All right. Come along."

Anya swept along at his side, the crowds parting before them like water. Briefly, Delaford frowned down at her.

"If you don't mind my saying so, you're more like your father than I expected," he said. "When they told me Lord Nevis had a Weatherell girl as his heir and was planning to steal her out from under the noses of the Elect, I thought you'd be . . . different somehow."

"I'm not like him at all," Anya said, lifting her chin. Ilva was following along, drifting through the revelers beside them, and her lips moved in a silent litany. "The best of me is like my sister, and the strongest of me is like my mother."

"And the worst of you?" Delaford asked lightly.

Anya caught his pallid blue gaze and held it. She thought of her stubbornness, in forever refusing to see good in the long march of sacrifices the Elect had orchestrated. Of her unforgivable cowardice in letting Ilva go to the god. Of the way she had lied and hidden, all the way across Albion. Of how she'd stood before the god of the mountain and driven twin blades into his heart. How she was somehow still alive, in the aftermath of that failure.

But mostly, she thought of the furious, foolish fire she clung to so tightly and was even now nursing back to life at her core.

"I don't think either you or Jonus could bear the worst of me, if I chose to let it show."

Delaford led Anya out of the manor house, the billowing sounds of merriment dimming as they emerged into the night. Before the estate lay a long sweep of gravel drive, lined with torches. Above it spread the stars. And beyond the drive, Anya could see only darkness and intermittent flame, which signaled the presence of the god.

Before, when she'd thought of him, it had been with mingled revulsion and dread. She had feared and hated him above all else and wanted no more than his downfall. Now, in the wake of her failure, the fear she'd felt was gone, burned away by her own unquenchable passion. The only emotion left when she thought of the god was wrath.

Her fear had died on the mountain. Anger, however, had survived.

Delaford stopped a few paces from the gate, where half a dozen uniformed guards kept watch over the place where the Astraea estate's walled grounds opened into the rest of the city.

"There you have it," he said, without meeting Anya's eyes. "Our protection against the god."

Anya cast a cursory glance over the guards. "They're not enough. You forget that I've seen him. Stood before him. Six guards could hardly set themselves against the terror that destroyed a Roman *centuria* in ages past."

"They're better equipped than you give them credit for," Delaford said, but he was no liar. Not the way Anya's thief had been. His gaze strayed to the estate's high stone walls, and impatiently, Anya slipped her hand from his arm, striding across the lawn and pushing apart the ivy that draped the stonework.

Bones.

Anya's ghosts flared to life all across the lawn as she stood looking at a wall where the thick mortar had been inset with bones. Weatherell ringed with bones. The Astraeas' gleaming and untouchable estate hedged in by the same. Bones lining the path to shepherd the god down from Bane Nevis, to the waiting city below.

Bones are for protection, blood is for ill luck.

Anya's heart leaped into her throat. She'd been a hair's breadth from success. All she'd needed was Ilva.

"Leave me," she demanded, turning on her heel to address Delaford. "I want to walk the grounds alone."

"But I—" he began.

Anya channeled Willem, cold and imperious.

"Leave," she snapped.

And to her shock, he left.

Gathering up her skirts, Anya set off across the moonlit lawns, away from the gate and its guards. It irked her, to be so visible in her fine and glinting gown. She'd much rather have been in her trousers and roughspun shirt, and able to melt into the shadows. It was cold after dark too, and the chilly night air had her shivering in minutes.

At the far side of the grounds, where a long expanse of secretive, tangled gardens lay between the wall and the back of the palatial house, Anya found the escape she needed. She came across a small and rusted back gate, and at this one, the lone liveried guard was slumped over, an empty flagon beside him, his breath deep and even with sleep. Hardly daring to hope, Anya picked her way delicately past him and tried the gate.

Locked.

With great care, she rifled through the guard's pockets, her heart nearly stopping when he shifted once beneath her touch. Nothing, though. No keys. No knife. Not even a pin with which she might try to pick the lock.

Moving back a little way, Anya glanced up at the bone-set wall in despair. It was thick with ivy here, too, and at the top, barely visible in the dim moonlight, was something that quickened her pulse and set the hope she'd tamped down arrowing through her again.

Draped over the wall lay a thin length of braided crimson cord.

Without hesitation, Anya gathered up her glistening skirts and knotted them around her waist, then set herself to climbing the ivy.

For someone forest-bred, who'd spent all her life clambering up and down trees in a vain attempt to keep pace with Ilva, it was the work of moments to reach the top of the wall, though the gown she wore caught and tore more than once.

Atop the wall, Anya cast about herself, and for a moment it seemed her flight had ended, and there was no way down. The wall's far side had no accommodating ivy, and the barrier was fully twelve feet high. Anya could not afford to turn or break an ankle in her descent—Lord Astraea or the Elect would collect her within an hour, if she was forced to limp about the city. But then, in the shadows, she saw it—an old and half-rotted wooden ladder, leaned up against the stone. Making her way along the top of the wall on hands and knees and hardly daring to breathe lest someone catch sight of her shining like a fallen star in the moonlight, Anya reached the ladder. It groaned and creaked in protest but held her weight, and at last she was on solid ground, outside the bounds of Jonus Astraea's gilded realm.

Allowing herself a half smile, Anya bent to unknot her skirts, only to be nearly bowled over by a trio of familiar figures—Janie and Ella, who threw their arms around her and held her tight for a long moment, and a triumphant Midge. Though the dog kept silent, she put her muddy paws up on Anya's fine gown, adding to the damage. Warm tears slipped down Anya's face, but they had nothing to do with sorrow and everything to do with glad relief.

"You look radiant. And miserable. And absolutely freezing," Janie whispered. "We ought to get ourselves away from here. El and me have been lurking for ages—I've slipped valerian to three guards in a row now, and we're lucky they're too embarrassed or too afraid to say anything about it when they doze off. Come on, we've only been waiting for you before we leave Banevale."

They were already leading Anya away from the Astraea estate, through the night-dark and empty streets of the beleaguered city. But at Janie's last words, Anya stopped.

"You were waiting for me?" she asked, not quite believing what she'd heard.

"Really, Anya, we know Matthias told you that you're family now," Ella said, and even her gentle voice held a mild reproach. "Won't you ever believe it? We don't leave family in trouble."

"Not even the ones who seem to draw trouble to themselves," Janie added with a smile. She held out a hand and Anya took it without hesitation. "Come on. We can keep you safer than anyone else in Albion, now you're clear of the Elect and Nevis. You'll be all right with us, Anya, we swear it."

It was almost unbearably tempting. Anya wanted nothing more than to accept their offer—to let herself be enveloped by the wanderers' affection and goodwill and care, and knit herself into their company until she became as much a part of them as Matthias or Lee or one of the girls. She didn't doubt Janie's assurance, either. She *would* be safe with them. She'd be all right. She'd be looked after, as she'd never been before.

And every day, her ghosts and her guilt would haunt her, no matter how long she lived. Anya would never really be free of Albion's god and the long shadow he cast, not so long as he still slept on his mountain. Her fate had been bound to his the day Willem gave her hands in exchange for the lives of the daughters she hadn't yet known she carried.

I don't want to go, Anya had said to Ilva, a lifetime ago. *But I don't want anyone else to go either.*

This is how things are, Ilva had answered. *This is how they were. This is how they will be. It's the way of the world, little moon.*

Well, from what Anya had seen of it, the world was broken. Worse than broken, it was burning. And perhaps it would take the fire within her to extinguish the ravenous flame at Albion's heart.

"I *want* to come with you," Anya said, and she meant it with every part of her. "But I haven't finished what I set out to do, and I'll never be able to rest easy until it's done."

"What will you give?" Ella asked, a pained look crossing her face.

In answer, Anya drew herself up.

"Nothing," she said, the word ringing with truth. "I've given more than any other Weatherell girl to the god on that mountain already. He'll have no more of what's mine. I mean to make an end of him, instead. I have never been a sacrifice."

When Janie smiled at Anya, it was a satisfied and sharp-edged thing.

"Good," she said. "But we'll be waiting for you—just be sure you don't take forever to finish what you've started."

Janie squeezed Anya's hand tight, and Anya nodded.

"I have to find Tieran," Anya said. "You haven't seen him, have you? He's got something of mine that I need."

Ella shot her sister a knowing glance. "You'd better come with us."

TWENTY-FOUR
Things Kept Secret

The abandoned mill Anya had camped in with the wanderers stood stark and black against the night. Janie and Ella led her across the empty, shadowed street and under the mill's eaves, flitting through the gloom like a pair of ghosts themselves. They gave a nearly inaudible signal, and the door swung open, revealing the wanderers and the low light of their small, carefully made fires. It looked for all the world as if Anya had just left.

Unconsciously, she began scanning the faces of the wanderers, searching for one in particular.

"You ought to have moved the camp," she fussed. "It's dangerous to stay here, when both the Elect and Nevis know it's where you were last."

"Unfortunately, we're stuck for the moment," Ella said. "Something's anchoring us to this spot. Look at her—she can show you what the trouble is."

Ella gestured to Midge, who was trotting purposefully across the mill floor, weaving her way between the wanderers' cook-fires. The dog stopped beside the door to the storeroom where Anya had parted ways with Tieran and glanced back as if to say, *Well, come along.*

Anya followed Midge, drawn across the mill like a lodestone, but Janie caught her halfway.

"Wait," Janie said, one hand on Anya's arm. "Look, since you left, we've been told some things about you. About your sister, mostly. And maybe I never met your Ilva, but I know what *I'd* have done if Ella and I were still in Weatherell, and not wanderers. I'd have gone to the god in a heartbeat to keep her safe. Even if it had killed me. I wouldn't have had to think twice about it.

"Tieran said it's haunting you, that she went when you stayed. But that's not fair to her, Anya. That makes her smaller, and less, to wish what she chose was undone. You being guilty and eaten up by what happened takes the point out of what Ilva did. Don't do that to her. I think I can promise you, that's not what she would have wanted."

A memory washed over Anya of Tieran's meeting with Ilva, and what her sister had said to him. That she wanted to get home. That she had someone who always looked after her and fixed everything she'd ever broken. For the first time, the heat growing within Anya felt less like vengeance and more like bravery. Like the courage she sought. As if, perhaps, she'd always been brave in her own way, just by looking at the world and owning to herself that it was broken and ought not to be so.

"I think you're right," Anya said to Janie. "I think I was lucky to have Ilva, and Ella's lucky to have you. And I think whatever comes, we're all lucky to have known one another."

Neither of them hesitated. Janie wrapped her arms around Anya and Anya hugged her back, and it knit something inside her together again.

"Don't take forever with what comes next," Janie said with a lift of her chin as they separated. "And don't forget what I said— we'll be waiting."

She turned back to Ella and moved toward her with outstretched hands.

The storeroom door before Anya stood slightly ajar, and through it she caught a glimpse of something so familiar, it felt like home. A small, smokeless fire, burning very low. A moth-eaten bedroll, spread out beside it. A bone charm, hanging from one of the rafters.

A thief, seated by the fire, staring into its embers with emptiness behind his eyes.

Overcome by an impossible tangle of emotions, Anya shifted, and one of her clumsy, bandaged arms brushed against the door.

"Leave me be, Matthias," Tieran said hoarsely. "Already told you, I'll sit here forever if she doesn't turn up. See if I don't."

The hinges whined softly as Anya pushed her way in and shut the door behind her. Tieran glanced up, sharp and fierce, but at the sight of Anya, pale and mud-stained in the ruins of her fine gown, his eyes went wide. The thief scrambled to his feet and backed away until there was only wall behind him, shaking his head as he went.

"Can't do this," he murmured desperately. "Not again. Not another ghost. Already had one and that was bad enough. Not looking. Can't see you."

"I'm not a ghost," Anya said, though she was sure she looked the part.

Tieran only grew more distraught. He was fighting harder to hold his shape than Anya had ever seen him do before—it wasn't just his hands shifting, but his face, his outline, his entire form.

"Makes it worse," he managed to get out. "If it's you in the flesh."

With an agonized sound, Tieran sank to the floor and curled inward, hiding as much of himself as he could. Deep shudders wracked him, and Anya could not bear it. However faithless he was, however disloyal when backed into a corner, it had never been in her to see him suffer. From the first moment she'd laid eyes on him, that had been the one thing she could not tolerate.

Crossing the storeroom in a heartbeat, Anya dropped down at Tieran's side. She reached out tentatively, fingers brushing the thief's hunched shoulders, and when he did not flinch or pull away, she put both arms around him, gathering him to herself.

"Oh, don't," she pleaded in a whisper, because he was sobbing, each breath dredged out of a broken place within him. "Please, Tieran, my heart."

She sat and held the thief until he'd grown a little calmer, and could bring himself to speak.

"Done a lot of bad things," he said, the words coming out muffled. "Some worse than you can imagine. You—you think I'm a thief, but that's not even the start. Nothing ever felt worse than leaving you, though. I *didn't want to do it.*"

"Then why did you?" Anya asked, but gently.

For the first time Tieran looked up, tearstained and wretched, and Anya knew she was lost. That she loved him with her whole being, and would do anything for him—anything besides turn away from her appointed task.

"Can't say," Tieran told her with a shake of his head. "There are things I've never breathed a word of to nobody, Anya. Not even Matthias. I'm too afraid."

Leaning forward, Anya kissed him, slow and soft and sweet.

"You don't ever have to be afraid on my account," she said. "Not afraid of me or afraid for me—whichever it is. I know the truth comes hard for you, but I want to hear it, if you can bring yourself to tell it. I'll start with mine, if you like—my name is Anya Astraea and I have never been a Weatherell girl. It has always been my intent to kill a god. First for my sister's sake, now for my own and everyone else's."

"Think I didn't know that?" Tieran grumbled halfheartedly, sounding a little more like himself. "Think you're smart? First time I saw you, I thought to myself, *There goes death in a red collar.*"

He shifted his weight, until they were both sitting with their backs to the wall, Tieran's arm around Anya's shoulders and his other hand caught in both of hers. There was a long silence, and for a moment, Anya was afraid he didn't have it in him. That whatever hidden things lay at the center of his being would stay locked away there forever, unknown to her.

But then:

"You remember what I told you about my mother? That she died in a fire?" Tieran said, quiet and hesitant, as if the words might come out razor-edged and cut at him as they went. "Well, that was the truth. Or some of it, anyhow."

† † † †

My mother was a Vestal—a sacrifice, raised by the Elect. They grow up cloistered, hidden away from the world until they're old enough to be given a choice. Leave behind everything you've ever known, and make your way with nothing and no one, or stay with us and become a sacrifice. Think you know a bit about choices like that.

Only their sacrifice isn't your sort of sacrifice, Anya Astraea. Vestals are for something else. Grayrobes call them the little brides, *and most of them don't live. A few make it back down the mountain, but not enough that they expect to. The ones that make it mostly die later, burned up from the inside out, all because the Elect aren't happy with their god. Not that they'd ever say it to an outsider, or let someone like you know, but you seen it—he's difficult. Doesn't do their bidding, and it costs to keep him quiet, or to show his wrath. They want a god they can order about.*

So they been trying to make one.

Sometimes they got close. Sometimes a little bride lived for months after coming down from the mountain, and the Elect started hoping, but they all died too early. All except my mother. She lived and lived, even though she was burning. She lived so long that she started begging to die, and when she finally got what she wished for and left this life in agony, she'd hung on so long that the Elect got what they wanted, too.

They cut the bastard offspring of a Vestal and that horror on the mountain out of my mother as the breath left her body, and were pleased with themselves.

First thing I remember is her ghost. Was in one of those rooms they kept me in—all white, so they could see the scorch marks if I lost my temper—and they'd just done something I was a bit low about. They were always doing things to push me. Giving me some comfort I'd take a liking to—a blanket, or a soft toy—then taking it away. Not bothering to send in any food for a day or two. That was in the early days, before it got worse, but I was barely walking and it all seemed hard enough.

So I was sitting in a corner, feeling sore over everything, and she just . . . appeared. Didn't look right—looked like a girl what got burned to death from the inside out, which she had been, but I didn't know none of that yet. And I didn't get much company. No one ever stayed with me long, so I started talking to her. The more I talked, the longer she'd keep visible, just standing there and listening, with a bit of a smile.

Wasn't long after that, things started to get worse. Back then I didn't look like this. Didn't know how to take a shape and hold it. I was always just burning, like my mother had been, like my—like the god what sired me still is. Only difference was, I never died of it. And I'd never touched nobody. Never got close enough, the Elect made sure. Because once the god on the mountain touches someone, they've got to do his bidding if they hear him speak. They weren't ready to test me on that yet. They wanted to go slow, be cautious.

So they gave me a dog.

It was a little mongrel off the streets, scared and mean. I loved it, meanness and all. Thought it was the best thing that had ever happened. Gave it scraps, talked to it, left my own blanket in a corner so it'd be comfortable. It got braver and braver, coming nearer to me a bit at a time. Things were going so well, but I wanted more and I didn't know better. So one day, when it was lapping water out of a bowl, I reached out and put a hand on its back.

Could see right away that what I was doing was hurting it, but I couldn't stop. It felt good and right and perfect, having a living thing in my power. So I kept my hand where it was, until the dog's fur had burned away and its skin began to char where I'd touched it, leaving an awful burn. Guilt set in then and I took my hand away, but the damage was done. I hadn't just hurt the dog, I'd changed it somehow. It wasn't scared or mean anymore, just small and broken and sad, though it didn't seem to remember a bit of what I'd done. And from then on, the dog would do anything I asked it to, the moment the words were out of my mouth.

For a few days, I managed to keep myself away from it. But on the third I couldn't stand it anymore. I sat down and called that dog over to me. I took it onto my lap and held it close, and I'd never felt anything worse or better, even as it stopped moving and I knew I'd killed it.

Got awfully low after that. Didn't want to eat or drink or do nothing. Would've stopped breathing if I could. But she talked me through it—my mother. It'd only ever been me talking to her until then, but after she saw what I did she started speaking. Told me over and over again that I didn't have to be whatever the Elect was trying to turn me into. That I could do better. The Elect sent people in often enough to tell me things to the contrary that I didn't much believe her. But it meant a lot to hear her say it. To know someone thought there might be even a bit of good in me.

She was wrong, though.

Awhile after the dog, I woke up and found a basket in my room. There was . . . a baby inside it. This tiny, perfect thing. I begged the Elect to take her away, and they wouldn't. Told me I'd look after her, or she'd starve. So I did my best. I gave her the milk they brought and kept her swaddled in blankets, so I wouldn't touch her by mistake. I wanted to touch her soft hair more than anything, but I didn't and I didn't, and it kept getting a little easier not to until one day when I was changing her, being as a careful as always, she reached out and took hold of my finger.

I was still trying to pry her hand off me when she died. I'd tried so hard not to hurt her, but I had in the end, and there was still that piece of me what was happy about it. What thought, Yeah, this is how things should be. There should be death in our presence, because we're different and stronger and we deserve it.

My mother didn't say much after that. Didn't bother telling me it was an accident or that I could have done better. She just sat in a corner, smelling of smoke and heartbreak, and singing. Old folk songs mostly, or sometimes music without words. She never did hymns, even though I expect that's what she knew best from growing up with the Elect.

I was grateful for that.

Sometimes it all stopped. Like the Elect just forgot about me. I know they didn't—know there's always a reason for what they do—but it felt like being forgotten. Everything would get dark and quiet. No visits from sharp-tongued or worshipful grayrobes. No living things left in my care. No food. No water. Just days of emptiness. Sometimes it would go for so long I got afraid they'd all left. That I'd die locked in that room, on account of having been less than they wanted. That was the only thing that seemed worse than killing, because even the bad part of me wasn't happy about it. So when they'd come back, I'd try and do whatever they wanted. By then they'd started sending in their own, ready for a sacrifice.

I knew what the Elect were looking for from me, and I didn't want to die on my own, locked in that white room I'd never seen the outside of. So when they sent a sacrifice in, I'd . . . be cruel to them a bit. Not kill them outright at first. Just hurt them, and order them about. Make them pray or beg or do some sort of pointless ritual. Sometimes I'd make them hurt themselves, because none of it seemed to matter anymore. Went on like that for a while, getting worse and worse. And then one day when I woke up, it wasn't a gray-robe waiting for me, or some helpless creature.

It was a boy. A ragged one fresh off the street, maybe ten years old, same as me. There was fear in his eyes like I'd never seen when I got near him. And I couldn't do it. Even halfway to the monster they wanted me to become, I couldn't hurt him. But I couldn't talk to him either, to tell him who I was or why he'd been brought in or that I didn't want any harm to come to him. I only had Divinitas, and he only had Brythonic.

I held off for days, until the Elect stopped coming. Stopped feeding us. Stopped bringing water. I knew what they wanted from me, and a lot of me wanted it too, but I dug in my heels. Wasn't gonna do their bidding no more. Wasn't gonna be what they set out for me to be. Not even if it meant dying to get clear of them.

Trouble was, that boy off the street was already skin and bone when they brought him in, and he started his dying first. I was jealous. Didn't have room left in me for anything better or softer by then. I sat there and I watched him die. It took ages and it hurt him and I could have made it quick, but I wouldn't give the Elect the satisfaction.

Only when he'd gone, I realized what they'd done. That I was a monster now, whatever I chose. Even without being the one who'd done the killing. Didn't have an ounce of mercy left in me, and I hated it. I hated them. Hated everything, even that fool of a boy who'd been too soft to avoid getting caught.

Hated the ghost of my mother, who'd watched it all happen and never gave me any help besides what she was doing right at that moment—whispering that I could do better, that I could be different, when I knew that was a lie. Knew I couldn't change, no matter how hard I tried.

I wanted to change. Wanted to change more than anything else. It's what I was thinking of, when I reached out and touched that boy's face, knowing I couldn't hurt him no more on account of he was already gone. It pained me, touching him. Not just in the soul, in the body. But I didn't take my hand away and I kept wishing for a change with everything in me. Didn't matter what sort of change, really. Anything would be fine, because the way things were was intolerable.

When I stood up, I was still hurting, but I deserved the pain so I bore down on it and let it be. Let it get bigger inside me, till I thought maybe it'd be what killed me, which would be all right. Only it didn't. It got smaller again and I was going to lie down when I saw another ghost.

The boy this time, looking whole and well enough, like he had when they first brought him in.

I went toward him and he came toward me. I raised a hand and he raised a hand. Was then I realized, I wasn't seeing a ghost at all. It was my reflection, in a mirror the Elect kept in my room so I'd have to see what a monster I was. Only now I wasn't—I'd changed, just like I wished to. That boy had died on account of me, and then I'd stolen his face.

The shock of it threw me back into my own shape, but I went and knelt by him and did it again, and then again, and once more just to be sure. My mother watched the whole thing, and after that last time, she came and took me by the shoulders. Couldn't recall her ever doing that before, and her hands were the coldest thing I'd ever felt.

Wear your face and wait, *she said, and I did as I was told.*

Took another two days for the Elect to come back. Think they were punishing me, for not doing what they wanted and killing the boy. When they finally sent someone in, I realized they'd got awful careless. A pair of grayrobes came in, talking with each other and mostly ignoring me, and they weren't even worried. Didn't pay attention. Left the door ajar behind them. They really thought I'd never try to bolt, because I hadn't done it yet. Because I knew what they said was right—no one who looked the way I did would get far in the world, or be able to hide from them.

But now I could.

And so I ran. I left my mother's ghost behind in that white room and ran like I'd never been able to do before. The Elect didn't know which way was up—hadn't ever dreamed I'd do something like that, or prepared for it at all. I gave them the slip and the moment I was on the streets, I changed my shape and disappeared. Stole what I needed to get by and ended up in Londin eventually. Learned Brythonic, just by listening to what I heard on the streets. Got mean, and flighty, but better than I was before. Found that if things were really bad—if I wanted more than anything to shed my shape and be the one I was born to, the one where I could lay my hands on someone and have them in my power—I could do other things. Could lie and steal and it'd take the edge off. Not saying those things are right, mind. Not saying I don't try to find other ways of keeping myself tamer, but sometimes being what I am gets around me. Sometimes I do the smaller wrongs to keep worse things from coming about. Not defending it, but it's who I am.

That's who and how I been since Matthias found me and took me in. Since you met me and we fell in together. Not a soul knows any of that, Anya Astraea. I never breathed a word. But I'm scared every day—that the

Elect'll find me, and put me back in that room and finish turning me into the monster they wanted. Or that maybe they did finish the job, and I never noticed. Maybe one of these days, the smaller wrongs won't be enough, and I'll do something really unforgivable.

Even if none of that happens, though, I don't know how to not be afraid. Because everyone I get close to writes me off in the end. Oh, that's just Tieran. You can't trust him. Can't depend on him. Can't turn your back on him. *And they're not wrong. Trying not to be a monster doesn't mean I been good. Don't know if I ever can be.*

And that's me. That's the start and the end, and I don't know what else to say.

TWENTY-FIVE
The Ghost Path

All the while, as Tieran spoke, Anya had stayed resolutely close to him. She'd kept her head on his chest, listening to the familiar beat of his heart and breathing in his reassuring scent, remembering over and over that he was who he'd always been. She could feel the fear in him—in the rapid pace of his pulse, in the tension singing through his body. And she hated it, as she had always hated knowing he was hurt or afraid.

When he fell silent, Anya shifted, inching away and getting to her feet. She stood for a moment, looking down at the disreputable thief, and he would not meet her eyes.

"Get up," Anya said softly.

With a nod, Tieran did as he was told, gaze still fixed on the floor.

"Show me," Anya said.

Tieran drew in a quick breath. "Don't think that's wise."

"Why?" Anya asked, still gentle, though he seemed not to notice her gentleness. "Will you hurt me?"

The thief flinched.

"No," he swore. "Never. Rather die, Anya Astraea."

"Then show me," she said once more.

Reluctantly, Tieran nodded.

He changed so quickly it made Anya's head spin. As if he was always holding this other version of himself at bay and it only waited to resurface. One moment it was her thief standing before her. The next it was someone and something else entirely.

This Tieran was a luminous and deadly thing, with fire flickering perpetually beneath the thin web of his skin and eyes like embers. As with the god of the mountain, Anya was overcome by a sudden compulsion to kneel. But she did not. She'd stood before Albion's great terror—driven a knife into him, too. She would not worship at a lesser altar.

And as she stepped forward, she realized her first impression had been wrong. Perhaps this was not Tieran as she'd ever seen him before, but no matter his shape, she'd learned him well enough that he was not unrecognizable. She could still see his sharpness and fear, his anxious way of carrying himself, and whether his gaze was hazel or flame, the same cleverness and anguish lurked behind it.

"Tieran?" Anya said.

He nodded uncertainly, and even like this—especially like this—his hesitance cut at her.

"I love you," Anya said, her eyes never leaving his. "I didn't get a chance to say so before, but there it is. I loved you while you were telling me who you are, and I love you standing here and seeing it now. I loved you while you were leaving me, and I will love you if you go again because I know you feel the same, and I think we'll always find our way back to each other. Maybe your life has been a sad story, but when I look at you, I see something beautiful. I watch. I've seen. I know how hard you try to be better. And everything I am loves everything you are."

Tieran did not struggle with the change this time—at least, not the way Anya had seen him do before. Instead, he forcibly dragged himself into his chosen form, becoming the boy she knew with a sudden and supreme effort. He stepped into Anya's open arms and she held him close, and though he shook, it was not from the difficulty of holding his shape—his hands did not waver at all.

"You're going back up the mountain, aren't you?" Tieran said at last.

Anya nodded. "I'll be needing my bone knife back. This is what lies under *my* skin, you know. I've never wanted to be an offering, but I've never wanted anyone else to go either. So it's time for me to finish what I started and fix what's broken, like Ilva thought I could."

"Gonna come with you."

"Oh, Tieran, you don't have to—"

"Yeah. Yeah, I do."

† † † †

It was entirely different, climbing the mountain in the clear light of morning. Though the signs of the god's recent passage were undeniable—smoking rocks and charred grasses made a scorched path all the way to the bare and rocky summit—Anya was quiet and resolute, moving along with Tieran at her side and, on the easier stretches, with his hand in hers. The morning was fine, the air sweet and mild with the last taste of summer. It would have been beautiful under any other circumstances.

It was still beautiful.

Bones are for protection, Anya thought, feeling the familiar and comforting presence of the blade strapped to her thigh. In the end, she and Ilva together would have to be enough. Not for an offering, but for the remaking of the world. If necessary, Anya would die to ensure they became so, and to see that her sister was remembered not as a failure but as the last and greatest of Albion's Weatherell girls.

Halfway to the summit, Anya and Tieran stopped for a few moments on the shore of the narrow lake, which shone dazzlingly bright under the morning sun. The grass was green and soft, the sky a far perfect blue with white clouds scudding across it. Anya sat and watched the shadows of those clouds pass over the country below, moving across the distant expanse of Banevale, while Tieran looked over his own knives beside her. Up above them somewhere, a lark was singing, its song a glorious fall of liquid music.

"Tieran?" Anya said suddenly. "I'm happy. I'm happy to be here with you. I can't remember the last time I felt this way."

"Glad you're happy, Weatherell girl," he said, still bent over his knives, testing their edges and weights.

"Aren't you happy?" she pressed.

Tieran glanced up, squinting at her in the full sun. "Gonna be happy if we're sitting here again on our way back down the mountain. Not holding my breath on that score, though."

"Come over here," Anya said, patting the turf beside her.

"But I got to—"

"Come over here," she insisted.

With a sigh, Tieran joined her.

"Look," Anya said, pointing to the endless view before them. "Isn't that something?"

Tieran gave it all a cursory glance. "Yeah, that's something. Now can I—"

"Kiss me," Anya said. "Unless you've got something better to do."

"No." Tieran flushed. "Nothing better to do than that."

"Well, all right then."

Anya shifted closer to him and turned her face up to his. When Tieran kissed her, she let her lips part softly and her hands move of their own accord, one at the back of his neck and one at his waist. They were perfect together, the best thing she knew, and Anya kissed Tieran until she was sure he'd forgotten about his knives and what was to come. Until there was only the two of them, alone on a hillside, absorbed in the straightforward joy of being with each other.

When Tieran stopped for a moment, breathless, Anya tucked a strand of dark hair behind her ear and smiled.

"I think I asked you about being happy?" she said.

Tieran attempted to look sullen, and failed.

"Getting happier," he admitted. "But we got to go."

"I know," Anya said reluctantly. "But wouldn't it be nice if we could stay here like this forever?"

Leaning forward, Tieran kissed the tip of her nose. "Not nice. Perfect."

He gathered up his knives and gave several to Anya and then, as if noticing it for the first time, shook his head over her ruined gown and thin dancing slippers.

"It's cold up top, you're gonna freeze in that," Tieran said disapprovingly, and Anya loved him and all the wanderers for seeing only impracticality where others saw what was rich and fine.

With a motion that felt like habit between them, Tieran shrugged out of the oilskin coat. It still smelled of smoke, but since the last time Anya wore it, the sleeves had been carefully patched and mended. Helping her into it, Tieran fussed over the buttons.

Fog rolled in as they climbed the latter half of the mountain, working toward its summit. Mist made a ghost of all that Anya had found beautiful, and her own ghosts slipped through it, flitting across the path, appearing in open spaces cleared by the wind, whispering, whispering, whispering, of wordless things and forgotten offerings. Everything grew damp and cold and dim, and Anya clutched Tieran's hand whenever she could, wanting the reminder of something living and real.

At the peak of Bane Nevis, where the mountain plateaued, its beehive cairns with their thousand bones loomed wraithlike in the fog. Ghosts ringed every one of them—girls dressed in white, with pieces of themselves missing, and as Anya began to cross the summit, they stepped forward to line the path, reaching out to her with icy hands.

Don't go, they sighed. *Don't let anyone else go.*

Anya's ghosts breathed the words like a prayer, like a hope too dear to have reached for in life, a hope that only bloomed pale and spectral in the last darkness of the grave. They ran their soft, yielding hands over Anya until she was cold as the bones they'd left behind, but she would not have stopped them. Not for all the world.

"Can you see them?" she asked Tieran, halfway across the rocky, fogbound summit. He was watching her closely and shook his head.

"No. That don't mean anything, though. If you can see them, I know they're there."

By the time they reached the entrance to the god of the mountain's lair, Anya was shaking with cold, and Ilva stood waiting. She smiled, decaying skin pulling taut across her beloved face, and kissed Anya's forehead. Anya swallowed back tears.

Be brave, Ilva echoed. *Be brave.*

And the image of her faded away.

Anya reached through the torn and fraying fabric of her skirts, gripping the last piece of her sister, once more in its hidden sheath on her thigh. It felt like the only thing still tethering her to the world, small and frail and poorly crafted as it might be.

"Ready?" she asked Tieran, and glanced over her shoulder as one by one, the ghosts gleaming along the mountaintop winked out. Their ice had worked its way so deep into Anya, she thought she might never be warm again. Still, the flame within her burned at the heart of that ice, and so long as it was unquenched, she would carry on.

"Ready," Tieran said, though his voice was uncertain.

Then there was the twining, torchlit stair, with its over-powering smells of ash and flame. Near the base of the steps, where the hellish glow cast off by the god himself illuminated the walls, Tieran stopped. He was sweating with the effort to hold himself to his shape, hands shifting wildly, and Anya could read naked fear in his eyes.

"Maybe this is far enough for you," she said. "If I were really a Weatherell girl, I'd be going by myself. I don't mind. Truly, I don't."

"I just . . . need a moment." Tieran's eyes were fixed on the stone floor, his breath ragged. "I'll catch you up?"

"Of course." Anya nodded, and much as she tried to sound easy, she couldn't keep a note of sadness from creeping into the words. Tieran, for all he held her heart, was not someone she relied on when it mattered. There was only her here, and the last of Ilva.

Rising on her toes, Anya kissed the thief's cheek. He was flushed and miserable, and held her hands tightly.

"I'll be back, I hope," Anya said. "But you don't have to wait for me. If you have to go, I understand."

Squaring her shoulders, she stepped forward, out into the echoing cavern that housed Albion's terrible god.

TWENTY-SIX
Anya Among the Gods

Immediately, a wall of blistering heat slammed into Anya, dashing her hopes that she'd catch the god at rest. The blast forced her eyes shut and once more, overwhelming awareness of the god's presence drove her to kneel. Anya fought against it, striving for vision, for clarity, for steadiness. In only an instant she had her eyes open, but the god already loomed over her, a vast and fiery menace.

Anya stayed on her knees, even as his voice scorched at her.

"So, a scapegoat returns from the wilderness it was sent out to. You should have valued your freedom and your life more highly, little heretic. You will not leave this place with both of them a second time."

Keeping her head bowed contritely, Anya reached inward. She drew on every moment of penitence and every lie she'd ever told and twined them into a false confession fit to beguile a god.

"Not a scapegoat," she breathed. "Not that, my lord. An erring lamb, rather, who has seen her folly and hopes her repentance does not come too late."

"Pretty lies," the god scoffed. *"But you have lied to me before."*

"I have never lied to you before now," Anya swore, truth ringing through her words. "All I've ever done is give you pieces of myself, over and over again. You have taken things that were dear to me since before I left my mother's womb, and it was too much, for a moment, for me to bear up under. But I've found my courage, and am prepared to suffer for you a final time."

"She who has a deceitful heart finds no good, and she who has a perverse tongue falls into evil."

The god was circling Anya now, slowly taking the measure of her, and she was dizzy and sick with his nearness. But she had not come so far only to fail a second time. With a decisive motion, she slid the oilskin coat from her shoulders, revealing the tatters of her gleaming, milk-white gown and the completed prayer the Elect had inked into the skin of her back.

She could sense the moment he saw what she'd become— both prayer and power. The moment he realized that what she offered was unlike anything a Weatherell girl had offered before.

"My Arbiter once told me," Anya said, her voice low and sweet, "that the god of the mountain and his righteous Elect rejoice more over one straying lamb who returns to the fold than over all those who remain true. I have strayed, yes, but here I am. Not just a lamb, but a moon that moves in brightness. I have been offered the world and given it up to kneel at your feet. No sacrifice has been tempted as I have and still presented herself before you in the end. I swear it on my mother's hands. I swear it on my sister's bones."

The god had stopped his prowling and stood behind Anya. She could feel the intolerable heat of him, his attention fixed on the prayer she bore.

"*Fair as the moon,*" the god muttered, the words like ash and embers. "*Clear as the sun. You are all fair, my love, and there is no spot in you.*"

"None," Anya answered. "Whatever my flaws, I have burned them from my soul with fire, so that I might be fit to come before you again."

When Anya held out her hand to the god of her own volition, his touch did not burn. He raised her to her feet, and like a nobleman escorting a dancer across Lord Astraea's ballroom, led her to the stone altar at the sanctum's far end.

Anya fought to remain serene. She let not a hint of the fear raging in her show as she climbed the slick footholds left by countless Weatherell girls who'd gone before. Though her pulse raced like a wild thing, she laid herself down on the altar's worn and uneven surface, refusing to allow her gaze to drift to the heavy shackles that had once chained a god. They were broken and twisted now, useless and stained with rust the color of blood.

Or perhaps it was blood—Anya supposed either was just as likely. She kept her hands at her sides, not daring to reach for her bone knife until the last possible moment, for she could not afford to fail again. Above her, the god bowed low, hunger written across his brutal face.

"*Are you ready at last, little moon?*" he asked, his voice a flame. "*It is for me to name my requirement now, and for you to give.*"

Inside, Anya writhed with fury at the sound of Ilva's nickname coming from the god of the mountain's abominable mouth. Outside, she only nodded.

The god's hunger grew sharper, thicker, a palpable cloud. It was written all through him—in his posture, in the flames that licked faster and hotter across his ashen skin. For a moment, he said nothing, and Anya realized with a pang of horror that he was warring with himself, overcome with his wretched lust for the piece of her he would require. He was utterly abhorrent to her, not because of his shape or his fire, but because of his nature, his temperament, his repellent appetites.

"*I would have your heart,*" the god said finally. "*I would have the devotion you have thus far denied me. Not taken from you by my touch or my word, but freely given.*"

"What will you do with it?" Anya could not help asking. She had no intention of giving what he desired, but she wanted to know what he would have made of her, had she done her duty and no more. Had she been the offering she was meant for.

"*I will make you the greatest of the devout,*" the god said. "*A voice crying in the wilderness. A reformer, who returns Albion to its old righteousness. Offertory villages will mark this land like stars, and you will oversee them all, shepherding the purest and most perfect of their offspring along the path to my altar. I will feast and sleep, and for as long as you live Albion will prosper, in a golden age brought about by my benevolence and the gift of your heart. You will be seen as a saint, and your fire joined with mine will cleanse all this land we dwell upon.*"

This time, Anya could not fully suppress the shudder that

ran through her. But she fixed her gaze on the baleful god of the mountain and inclined her head.

"Do with me as you will."

He was an inferno now, the heat of him scorching Anya's skin. As he began to bow still lower over her, she let her hand creep, inch by inch, to the hidden sheath on her thigh. To the last piece of Ilva.

Bones are for protection.

She could not help the way her gaze cut to the god's stained and long-broken shackles.

Blood is for ill luck.

Anya's fingertips closed around the rough cord handle of her knife. She eased it from the sheath as the god swam above her, gone hazy and indistinct in the waves of his own cast-off heat.

Bones are for—

"Stop."

The god's voice ground out, potent as an earthquake, and Anya found herself pinned to the altar. It was as if the shackles he'd been freed from had wrapped around her wrists, her ankles, as if chains looped around her waist. His word was undeniable—she'd felt his touch before and could no longer avoid a direct command.

Dispassionately, the god took a heavy step back. His gaze raked over Anya, motionless on the altar, the bone knife clearly visible.

"*All of Albion in exchange for such a little thing—only your heart. And you, in your rebellion and arrogance and spite, choose death, not for yourself alone but for so many others. Never have I been sent an offering so rotten to her core.*"

The god's hand snaked out and gripped Anya's throat, and this time, his touch seared her. She cried out as her skin blistered and scorched, and then there was a blinding flash of light, and he drew away.

At the sanctum's heart stood Tieran.

He'd lost his frail human shape entirely, but even as a living flame he stood with shoulders hunched, head down, looking for all the world as if he were about to be chastised by Matthias or Lee. An attentive watchfulness swept over the god of the mountain, as if he could not make sense of the boy before him.

"Not gonna let you touch her," Tieran muttered.

The god tilted his dreadful, inhuman head. *"But I already have. And so your concern comes too late. Her pain is my pleasure, her will mine to bend or break if she can hear my voice.*"

Anya shrank within herself as the god turned his attention to her.

"Is that not so, child?" he asked, his words like the earth itself shifting.

And to her horror, Anya found herself nodding, her lips forming an answer of their own volition even as she fought for silence. "Yes, my lord."

Tieran glanced back at her, every line of him speaking of anguish. Anya knew what he must be thinking of—things he'd done at the goading of the Elect, times he'd subsumed others' will beneath his own, just as the god did now.

"You don't have to listen to him," Tieran told Anya desperately. "Don't have to do nothing he tells you. He's not greater than you, Anya. He's not anything, compared to who you are."

But Tieran, with the rigid control he exercised over his inmost self, had no power to order or free Anya. He had never touched her as a flame—had always held her will sacred. And so the god of the mountain's hold over her remained complete.

"Stay silent, wayward lamb, and wait as you are," the god commanded.

The invisible bonds that held Anya tightened, but she kept her eyes fixed on Tieran. He seemed unbearably small, standing before the towering god, but still her thief shone like a defiant star.

He is beautiful, Anya thought, a splintering sensation rising within her. *He is always beautiful to me.*

Amid the fierce gleam of Tieran's unleashed fire, another light arose. Something sharp, and cold, and steely. His blade glittered in the air, casting off light and arcing toward the god of the mountain. The moment it reached its target, Tieran threw himself forward, giving no quarter, all fury and flame. The brightness of them grew intolerable, and Anya was forced to glance away. She could not call out to warn Tieran that steel held no power to harm the monster he'd pitted himself against—the god had bound her to silence, and she could not make a single sound.

When she looked back again, the god of the mountain still stood at the cavern's heart, seemingly untouched. Tieran had drawn back ten paces, breathing heavily, and the light in him was dimmer than it had been at first. He held himself awkwardly, and the god tilted his head to one side.

"One of mine," he said, as if to himself, not to either of the intruders in his sanctum. *"One of mine raised up for a challenge. And a callow, upstart thing at that. Do the grayrobes mock me?"*

"Leave him be," Anya managed to get out, now that the god's attention was wholly absorbed by Tieran. She sat at the very edge of the altar, forced by his injunction to keep contact with it, but fulfilling only the bare letter of the command. "He's hardly worth your notice, like you said. But I've come back to you—a prodigal and a heretic of the worst sort. Come and claim me."

She could not keep her voice from shaking as she made the invitation, and the god of the mountain shot her a look of fathomless disdain.

"Did I not order you to silence and stillness?" he rumbled. *"I grow weary of your interruptions. Do not speak again, until the business of your betters is done."*

Anya's insides twisted and her tongue cleaved to the roof of her mouth as the god turned back to Tieran.

"You want this lamb for your own, little godling?" he said. *"Then prove yourself divine. Wrest her from me."*

Pleading with her eyes, Anya shook her head. But Tieran blazed, steel glinting in his hand, and once more the gods were met. Their coming together was a terrible thing that shook the earth and set loose stones crashing from the cavern roof in a deafening rockfall.

When the dust cleared, the god of the mountain stood

triumphant. He was an avenging inferno with Tieran at his feet, the thief looking small and broken, all his lesser light gone to shadow. As a last defiance, Tieran dragged himself back into his human form and set his jaw. Anya could see where the god had wounded him, though not how—a terrible, rust-red slick was spreading across his ragged shirt, plastering it to his skin.

"You come against me with steel and flame," the god of the mountain scoffed. *"I am greater than you can fathom. Ageless as stone. No blade forged by men can wound me, and fire is my domain. But you are less and fragile and weak where I am strong, and I will wipe even your memory from the face of the earth. Then there will be a reckoning for the grayrobes, for only fools believe they can raise up a power to rival me, and I do not suffer fools."*

Anya could not look away from Tieran. She scrabbled helplessly at the stone of the altar, tearing the skin from her fingertips and splintering her fingernails in an effort to break the god's command. But his word held her fast and after a moment she grew quieter, her breath coming in great, desperate gasps.

Still, her fingers probed the crevices and fissures of the altar, which had seen so much of sacrifice and blood. At last, as the god bent slowly over Tieran, she touched something strange and cold and smooth.

A hint of metal.

Grasping for it, Anya drew something from the rock she had never expected to see again. Ilva's little sufferer—the pendant she had worn to the god's mountain and returned home without. Every line of it was familiar—a reminder of who Ilva had been, bright and brave and beautiful, unshakeable in her choices, unrepentant in her boldness. A shining image rose up in Anya's mind, of the last time she and Ilva had stood together in Weatherell's final clearing. Before the god of the mountain tore out Anya's beating heart.

Inside Anya Astraea, the flame that had plagued her all her life grew into a towering inferno. It sent rage scorching through every inch of her, and perhaps the god of the mountain and Tieran the thief burned visibly, but Anya was no less a living fire because her fury burned unseen.

With a wrenching effort, she broke free of the altar and of the god's command, and flew across the cavern to stand between Tieran and the god.

"He never wanted to come to you," Anya said, her voice ringing with defiant truth. "It was his intention to stay clear of you forever—to haunt the edges of Albion in his human form and never set himself against the greater power that began him. *I* brought him here. *I* crossed this whole land intent on harming you. *I* defied the grayrobes and drew the offspring they raised for you into my schemes. If you have any enemy in this world, it is me. It will always be me, for as long as I live."

The god bent low over Anya to peer into her face. Flames filled her field of vision.

"*Who are you,*" the god said wonderingly, "*that you come against me again and again?*"

Anya glanced back at Tieran. He was pale as weathered bones now, eyes shut, chest barely rising and falling, and blood pooled on the cavern floor beneath him. Everything in Anya hurt at the sight and recoiled from the thought of facing another heartbreak.

It had been like dying herself, losing Ilva. It was still like dying, piece by piece, one fragment at a time. But she had grown strong on the road—flames were consuming Anya despite her worry, roaring through her blood and bones. Despair and fury, sorrow and rage, all tangled up within her. She loved Tieran, loved Ilva, loved Willem and Philomena and Sylvie and the memory of every girl who'd gone before. She loved her own life. Loved the intolerable force of her anger. Loved the brief and tantalizing glimpse she'd had of freedom.

Don't go, Ilva whispered, from somewhere and nowhere and everywhere at once, her voice so soft the god could not overhear. *Don't let anyone else go.*

Anya envisioned Ilva, lying on the god's fearful altar, denying him his first request. She had refused him when asked for the memories of her sister, though doing so led to her own destruction. She had not shied away from hurt. She'd held fast to what she knew was good and right. Even now, the recollection of Ilva's courage and conviction robbed Anya of her breath. Into death and beyond, Ilva had kept her fire and refused to falter.

Bone of my bone, Anya thought. *Flesh of my flesh. I can do no more or less. Can be no more or less than she was.*

With her left hand, Anya clutched the little sufferer. With her right, she reached for her other relic—the final remnant of Ilva Astraea, which she'd carried from Weatherell to the mountain.

"I am the last offering," Anya answered softly, so quiet and meek that the god was forced to stoop lower still. "The one that burns so fiercely, it will sate you forever. My sister was the spark that kindled me, but I am a consuming fire."

And with all that burned in her, all the anger and conviction and heartache and grief, she took her bone knife and drove it into the god of the mountain's throat. Wrenching forward with every muscle, Anya felt whatever fiber the god was made from give way and rend. Steel was not enough to mar him, but Ilva was. Anya was. And together, they left a killing wound.

Molten blood fountained over Anya and she darted away with a cry, frantically wiping at it before it could burn too deep. The god clutched at his throat and the sound he made was a nightmare, a whole world ending. His death rattle shook the cavern, and when he fell back upon the altar, the massive stone of it split in two.

The heat in Anya was an inferno, an incandescent storm. She stood above the god of the mountain and stared down at his ruin, as he must surely have stared down at her sister. At her mother. At scores of other girls.

"I was never a lamb," she said furiously as Ilva's ghostly hand settled on her shoulder, a benediction made manifest. "I was never an offering. And no one else will be made so *ever again.*"

TWENTY-SEVEN
The Ones Who Went

Thought I was the frightening one," a weak voice said from behind Anya. "But that's not true. You're much more frightening than I am."

Anya whirled, the burning within her dimming at once, and found Tieran pushing himself upright with a pained look on his face. He was a disaster in his human form, all blood and soot and alarmingly pale skin, but a bit of his color was returning, and for Anya he managed a rueful smile.

"What are you doing?" she asked, unable to hide her shock. "I thought he'd killed you."

Tieran stifled a groan and attempted, unsuccessfully, to stand. Anya was at his side in a moment, keeping him seated with gentle hands.

"Ridiculous boy. Don't get up."

"I'm all right," he insisted. "Or I will be in a minute. Don't you know it takes some doing to kill a god, Anya Astraea?"

"You're not a god," she scoffed, though tears were blurring her vision. "And killing one was straightforward enough, once I really got down to it."

She fixed her eyes on Tieran, and he must have seen the fear still lingering in her—that she would suffer one more loss, and it would be him, and she would not be able to bear up under it.

"Don't look so," Tieran said softly, brushing the tears from her face with his thumb. "We're gonna be just fine, you and me."

Anya nodded, but despite her resolve, she'd never really expected to succeed in the task she'd set for herself—it wasn't for Weatherell girls to triumph. They broke, or sometimes died. They did not emerge from the cavern of the god whole and victorious. It would all take a great deal of getting used to.

"Do you have another knife?" she asked.

Tieran's smile widened. "Course I do."

"A big one?"

Fidgeting, Tieran procured a blade that was halfway to a short sword.

Anya frowned. "Where did you—no. Never mind."

Squaring her shoulders, she returned to the remains of the god and stared down at them dispassionately for a moment. He had only been a monster, after all. Only a twisted thing made of malice and lust for power, without anything truly divine at his core. He had not been enough to stand against her, and had never deserved the pure-hearted sacrifices of all the Weatherell girls who came before. Had not deserved Willem, or Ilva, or any of the others, or the piece of Anya's heart she'd never regain in the absence of her sister.

Stooping, Anya gripped Tieran's keen blade tight and cut the god of the mountain's head from his shoulders.

"I'm not finished yet," she said to the thief, heaving the god's head up by one curling horn. It was ponderous and awkward and would be a burden to drag down the mountain, but the god weighed less on Anya in death than he had in life. "There's still something left for me to do."

"Frightening," Tieran muttered. But there was devotion in his eyes when he looked at Anya, encumbered by the weight of the god, and she knew there was boundless affection in hers when she looked back at him.

† † † †

At the center of Banevale, as in most cities or towns across Albion, there lay an open square. It served for a market and a meeting place, where the Elect taught or dealt out judgments and itinerant preachers spoke of wrath and fire. Lackeys of Lord Astraea levied taxes there or enlisted new youths for his private guard. People learned their news in the square; they conducted business and gossiped and bickered and wooed one another within its busy confines.

At the edge of that square, Anya hesitated. Though they'd passed a day and a night on the mountain and it was only a little after dawn, a crowd milled about already. A motley assortment of hawkers and the working poor and girls with half-healed burns, of well-clad merchants and gray-robed Elect, of liveried guards and, on horseback, tending to some unknown business, Anya's father himself. The moment she stepped out of the shadows, Anya knew every gaze would be trained on her. Every listening soul would hang upon her words.

Her hands began to tremble and her stomach to turn over.

"Tieran, I'm afraid," she breathed.

"I know," he said reassuringly. "I know, but you can do this. You got to do this—if you don't get up there and say something, Lord Nevis or the Elect'll do it for you. They'll twist what you done, and find a way to use it to their own ends. But I'm right here. Be waiting for you and watching you, all the time."

Anya shut her eyes for a moment, wishing the crowds would be gone when she'd opened them. But the waiting masses remained resolutely there, along with the increasingly burden-some weight of what she'd taken from the god of the mountain, now wrapped in her indispensable oilskin coat.

Fanning the embers of her courage to life once more, Anya stepped forward.

The crowd parted before her like water, leaving a broad clear path for Anya to travel. At the center of the square stood an empty and unattended wagon, and Anya scrambled onto its bed. She got to her feet and pulled the oilskin from the god of the mountain's severed head, then let it fall onto the wooden plank-ing, which it hit with a low, thunderous sound, as if it still held the power to shake the earth.

But there was nothing of life in it, and no fire gleamed from those filmy, dead eyes, which had once beheld so much of sacri-fice and done so much wickedness.

Anya cleared her throat and clasped her hands before her, so that the gathered watchers would not see how they shook.

"This is your god," she said, and it seemed a miracle that her voice rang out clear and true. "My name is Anya Astraea and I crossed Albion for a sacrifice. My mother, Willem, and my sister, Ilva, both went before me. My mother gave her hands to the god of the mountain. My sister's life was stolen by him. So I set out on my sister's behalf, to make right what others have called her failure. But I never intended to serve as an offering myself—my intent was always to exact one, on behalf of every girl the god has marred or broken. So here he is, what's left of him, and here I am. Maybe it was blasphemy, what I've done. But my Arbiter spoke of how someday, justice would run down the mountain like water, and righteousness like a mighty stream. I think what I undertook was right and just, and if it was wrong you can lock me away but you can't undo it. I'm glad of that. Right or wrong, I'm glad no other girl will ever have to make that climb and give up some of who she is to buy peace for us all."

Anya caught her breath and for a moment, the square was utterly silent. Orielle had appeared at the head of the crowd, her expression unreadable, and Jonus Astraea watched Anya from astride his tall black horse, with something calculating behind his eyes.

"Anyway, that's everything," Anya said, with a trace of Tieran's stubborn sullenness. "I've done what I came to do. Whatever happens next is up to everyone else."

Turning, she scrambled back down from the wagon box.

Every soul in the square stayed rooted to the spot, their eyes fixed on the remains of the god of the mountain that Anya had left behind.

"Was that all right?" Anya whispered to Tieran as she reached him at the edge of the square.

"Yeah," he said anxiously. "It was perfect. You were perfect. But we got to get going, I think we only got a moment before—"

He grabbed Anya's hand and broke into a half run, away from the square and its crowd as ripples of raised voices began to spread. Like wildfire, pandemonium broke loose, but Tieran was quick and clever, and had them away before it had truly caught. Flurries of running feet and shouts echoed here and there, but the thief dodged through the streets with Anya in tow, until they reached a shadowed alley and an even dimmer recessed doorway.

"Got to get you out of this city and off the high roads," Tieran said, half to himself, as they stood huddled together. "Lucky for us I know some people what take care of that sort of thing."

"Tieran?" Anya said.

"Hm?" He glanced nervously past her, at the head of the alley. But there was no one there besides a shadow that resolved itself into Midge, brought to them by her incomprehensible internal compass and transparently happy as she pressed herself against Anya's legs.

"Tieran?" Anya said again.

"Yeah?" This time it was the boarded-up doorways the thief scanned, as if a contingent of guards or flock of grayrobes might come pouring out of a hitherto abandoned building.

"Tieran," Anya insisted.

His sly hazel eyes met hers at last, and both of them stilled.

"If I go back to my Weatherell, and to the others, would you come with me?" Anya asked. "I don't expect you to stay, not always. But I need to see my mother and tell everyone what's happened—they won't let all the other girls brought up for sacrifice know otherwise, I don't think. I want to be with you, though, whenever and wherever I can. And maybe later, to be with your wanderers."

Tieran nodded. "Where you go, I go. That's it for me from now on. Never gonna want to stay long in a place if you're not there. Can't promise I won't disappear for a day or two now and then, but I'll come back. I'll always come back to you."

"I love you," Anya said earnestly. "All of you."

The thief grinned. "And I think you're all right, Weatherell girl."

With Midge lying watchfully at their feet, Anya stood on her toes and kissed Tieran until his smug look and underlying wariness had gone and he was aware of nothing but her. For her part, Anya sank into the warmth and light being near him woke at her center. Only for a moment did her attention waver, as a pale glow flickered to life across the alley.

Ilva stood there, and her ghost was no longer a gaunt and decaying thing. She looked as she had the day she set out from Weatherell—eager, and full of expectation. As her eyes caught Anya's, she smiled, raising a hand in farewell.

Be brave, little moon, the air itself seemed to whisper. *Hold on to your courage without me.*

Then Ilva faded, and for the last time, vanished.

The sorrow that rose in Anya as she went was no longer enough to overwhelm. It came with a bittersweet pang and softened into the comfort of memory, and left Anya hungrier than ever for the business at hand.

For life.

For joy.

For an ending that might, perhaps, not always be happy, but that she knew unshakeably was just, and right, and good.

ACKNOWLEDGMENTS

Every new book I write is the product of a holy trinity of creative input: it starts with me, but there are two other integral parties. For *A Consuming Fire*, the first is Nicole Fiorica, my deeply talented and sympathetic editor. She takes the rough, vaguely book-shaped things I come up with and makes them shine. She's a staunch advocate and a wonderful publishing-world partner. I'm so grateful to have her in my corner and hope we'll be making novels together for years to come.

The second indispensable participant in the creation of my books is Lauren Spieller, literary agent extraordinaire. Lauren reads everything first, she helps me hone my ideas, and she turns them from something nebulous and plotless into actual cohesive stories. She is so, so much more than someone who just handles the business end of things. But she knows all that, so I'll just say, Lauren, you're the best. Let's keep doing this forever.

They say you can't judge a book by its cover, but I happen to be a person who often does. I've been privileged to have my worlds and characters brought to life by incredibly talented cover artist Kim Ekdahl for two consecutive books now, and I am so appreciative of her creative genius and thoughtful compositions.

When my stories are in their infancy, there are two people I entrust them to before anyone else: my mom and Steph Messa. They're the people I consider my alpha readers—beloved cheerleaders who provide enthusiasm when the books I write are still kind of a hot mess.

And speaking of hot messes, I myself am one on a regular basis. Any functionality I possess is brought to you by my emotional support writing group, affectionately known as The Pod: Steph Messa, Anna Bright, Hannah Whitten, Jen Fulmer, and Joanna Meyer. I would bury a body for any one of them, no questions asked, and know they'd do the same for me.

Writing books takes a lot of time. It means a lot of sitting in a room with the door shut, being completely unavailable because frequent disturbances and creative flow are mortal enemies. Thank you so much to my person, Tyler, and my darling changeling children for being understanding when I shout "NO INTERRUPTIONS" with a wild gleam in my eyes and hole up at the far end of the house for entire afternoons.

Lastly, and most importantly, thank you to my readers. To those who've just joined me, and those who've been here for a book or two, and those who've traveled with me through all four stories—you are the reason I do what I do.